I AM THE
BLADE

J. P. BUXTON

Hodder
Children's
Books

A division of Hachette Children's Books

Typeset in AGaramond by Avon DataSet Ltd,
Bidford on Avon, Warwickshire

Printed and bound in Great Britain by
CPI Bookmarque Ltd, Croydon, Surrey

The paper and board used in this paperback by Hodder Children's Books
are natural recyclable products made from wood grown in
sustainable forests. The manufacturing processes conform to the
environmental regulations of the country of origin.

Hodder Children's Books
a division of Hachette Children's Books
338 Euston Road, London NW1 3BH
An Hachette UK company
www.hachette.co.uk

For Sara Fisher

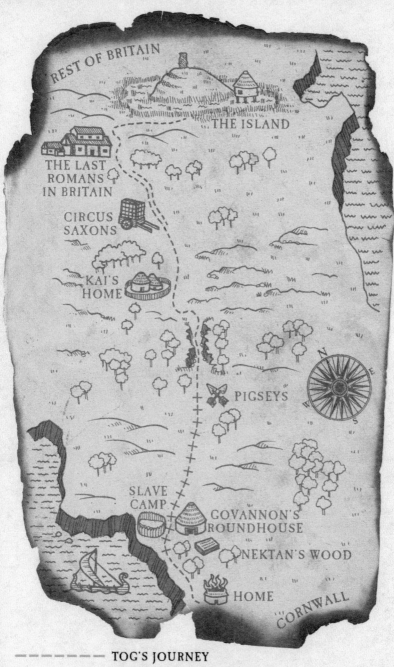

REST OF BRITAIN

THE ISLAND

THE LAST
ROMANS
IN BRITAIN

CIRCUS
SAXONS

KAI'S
HOME

PIGSEYS

N
E
W
S

SLAVE
CAMP

GOVANNON'S
ROUNDHOUSE

NEKTAN'S WOOD

HOME

CORNWALL

-------- TOG'S JOURNEY
++++++++ WITH CROTUS'S PILGRIMS
======== WITH CIRCUS SAXONS

Oh little shining thing
My little tinny thing
Make me a king.

Oh little shining man
As your start was stone
Water is your end.

Who's the little blade?
I'm the blade.
Who is the blade?
I am.

(repeat)

Cornish, traditional,
800 BCE approx

I

Full

'Translate,' the woodcutter barked.

'I don't like this bit.' Tog blushed invisibly. It was dark outside and almost as dark inside the small, round hut. The only light came from the fire in the middle of the floor and the twitchy flame of a pig fat candle on the table.

'Do it anyway.'

'Chapter Four, Verse Five,' Tog hesitated, swallowed, then hurried on: '*Duo ubera tua . . .*'

'Just get on with it.'

'*Duo ubera tua . . .* your two . . . chests. But this doesn't make sense.'

'Breasts, boy! Breasts. They're only natural.'

'Not these ones,' Tog muttered. '*Duo ubera tua sicut duo hinuli . . .*'

'Yes?'

'Your two . . . breasts are like two young deer . . . *capreae gemelli* . . . twins of gazelle . . . *qui pascunter in liliis* . . . which are fed on lilies. See?' Tog protested. 'If you fed on lilies you'd be sick – I'm sure of it – and how can anyone's breasts be like deer unless they're . . .' he sniggered, 'hairy.'

The woodcutter's mattress of dried bracken rustled as he shifted. Tog sensed a raised hand and said hurriedly: 'All right, all right, I'm on to it. *Donec adspiret dies et inclinentur umbrae* . . . Until the day breaks and the shadows flee away . . . *vadam ad montem murrae at ad collem tur*—' he paused as the woodcutter belched, '—*IS* . . . I'll go to the . . . What's "murrae"?'

'Myrrh.'

'And "*turis*"?'

'The other one.'

'So . . . I'll go the mountain of myrrh and the hill of the other one.'

Silence.

'It's what you told me,' Tog said. 'Oh all right: *The hill of frankincense*. Is that better?'

'I'm afraid I have overestimated you,' the woodcutter said with an attempt at frosty dignity. 'I thought you were mature enough for the *Song of Songs*, which describes the

2

passion King Solomon the Great felt for the Queen of Sheba. But you're obviously just an overtired, snide, sniggering child and not ready for it at all.'

To change the subject Tog said, 'I saw soldiers again.'

'How many?'

'Seven or eight.'

'That's a number?'

'All right, eight. Mounted. Going into the castle.'

'Better.'

The castle stood on a headland, pinched, where it joined the cliffs, into a narrow waist. Surrounded by sea on three sides and with an entrance that was only one man wide, it was easily defensible.

The woodcutter took another long pull from a stoneware pot containing the water of life. He wasn't much of a woodcutter and the poison he brewed certainly wasn't the water of life. A few years ago, he had ended up on the outskirts of the village with a half-baked grasp of distilling spirits, a woman and a baby that wasn't his. He claimed to be a fallen monk but Tog thought it more likely he was ex-army. Disgraced probably. A deserter. The hills and valleys of Cornwall were salted with the bitter remains of various beaten armies: angry men who sat in their huts and muttered about past glories and horrid incomers.

When the woman died, Tog was brought up by the

woodcutter, who sold whisky to the villagers and the castle, drank even more of it himself and, when he was sober, hewed wood for the queen's smelting ovens.

Tog was a slow learner where woodcutting was involved. However, he was well advanced in Latin, and, if he was given a smooth slate, had passable handwriting. He had also learned to fight a bit and had just begun beating the woodcutter. Tog reckoned that this was making the old man withdrawn and moody. In fact, he had been in a filthy mood since midwinter.

'Anyway,' Tog said. 'Someone was looking for you this morning.'

'After my whisky?'

'I don't know. The hogman told me and that's all he said.'

'What did he say exactly?'

'Nothing. Just that.'

The woodcutter cuffed Tog on the back of the head. 'I don't want "nothing" and I don't want "just that". What did the hogman say?'

'I'll tell you if you stop hitting me! The hogman said, quote: "You goes and tells that ole woodcutter loick, that a stranger's bin a pokin' around the ol' village and's a-looking for he." Unquote.'

'And did you see this stranger?' The woodcutter must

have been preoccupied or he would have hit Tog again.

'Me? No. I was down on the cliffs. There was a foreign merchant ship just beyond the bay and a boat pulling out to it.'

'Lying little toad. It's too early for traders and you know it.'

That was true. It was early but that didn't mean the ship hadn't been there. The traders that landed on the castle's sheltered beach came mostly from Brittany, just the other side of the Channel, sometimes from Massilia, which was further away, and occasionally from Constantinople which was very foreign indeed. Tog thought this ship had a Constantinople-ish look, but he knew the woodcutter hated speculation.

'Queen's run out of booze,' he said. It was an uncontroversial statement. Once the queen had been married to the Dux Britanniorum, or high king of Britain, but he'd dropped her when their baby died, people said. She'd moved back to Cornwall and now hardly ever left the castle where she grew richer and richer on the sale of tin and copper, and drunker and drunker on red wine. The high king encouraged this – he didn't care how drunk she was, or how rich, provided she didn't make trouble. Anyway, most of her garrison were king's men. She was practically under arrest.

The woodcutter ignored Tog's comment. 'What else did the hogman tell you?' he pressed.

'Oh for God's sake—' Tog began and was felled by a buffet on the side of the head.

'DON'T BLASPHEME, DON'T GIVE ME CHEEK AND DON'T PULL THAT FACE,' the woodcutter shouted. 'What else did he do?'

Tog jumped up, shouting, 'YOU NEVER DID SAY ANYTHING ABOUT SINGING, YOU FAT OLD IDIOT!'

He braced himself for another buffet but all the woodcutter said was, 'Singing?'

'The hogman said the stranger was singing under his breath when he didn't think anyone was near, though how he could have missed the hogman . . .'

'What?'

'Because the hogman's so RANK!'

'What was he singing?'

'A baby song.'

'Which baby song?'

Tog sang:

> Oh little shining thing
> My little tinny thing
> Make me a king.

Oh little shining man
As your start was stone
Water is your end.

Who's the little blade?
I'm the blade.
Who is the blade?
I am.
Blah blah de blahblah

Now the woodcutter was blinking in shock and suddenly Tog was worried. He had never seen him like this before. If he could provoke the woodcutter into having another go at him, it would mean normal service had resumed, so he whined, 'I still don't see why I can't work at the castle. You never explain anything.'

The woodcutter rose to the bait, perhaps grateful to change the subject. 'Never explain? How many times have I told you how they treat the locals?'

'You'll just lose your source of unpaid labour,' Tog sneered.

'As if you ever did a stroke of work for me. What about your lessons? What about the Latin?'

'I wouldn't have any, *Deus vult*,' Tog snapped back. 'Latin's just an elaborate form of torture worked out to punish bastards like me for the sins of their parents.'

'Don't you talk about your mother like that!'

'But it's literally true,' Tog yelled. 'I am a bastard, aren't I?'

The woodcutter blinked again and chewed a nail. When Tog was feeling vengeful, he liked to say things like this. It hurt him and for some reason, seemed to hurt the woodcutter. He had no idea who his father was, though the chances were that he was one of the queen's soldiers; the village was full of castle-bastards. Another theory was that the woodcutter was his natural father but too embarrassed to admit it.

Often, when Tog went on and on about it, the woodcutter would drink himself senseless. However, on this occasion he recovered quickly. 'Let's address the original point. You know my views on the castle. If you got in, you'd be the lowest of the low. A slop boy. No – you'd be the slop boy's boy. *If* you were lucky you might be allowed to eat his crumbs and wipe his . . .'

'Shut up!'

'. . . nose.'

Tog breathed out fiercely, enjoying the pointless argument. He had been brought up to loathe anything to do with the castle and found it quite easy to do so. The only thing the queen had going for her was her

Cornishness. That apart, she exploited the people whose taxes paid for:

a castle they couldn't live in,

feasts they couldn't eat,

horses they couldn't ride,

and the very weapons that were used to keep them down.

And although she was rumoured to be so full of magic that she practically leaked the stuff, it did no good at all. The harvest had failed two years running and Irish pirates had started to raid up and down the coast, burning villages and taking slaves at will. Of course, the local warlords could bypass her and appeal to the high king directly but they wouldn't. He was half Roman, people said. Not one of us. Give him an inch and he'd take a mile, like all incomers.

'Well,' the woodcutter said. Making an effort to seem normal, he joined Tog on the log that was drying out next to the fire. 'I don't know why anyone would want to see me.' With no more nails to chew he started on his cuticles. 'Tog, I know what you want. You want to know about your parents. Believe me, I . . .'

'Oh, here it comes,' Tog said, suddenly terrified. 'More of the same old same old.'

The woodcutter rolled his eyes upwards and said, 'Oh Lord, what do I do? Can you give me a sign?'

A bang on the door. Some knocks say: *Are you there?* This one said: *I'm here.* It cut off Tog's sarcastic reply and the woodcutter jumped up.

'Who's that?' he called. Occasionally someone would want a pitcher to be filled with hooch, but their knocks were rather quieter, as a rule.

The knock came again, even louder this time.

'Open the door and get out,' the woodcutter hissed. Tog thought he sounded jittery.

'Why?' Tog hissed back. 'Worried your wicked past's catching up with you? Remember the sins of the father . . .'

The woodcutter made a strangled sound in his throat and aimed a kick at Tog's leg, which he dodged. 'Go on! Do as I say! Sleep in the woodshed and if I find you've been listening I'll thrash you silly.'

Tog did not want the thrashing. The woodcutter thrashed like he was making up for all the wood he avoided chopping. It hurt for weeks afterwards. But even so, after he opened the door he paused to see who had come knocking.

The stranger was wearing a heavy, brown, hooded cloak over a grey tunic and warm-looking leggings. Soft leather boots, mud spattered, came up to his knees. His leather gloves were beautiful. He was young and had a young man's transparent beard. His eyes, which were blue and level, took in Tog at a glance and then slid past him to range around the hovel.

'Not a night to keep a man waiting outside,' he said.

'No,' Tog said. 'It's not.'

'Go away,' the stranger said, as if he meant it.

Tog went.

With the door firmly shut behind him, he almost decided to put his ear to it but then he decided he was too annoyed with the woodcutter to care what he was saying. And then there was the thrashing. Anyway he was tired and it was warm in the woodshed, a lean-to where they kept the bracken and heather for their bedding. He often wondered why they didn't just live there instead of the smoky, cluttered hut.

But in the middle of the night, he remembered. The wind changed direction and, instead of blowing against the lean-to's sloping roof, scoured right through it from end to end, bringing with it the smell of the hut's log fire. Tog burrowed as far as possible into the pile of bracken but could not get warm. He could not stop thinking that the woodcutter would have thrown a couple of extra logs on to the fire by now. He gathered himself for the short dash to the hut. When he opened his eyes and saw the flames, he ran.

They were leaping out of the smoke hole in the hut's roof and glowing through the gaps around the door. Tog stared for a second, trying to take it all in, then ran to the door, which was warping in the flames. He could feel his eyeballs drying and the heat tried to beat him back as he peered through a gap, searching for the woodcutter. Everything inside was flaming. A whisky jar exploded softly in a shower of blue.

'Woodcutter!' he shouted. 'Woodcutter!'

The door was jammed so he gave it a kick. The wall fell in and the entire roof collapsed, blasting him back and sending a twisting cone of sparks hissing into the sleety air. The door must have been holding the whole hut up.

As he retreated, his heels caught and he fell, scratching his hands on a gorse bush, then, over his desperate swearing, he heard something groan.

He leaned forward. He was lying across a small ditch with something soft in. He felt with his hands. Fabric. Skin.

'Woodcutter! Woodcutter!'

Another groan.

'I thought you were in the hut! I'll get the hogman. He'll know—'

'No time,' the woodcutter whispered hoarsely. Tog crawled round so he was facing the fire. He peered down into the ditch. The woodcutter's face was a big blister, dimpled around his features. When he touched it the woodcutter whimpered.

'Sorry, lad. Burned. Had to wait before . . . crawled out. No smoke on the floor – you remember that – but it was hot. Been stabbed as well.'

'But why?' Tog asked. 'What happened? Were you drunk?'

'No.' The woodcutter's hand twitched on his chest as he were trying to make the sign of the cross. He began to cough. Tog smelled the meat of his lungs.

'You . . . asked . . . That stranger. Wanted it.' He coughed again, more weakly. 'Secret . . . your . . .' His voice tailed off.

'What secret? What are you saying?' Tog protested. He felt lost and confused. The woodcutter blinked his eyes open. Closed. Shut. Each time they opened they had a bit less life in them.

'No time . . . explain. Stone . . . Full moon.'

'Stone? Full moon? What do you mean?'

The woodcutter cut Tog off with an impatient shake of the head as if he was altogether too cretinous for words.

Suddenly his body was wracked by a wave of shuddering coughs. His head jerked as blood trickled down the side of his mouth. Then the terrible, blistered mask fell back on to the ground.

'Take . . .'

His voice faded into a wet, rattling hiss.

'What?' Tog was crying.

'Little . . . man.'

The woodcutter's breath crackled once more.

'Oh, the orchards. Shine.'

His breath stopped. Crackled. Then stopped for good.

A weight slammed into Tog, knocking him flat against the woodcutter's body and winding him.

'You know where it is, you little catamite! Tell me!'

A man was lying on him, pressing him down, working his arm up his back until Tog thought it would crunch out of its socket. In front of his eye was a hole in the woodcutter's jerkin and behind it, the hole in his ribs.

'What?' Tog managed to get out.

'You know. You're the dog returning to its vomit. Now where is it?'

'I don't know . . .' Tog squeaked, then gasped as his head was pulled back by the hair. His neck was a bow.

'He's got it. The treasure. What is it?'

'He never said.' Tog's clenched teeth hedged in the pain. He felt the warmth of his burning home on his face. He wriggled to try and move forwards. His hand caught in the woodcutter's jerkin and his fingers closed on the house knife that the woodcutter must have picked up as he crawled out.

Surprise them; attack them; leg it: the woodcutter's three rules of fighting.

Tog went limp and whimpered as if he had given up, then, as soon he felt the tiniest slackening of pressure, bent his back, got some purchase with his knees, scuttled forwards to take the strain off his arm, and whipped his free arm round, stabbing blindly. The first thrust hit bone; the second went in. The man screamed and let go of his arm. Tog twisted, jumped to his feet and scooted off, horrified and elated by his glimpse of the stranger dancing silently in the firelight. The blade, as far as he could see, had gone in through one cheek and out of the other. Not a mortal wound, he thought, but a good disabling one, God forgive him et cetera et cetera amen.

He bolted through the bracken and gorse to lie low in one of his boltholes until there was enough light to see. Then he could try and work out what to do next.

Tog shivered in his hideout, trying to force his mind to work.

Rather like Latin, you could take the woodcutter's dying words and put them together in any order. Also like Latin, no amount of rearrangement made particular sense.

Secret. Stone. Full moon. Little man. Orchard. Shine. Then the stranger had asked him about treasure. That just made things more confusing.

If there had been treasure why hadn't the woodcutter used it to make their lives less miserable? Or told him about it?

The words made no sense in the order the woodcutter had said them, so Tog let his mind hop around.

Full moon. No moon tonight but he knew it was two days past full. So the next full moon was a month away.

Little man. Shine.

That seemed to come back to the old nursery rhyme – the one the hogman had overheard the stranger singing. He'd always thought it was nonsense, not even fun, with an idiotic, sinister ring.

Oh little shining thing
My little tinny thing
Make me a king.

Oh little shining man
As your start was stone
Water is your end.

Mothers sometimes sung it to their sons, children

sometimes sung it to their dolls but in this context it sounded like a coded message. But what? And who for? The key to the secret.

Orchard. Stone. Well, there might be some clues there.

Orchard would have something to do with apples. The woodcutter loved apples and treated them with a sort of misty-eyed reverence: the sight of an apple tree in blossom was enough to make him stop in his tracks and start muttering to himself. Unfortunately, there weren't any orchards in the neighbourhood.

But there was a stone and the woodcutter had taken him to it last spring, almost exactly a year ago, in fact. They had walked the crinkled cliff tops, their feet light on the springy turf, and watched the slow explosions of the sea heaving itself into the black cliffs. They had called out the names of birds they had seen: choughs, any amount of gulls, rooks, sand martins, pintails, guillemots, scaups and even a dowitcher.

They had dropped down into a small bay where a small river ran into the sea across glittering grey sand. There the sea had been dark blue and the crests of the waves as white as the small clouds high above them. They had found a small saltpan in a rock, rubbed their bread in it and eaten it, watching the waves march on to the land, endlessly and breathlessly. Then the woodcutter had given

Tog the special tea he carried in a skin and walked him up the valley to the Bloodstone.

The Bloodstone was a grey lump on a cliff, with a mazy spiral cut into its surface. The ground all around it was worn and trodden down, so that you couldn't help thinking of all the other people who had worn away at the earth before you as they walked around it. When Tog traced the maze lines, the stone taught his fingers the way they must go and his skin felt the touch of every other person who had traced the maze, smoothed the stone into these dreamy spiral runnels. And as he did so, some truth seemed to grow in his belly – a truth about the stone and people, about change and about never changing, about choosing a path and following a path. The stone made the truth grow, but in the end the truth was like a stone: grey, hard and silent. It was in him, but not to be spoken.

On the walk back he hadn't said much, but everything – the trees on the hill, the cloud shadows chasing each other across the turf, the sparkle of the waves and the web of foam between them – seemed important. When swallows had flown overhead, Tog thought he saw them trailing glowing threads behind them. These threads were like a net that connected everything on earth, and when he blinked he saw the swallows were swooping through a golden maze in the air. He had opened his mouth to say something, but the woodcutter had smiled and laid a finger across his lips.

The wet dark of the late winter night seeped into Tog's brain. He didn't think he'd ever felt worse – even the time he'd tried to get in with the village kids by throwing stones at the woodcutter and calling him vile names. Lying in the cleft of the rocks, behind the spiked branches of a hawthorn, the memory gnawed at him like a rat. The woodcutter, he now understood in some dim yet huge way, had been his entire world. Now he was gone, everything was a decision, starting with the big one: what should he do next?

He could carry on chopping wood for the furnaces that burned morning, noon, and night down by the queen's mines, but he knew that without a protector, they'd just take the wood off him without payment. He could brew hooch if only he'd bothered to listen and learn. He could try for a job at the castle but he'd only be given to some lackey, like the chief midden operator's apprentice's assistant's slave's slave, and beaten into the middle of next week just for being alive.

Tog's stomach rumbled. Not to be disrespectful, but hunger made things a million times worse, he thought. Dawn couldn't be far off – he could see black branches silhouetted against the sky and an impression of cloudbanks rolling off the sea. At last an idea came – he'd walk to the village, tell them what happened and go on from there. To an orchard. Or a stone.

He detoured foxily around the embers of the hut and was moving silently alongside a drystone wall when he was grabbed for the second time that night, this time round the biceps, by two immensely strong, outstandingly filthy hands.

Automatically, he threw his weight one way then the other, swung his leg round and back to sweep his attackers' away but instead of that happening, he was kicked hard in the calf. Pain shot up the back of his leg and the grip on his arms tightened.

'Oi know thy little tricksies, boy,' a voice hissed in his ear. 'Don't try them on Oi or Oi'll snap thy little leggsies off and feed them to my great big bootiful sow.'

Tog recoiled from the smell. He opened his mouth to shout but a putrid hand clamped itself around his mouth and over his nose.

'Shut thy silly little mouth and harken with thy soft little ears!'

Tog heard shouting coming from the clump of huts that called itself a village. It grew louder and then one voice was raised above them all. It was thick and distorted as if the

20

speaker was having trouble forming his words.

'Murder! The boy murdered his master and then attacked me. Look! Here! The knife went right through my face. He killed his master and then tried to kill me and then burned the place down. I managed to drag the old man out before I collapsed. He's up there now, lying in a ditch, murdered like a dog.'

Tog began to wriggle. 'Not a word,' the hogman said.

Tog managed to hiss: 'He's lying.'

''Course he is. Oi sees that stranger jump yerse outside the hut, don't Oi? Hears him ask about treasure, don't Oi? Sees yerse run off afore Oi can foind yerse. Bin waiting since.'

'Let's go and tell them!'

'For a clever little runt, yerse as thick as pigswill. Oo'll they believe?'

Tog's throat strangled his voice. 'Me.'

'They'll believe that what suits 'em. Oi bets they're already divvying up the goodies – the axe, the pots, the whisky hut. If yerse the guilty party, they hangs yerse noice and easy and they gets it. If yerse bain't, they don't get nothing at all. Right now they'll be getting themselves all noice and excited so when they finds yerse, they strangles yerse noice and quick. Got it, boy?'

Tog was speechless.

'Now can Oi let yerse go?'

Tog twisted round and asked: 'That message I took to the woodcutter – was it a warning?'

The hogman said nothing.

'Did you know something? Was he in trouble?'

'Dunno.'

'Had he stolen treasure?'

'Ever know him do a bad thing?' the hogman countered.

'No.'

'Then do what he says.'

'What? He didn't make sense.'

'Then think. And don't tell me. Get used to keeping your mouth closed.'

For the first time in his life Tog looked properly at the woodcutter's favoured drinking companion. The hogman's hair was matted into long, flat worms; his face was lined and the lines filled with dirt; his hands were the colour of tree roots and there were no words to describe his tunic. His eyes were bright though, and when he next spoke, his voice had grown deeper, less surly, more commanding.

'Listen to me. You know more than the old witch ever knew.' The hogman jerked his head to indicate the castle. 'Talk Latin?'

'Yes.'

'She doesn't. Read?'

'Yes.'

'She doesn't. Write?'

'Yes.'

'She doesn't.'

'I can't – I thought the woodcutter was just bullying me. Why are you talking about the queen?'

'Fool. Listen to me. They're coming so I'll just say this once. What the woodcutter gave you is more precious than silver, more precious than pearls, more precious than gold. Do you understand?'

Confused yet impressed, Tog nodded.

'The rabble will hang around the hut for a while and then they'll come after you, so you've got a tiny fragment of time to get as far away as possible. Here.'

He reached under his tunic and pulled out a lump of meat. There were other things in there, hanging from strings and stuffed into pockets. 'It's bacon. If you're careful, it'll get you forty miles before you fall over. Go. Run! That stranger, he'll be after you soon as they find you're gone. And don't count on him not knowing where you're headed. He might have forced it out of the woodcutter.'

'But why wasn't I told all this earlier?' Tog asked. 'Why now?'

'The same reason I wasn't told. For safety. Now run!'

* * *

I have to get to the Bloodstone, Tog thought. The shortest route, the one they'd taken last spring, was out of the question. Even this early villagers would be working their fields. No, he'd have to go inland then cut back later. He started to run uphill, stubbed his toe, which made him hobble, and started to cry, which made it hard to get his breath. He got tired incredibly quickly. Tears and snot ran across his face and the general impression was that instead of running forwards, he was falling backwards into a large hole.

But then the ground levelled out and he began to find a rhythm. In order to keep out of trouble, he had trained himself to run faster than anyone else in the village so he reckoned that running on the road would give him the greatest advantage.

Like most of the villagers, he had never set foot on the road because you were meant to pay for the privilege with money and few of them had even seen a coin. It belonged to the castle, was unimaginably weird and a wonder that anything so thin and long could stretch so far without snapping. The villagers said it ran from the Land of Death in the west to the Land of Birth in the east – so if he went east, he'd be getting younger, Tog thought.

He put a foot on to the paved surface, almost expecting it to wobble, but it stayed quite firm. He took one step, began to run and then the road seemed to shoot him forwards with a great feeling of lightness. Wings grew on his ankles and the world blurred on either side of him.

He was brought down to earth by the shouts of men. In the grey light, he saw two riders forcing their horses up the hill. If they were from the castle, they would happily kill him for trespassing on royal property.

He couldn't go any faster but made sure the slap slap slap of his sandals never slackened. When a dip in the land hid him, he threw himself sideways into the roadside ditch and tried to disappear.

The horses' hooves were beating on the earth. The earth drummed back and Tog felt as if he were being bounced like a pebble on its skin. He gripped tight with his fingers and promised the earth some of his blood if it would protect him. The horses juddered past him but just as he was feeling relieved, the thump of their hooves stopped.

In their heavy breaths and creaking leather kit, Tog could hear his death.

'He must've run off here.'

'He can shift. I'll give him that.' Their accents were clipped and flat.

'Call him out.'

'Boy. Show yourself.'

Tog found himself standing. He felt as light as dust. His head was on a level with the horses' sucked-pebble-eyes and he could smell the fermented grass thickening their breath. Above them the men were fatty and fit and looked at him from under the low brows of their Roman helmets. Together, they reached behind their heads and unsheathed stabbing swords from scabbards slung over their shoulders.

'Come with us or we'll kill you,' one said.

'Are you after me because you think I killed the woodcutter or because I'm trespassing?'

'We're after you because some prat with a hole in his face is paying us. All right?'

'Oh,' Tog said. 'I didn't think you could pay people to do that. But I'm still not coming with you so you'll have to kill me. I think I'll turn around, if you don't mind. By the way, which way am I facing? I mean towards birth or death?'

The men started to laugh and when he saw the joke, Tog had to admit it was funny.

'Legs apart,' one of the men said. 'Stand solid. Make yourself strong.'

On Tog's right, the rim of the sun appeared between two hills, a tiny sliver of gold. Off to his left he could hear the sea and suddenly he decided not to die. When he felt the

26

breath of the horses on his neck, he darted back between them and jinked down the hill where the ground was littered with enough rocks to risk breaking a horse's leg.

The men took some time to turn the horses and cursed as they tried to pick a way through the boulders. Then one of them turned back to the road while the other found a path and cantered so he could cut Tog off from below.

Tog skipped over boulders, but now the horses were on open ground and it sapped his strength to see how arrogantly they moved. When the riders caught him the next time, they'd drag him behind them until he was a long red smear on the road.

The riders were shouting to each other and pointing. Ahead the ground dipped suddenly into a small wooded valley that ran down to the sea and Tog was sure the Bloodstone lay at its head. He put on a spurt of speed and had made about fifty paces when he realized what the men were shouting.

'Nemeton!'

The word held him. He looked ahead, his chest burning and his mouth bitter. The wood made a grey wall, just fifty paces away.

He broke the word's power and ran. The lower horseman saw what he was doing and regardless of the danger, forced his horse across the broken ground to cut him off. Tog

27

made it ahead of him and backed up against an old grey tree trunk. Its naked branches spread above him. The horseman would not even venture close.

'Stop!' The man's face was pasty. 'Didn't you hear me shout? That's Nektan's Grove – a nemeton. It's sacred. The whole wood's taboo. The god's returned. You must be mad.'

'Maybe, but I'm alive,' Tog panted. He looked into the gloom. Lots of brambles in there and brambles were a bad sign. Pigs would keep them down and no pigs meant no people, which meant the wood really was taboo.

'Not for long. Look, spare a thought for us,' the soldier said. 'You're good as dead now for just touching that tree, so why not do everyone a favour and give up now?' He unslung a rope from his saddle. 'Tie this round your neck so you can't scarper again.'

'But you said I had to come with you or you'd kill me. Well, I've run away so that means you've got to kill me now, except I think I'd prefer to live. If you see what I mean.'

'It'd be kinder if we killed you. Put one foot in the nemeton and you'll get followed to the ends of the earth by woodwoses – they're sort of hairy men but instead of proper heads, they've just got huge jaws at the end of their necks, and they'll pin you down and bite chunks off you bit by bit. And if you think that's a horrible way to go, it's nothing compared to what'll happen if the Old Man catches you. He'll nail you between two trees like a starfish, split you open but you won't die. You'll get ants inside you and flies and all that kind of stuff, birds and things, but the worst is what happens to your spirit. He'll pull it out of you – and that hurts, I can tell you – and leave it to wander. You'll be alone. No home. No family. Unspeakable hunger, terrible thirst and no other feelings. For ever.'

'That's what will happen to me if I go into the wood?'

'For certain.' The soldier lowered his sword like a spear.

'I'll take my chances,' Tog said, dodged round to the other side of the tree, saw a gap in the brambles, and jumped in. He knew the rumours: the druids were back, had declared the old woods taboo, and dank clearings in the old forests now were home to old practices you didn't want to think about. On the other hand, the woodcutter had taught him to ignore such things and he felt it would be honouring his guardian to break the taboo.

However, the gap of brambles did not last long. They massed on the ground, never less than knee high. Within minutes Tog's legs were streaming with blood and his eyes were streaming with tears as the barbs tore him.

He stopped. The soldiers' shouts had grown no louder so they were no closer, at any rate, but what could he do?

The brambles writhed away as far as he could see. He

found that if he lifted his feet straight up and put them down very carefully, there was less scratching but even so, it was pretty bad. Far above Tog saw blue sky but down here the clammy gloom was trapped by the net of bare branches.

Whenever he stopped moving, he thought he could hear things moving.

He walked on slowly, concentrating on putting one foot in front of the other, trying to ignore the pain.

Then suddenly the brambles ended.

A carpet of thick leaf mould now lay under his feet. He heard the sound of rushing water and headed for it. The trees grew sparser and he saw clear sunlight ahead.

He slid down a steep bank and stopped dead.

Above him, a small river plunged down a cliff and poured through an arch in a rock before splashing into a deep pool.

He hobbled in. The water stung but felt clean after the vicious pricking of the bramble thorns. He watched the blood eddy round his legs and swore he'd stand there until it ran clean, offering up his blood as thanks. After a while, however, he began to shiver so much he felt ill. He splashed his way back to the bank and started to squeeze thorns from his feet. When he was finished, he tore off a mouthful of bacon with his teeth and chewed. After he had taken a few mouthfuls, he noticed something very disturbing.

Around the pool a circle of thick wooden stakes faded in and out of the shadows. They stood between the clearing and the trees, a barrier and a bridge.

They were old. Some were leaning over at crazy angles, some had greenish skulls balanced on them and all were blurred with thick moss and winter ferns. The skin on Tog's head tightened and prickled. He found he was holding his breath. This had to be the heart of the sacred grove. In spite of everything he had been taught, he could feel the power of the place.

Time slowed. Spray drifted. The waterfall roared in wet, giant breaths and by its side, halfway up the bank, a pattern of leaves and branches sharpened into a face.

Tog bit his knuckles as the god of the wood rose and glided down the slope. There was moss in his beard, grass in his hair and the colours of wood and water glinted in his eyes.

Tog fell on his belly and waited like a good dog waiting for the knife. The god prodded him with a horny toe. When he didn't move, the god crouched by his side. Tog squeezed his eyes tight but couldn't avoid feeling the god's hands running up and down his legs, and hearing him tsk tsk before stumping off.

31

Between slitted eyelids, he watched the god deftly work thick pelts of moss from the sacred posts. When he had two good patches, he came back and wrapped them, outside in, around Tog's calves. He secured them with sacred ivy yanked off a sacred tree. Tog had to admit his new bandages felt cool and wonderful.

'There,' the god said in a slightly cracked voice. 'You can stop shaking now and try to stand.'

Tog stood. Moisture from the moss trickled down his shins and tickled his feet.

'Better?'

Tog fell to his knees and grovelled. 'Nektan, Nektan,' he gabbled. 'I thank you. Do whatever you want with me but do not make my spirit wander.'

'Very good,' the god said. 'Your request is granted on condition you stop this grovelling.' Tog stood up again. 'Now, what shall I do with you?'

'Whatever Nektan wants,' Tog said, hanging his head.

'Can't hear you.'

Tog lifted his head and repeated.

'No, no,' Nektan snapped. 'Whatever *you* want.'

Tog thought it best to contradict the deity as politely as possible. He winced when the god frowned but all Nektan said was: 'Do I smell bacon? No, no. Don't tempt me,' as Tog put his hand inside his tunic. 'I gave up meat for Lent.

You go ahead, though.'

And he made his way up the side of the waterfall, returning with a rough wooden bowl that contained a blob of honey and some flat chestnut bread.

'Go on, go on.'

Tog fingered honey into his mouth and broke off a lump of bread.

'That should keep you going,' Nektan said. 'Build you up.'

The bread and honey turned to glue in Tog's mouth as his saliva dried up. He stopped chewing.

'What is it now?' Nektan asked. 'Honey not to your liking? I swear this charity business would test the patience of a saint. I order you to talk!'

Tog chewed and finally got the mouthful down with a scoop of water from the sacred stream. 'Erm, for what does the god want to build me up?'

'For whatever you're going to do next, of course.' The god seemed genuinely surprised.

'You're not going to . . . kill me then?' Tog asked.

'Not yet,' Nektan said grimly, then exploded: 'After I've tended to your bloody wounds and fed you?'

He made the sign of the cross and Tog made it back.

'I see you've been brought up a Christian,' Nektan said grudgingly. 'I'm giving it a go of course but what with the pagan revival everyone's talking about it's hard to know what's for the best. Take you for example. For setting foot in the sacred wood, the druids would recommend splitting open your miserable chest, removing your guts and so on. The Christman, on the other hand, says bind up your wounds, feed you bread and honey, bless you, anoint you with unction, and send you on your way. You see the problem?'

Tog pretended to consider. 'If I were you, I'd go with the Christman. Definitely.'

'I bet you would. What is unction, by the way?'

'A sort of ointment, Lord,' Tog said modestly.

'Ointment now? It just goes on and on. Anyway, perhaps we should begin again – establish where you're from and where you're heading.'

'I'm heading for the Bloodstone.'

'And I thought you were a Christian.'

'I was told . . .'

'No, no. I don't want to hear your excuses. It's downriver.'

Tog set off.

'And don't bother to come back this way!' the god shouted after him. 'I've just decided to become a hermit.'

The valley lightened as trees gave way to scrub. Close to the Bloodstone Tog made a circuit of the site. Someone else had been there not so long ago. By the stream, the sharp-edged print of a studded boot had filled with water. The well-dressed stranger had worn boots.

So, Tog thought, the stranger came here, looked for something, did not find it and went off to torture it out of the woodcutter. He felt sick and knelt by the maze, as much to get close to the woodcutter as to see if it would give anything up to him.

Nothing. The stone was hard and cold. Tog began to trace the stone groove with a finger, but the images didn't come thick and fast nor even thin and slow. A robin cheeped in a bare bush, but it was a melancholy, wintry sound that led nowhere. Nothing happened at all.

He tore the god's dressings off his legs, suddenly furious with the woodcutter for sending him here and furious with the god for dressing his wounds. He wanted his legs to hurt because it stopped him hurting so much inside.

He stumped back up the river to find the messy old god sitting on a rock in the mouth of his cave.

'Nothing,' Tog said. 'I don't know why the woodcutter sent me there.'

The god made a great show of cleaning out his ear. 'Eh?' he said.

'I don't know why the woodcutter told me to come to the stone.'

'Woodcutter? Why didn't you tell me? He used to come here.'

The lined face was impossible to read.

'He was my guardian,' Tog said. 'Last thing he told me to do before he died.'

'He's dead?' The god looked shocked and crossed himself inaccurately.

'He was murdered last night,' Tog said. 'Tortured for what he knew. Trouble is, he didn't tell me.'

The god chewed his lip. 'He mentioned you once or twice.' He darted a sideways look at Tog. 'Used to come here to meet someone.'

'Who?'

A shrug. 'I kept away but I know where. It's another stone. A secret one. A hundred paces up river, left-hand bank. Scramble up. There's a barrow – an old tomb. Right on the top, you'll find it. Flat, it is, and edged. Off you go.'

Tog was off, then stopped. 'There may be someone following me,' he said. 'He killed the woodcutter. Keep out of his way.' The riverbank was bare under the leaf mould and Tog scrambled carelessly up it, feet scarring the red earth. A secret stone. So that was what the woodcutter had been trying to tell him, and he only found it out by accident.

The barrow looked low and frightening. Once it would have stood in a clearing but trees had encroached. Most barrows had been robbed long ago – they were an easy target – but a barrow that was protected by a nemeton was a secret worth knowing about. Tog thought of ingots of copper, rings of brass, bracelets of silver and crowns of gold. He blessed the woodcutter: the old tomb was going to make him rich.

On the top of the mound, Tog felt the earth tremble, heard a slight hollowness in his footsteps. He stuck his hand through last year's brown leaves to the musty slime of countless autumns and cleared a space back to the stone. In the runnels, the leaf mould had turned to earth. He cleaned them with a stick, exposing bright pink worms and harder, straighter lines than the Bloodstone's.

He ran his fingers over the maze, waiting for the hope that swirled inside him to gather into something more substantial.

The world dropped away. Tog's breath thickened and he heard a rushing in his ears. Something he knew was making itself known. Now. Now.

Not a maze: carved letters.

eXq
UO
ndamre
xquefut

eXq? The letters meant nothing, but he was certain that they wanted to talk to him. He scribbled them on the stone, the end of the stick scraping through the dirt. EXQ UO

A word seemed to flit into his mind, like a sparrow just seen out of the corner of his eye. eXq?

Wait a minute. There was a word in there but it was divided. *Ex* was a Latin word, and if you took the q and ran that over into the next line you got *quondam*, another one. Take the r and e from that and add to the x on the following line, and you got *rex*. Then *que*. He scraped more dirt away from the end to find *urus* to add to the last word: *futurus*. As an afterthought, he looked in front of the e of the first word and uncovered an r. Hah!

Now to translate.

Rex meant 'King'.

Quondam meant 'in the past'.

Rex (again) meant 'king'.

If you added *que* to the end of a word, it meant 'and'.

Futurus meant 'the future'.

Run them all together and you got *rex quondam rexque futurus*.

King in the past and king in the future? That was relatively straightforward for Latin.

He was stiff and sat back on his heels to think, but before much thought happened, the stone wobbled, tipped and dropped him into the darkness, into the old tomb.

A ragged hole of light had been torn in his head and he couldn't breathe. His back hurt and something was going whoop whoop whoop quietly in his ear.

Bit by bit, all these things came together.

He was going whoop whoop whoop because he was winded, the light above him was the hole he had fallen through and his back hurt because he had fallen on it – not from the full height above: he had landed feet first on the edge of a raised stone slab and then fallen backwards off that.

Tog pushed himself up. He had landed at one end of the chamber, which was about twice his height, ten paces long and five wide, much smaller than the mound. The walls of the tomb were lined with flat slabs of stone, each with a small niche set into it at floor level. Old tombs were often used for more than a single occupant and the old bones were piled in the niches.

A typical tomb then, just like the ones kids play in

everywhere, apart from the stone slab. Slanting light picked out peculiar things arranged on it. They were:

a mummified baby wrapped in a stiff red cloak;

a short, straight sword in a mouldy leather scabbard laid sideways above its head;

above that, almost invisible, a gold half disc not much bigger than a thumbnail.

All were covered with a thin layer of dusty earth.

Tog walked round the arrangement, trying to make sense of it. Why lay the baby out like that? It was obscene, cruel. Cloak or no, it looked so cold and lonely that he wanted to do something about it.

He rubbed the cloak between his fingertips. Good cloth. Maybe Roman.

Rex quondam rexque futurus.

At a guess the tomb was much older than the baby but the inscription suggested the child was royal. The queen's? The one she had with the high king? Tog backed away. While the sacred grove held no terrors for him, a dead royal baby was to be respected in some very basic way. On the other hand, the woodcutter had sent him here and he really had to find out why.

He checked under the slab – nothing there – then turned his attention to the niches. They were just big enough to crawl into, small enough to make him feel trapped. Bones,

bones and more bones. He was just reaching into the back of the last one when a heavy dry clap of wings outside exploded into the silence and he reversed quickly. Crows started shouting. Tog grabbed the little old sword and the half gold disc and backed into the last niche, pushing the bones back out of the way with his heels.

A head blocked off the daylight. It was the stranger, dried blood clogging his beard and his head trussed up in strips of fabric like a boiled pudding.

He pulled his head back to give himself more light, cupped his hands around his eyes and peered into the tomb for a very long time. Then he went away again. Tog didn't dare move but looked desperately for another way out. White roots fringed some of the lining stones but the main roots hadn't broken in yet and the tomb looked strong.

There was a lot of cracking and crashing outside, then the bough of a tree plunged through the hole and on to the table. Daylight was blocked off as the stranger climbed down it, using the side branches like a ladder.

He smacked his hands together, poked at the baby with a finger, looked around and went down on all fours to look into the niche at the far end of the tomb. When his head was right inside it, Tog put the coin into his mouth, gripped the little sword, leapt on to the table and shinned up the branch, roaring with fear. He yanked the bough out of the tomb and ran.

The stranger chased him for two days but by the third, Tog was quite confident that he had escaped.

The first day had been an eye-opener. Tog had run, trusting that his speed, stamina and bacon would carry him away to safety but the stranger had not given up. He had nothing like Tog's speed and he ran like he was dying but he was scarily persistent. Once, when Tog had doubled back and climbed a tree, the stranger had passed not twenty paces away and although he looked dreadful – his puffed up face a medley of red and black and yellow – his eyes had been level and calm. He seemed to keep himself going by repeating the rhyme, thumping his feet down on the slow beat of the words:

> Oh little shining thing
> My little tinny thing
> Make me a king.

> Oh little shining man
> As your start was stone
> Water is your end.

He stopped and looked around. Up in his tree, Tog had

frozen and if the stranger had thought to look, he would have been trapped.

But the stranger didn't look up. He spat, half fell, groaned and then staggered on.

After that incident, Tog worked out some rules for himself.

Instead of feeling that he was pursued, he told himself that he was leading. Instead of being terrified that the stranger would catch him, he made himself imagine the stranger's pain at losing him. Instead of feeling he had nowhere to hide, he imagined that the whole of Britain was his: its mountains and forests, valleys and caves, fields and glades.

How could the stranger find him in all that?

The last time he had seen the stranger, he had been a dot on the side of a hill, weaving his way back the way he had come.

Now Tog was lying on his back in sight of the sea, holding the sword from the tomb up to the sunlight.

It was small, bronze and therefore old and not much good. The tapering blade was pitted and worn – bronze was soft compared to iron – but its last owner had given it a vicious edge before leaving it in the tomb. The metal hilt fitted his hand nicely and Tog had to admit it was well balanced. He wished he had had it with him when the soldiers from the castle were trying to kill him. Then again, if he *had* had it with him, he wouldn't have run into the woods, so he would never have found it. Make sense of that.

He was also trying to make sense of everything else. The way the hogman had changed from smelly yokel to something . . . different. What did the hogman do? He wandered all over the place. He talked to his pigs. People avoided him. He was invisible, in a way, but he saw things. He sent messages about strangers. He watched – that was it! If the woodcutter had a secret, then the hogman was his watchman. If the secret was treasure, then it was disappointing that it was just this funny old sword and half a gold coin.

He froze and held his breath. A voice!

He listened hard. It was getting closer and clearer – an Irish voice singing a nonsense song about some hero or other who hopped on one leg all day before killing a giant with a single blow and cutting off his hand to feed his hounds. Whose hand exactly, his or the giant's, was not clear.

Tog got up into a crouch to see who was coming.

There were four of them in a line: a grey-haired man leading, two slaves next, tied together with a rope around their necks and hands bound behind them, and a man with long black hair pulled into a tight ponytail bringing up the rear. He was singing and punctuating his verses by swishing at the back of the second slave with a knotted rope.

> *And if you don't do what I want*
> Swish
> *I'll beat you till your back is bleeding*
> Swish
> *And then you'll do it anyway*
> Swish
> *And I'll have made you cry again*
> Swish
> *Big Baby Big Baby Big Baby*

The slave looked the same age as Tog but he was taller than his captor. He had ash-blond hair and very red lips and was crying quite freely. In front of him was a girl with black matted hair and tattoos that swirled on her cheeks.

'So. We'll leave them here then?' the man with the ponytail said. 'And go and look for it?'

'Who said anything about leaving them anywhere?' the other replied in a gravelly voice. He had bandy legs and a beard that was plaited into two forks.

'Because then we'll be able to split up and find this blessed cove and if we find the blessed cove, we'll find the blessed boat and if we find the blessed boat, we'll be able to take our blessed cargo home and sell it which is the purpose of our blessed visit to this blessed place.'

'And if you'd bothered to remember where the blessed boat was going to land, we wouldn't be in this blessed mess.'

'And if you had bothered to remember too, we wouldn't be either.'

'It wasn't for me to remember. As you keep on reminding me, you're the brains of the outfit. I'm just the muscle.'

'But they told you where they were landing, you big eejit.'

'They said: "we'll have a meet before we drop them all off at the holding pen". But they never said where. That was for you to find out.'

'Well, they never . . . Oh, shut up, monster boy, d'you hear?'

This last comment was for the boy slave. In frustration, the young slaver tore out a clump of turf and rubbed it in the boy's face.

'OK – there's an old settlement up ahead,' the older one said. 'We'll leave them there and go looking.'

They breasted the top of a rise and the voices faded.

Tog held his finger up and waited for the sun to pass behind it, then followed.

* * *

The deserted village lay in a dip in the ground and was sadly settling back into the earth. Tog counted eight round buildings with turf roofs collapsing so the wooden beams were bared like ribs. Grass crawled up the rough stone walls. The slaves were in the largest hut, tied like chickens, still joined by the neck rope, but gagged as well now. They watched Tog silently as he went through a sack that the slavers had dumped just inside the door. He found a bag of oats, a wooden bowl, some dried fish and, joy, some turnips, albeit rather spongy; also a rough wooden box with iron, flint and tinder in it. Then he turned to contemplate the slaves.

He'd seen slaves before and completely accepted them as part of the landscape, so to speak, but it had never struck Tog until now that slavish was something you *became* rather than something you *were*.

The girl jerked him out of his reverie by kicking out. Tog knelt by her, and tried to untie the leather strap round her mouth but the knot was too tight and his fingers too cold. When he pulled out the sword from its scabbard the girl began to scream in the back of her throat. He tried to hold her down but she writhed too hard and he thought he'd hurt her. Very gently, so it was clear he meant no harm, he sawed through the boy's gag and ties. While the boy retched and spat out earth, he returned to the girl who now suffered herself to be freed.

From outside, they heard the voices of the slavers, carelessly loud.

Tog ran to the door and peered round. The sun was setting and the sky was red over the sea, dark over the land. One hard star glimmered in the east. He registered that it would freeze tonight; also that the doorway of the hut faced away from the sea so the men would approach it from behind.

The boy joined him in the doorway.

'We've got to go that way.' Tog gestured inland.

The boy tilted his head on one side, as if he didn't understand. Then he pointed and nodded.

The three of them hid behind the ruined hut next door. The voices again, much closer.

'So,' the younger slaver said. 'All's well that ends well, eh? Boat found, mates waiting and payday just the other side of the horizon.'

'Don't count your chickens. We've got to get this sorry pair to the holding pen first and the way our luck's been – what the . . . where—'

Now! Tog thought. Escape now while the men were in the hut.

'They can't be far. The ground's still warm where they

were lying,' the older one said sharply. 'Run up the slope! Have a look round.'

The voice was nearer.

'Come on now,' he called out. 'Where are you? I'm coming to get you and I'm not too pleased.'

Tog peered through a gap between the houses. He saw the old man stalking round another hut, his back to them. Of the younger man there was no sign. The older man went right. They went left.

'I heard a little rat!' He called out. 'My, my, or is it two little rats? Come on, little rats. Come out now and I won't hurt you.'

There was a rush as he ran into a hut. They heard him swear, then call out again.

'I won't hurt you if you come NOW. But if you keep me waiting, there'll be hell to pay.'

They ran round the back of the next hut, heading away from the sea. If they could make a break for it over the moorland, they would have a greater chance of escaping. And the further they led the men away from the boat, the greater the chance of them giving up.

'Oi, matey! Found anything?' the old man called.

'Funny you should say that,' the young man called back. 'Three little rats.'

Tog and the two slaves turned. The younger man was

looking down on them, a black shape against a dark sky.

'Leg it!' Tog yelled. They scattered. Tog broke right, dodged round the corner of a house and saw the old man heading across his path to try and catch the girl. Behind him he heard a shout and turned to see the older man break off from chasing the girl and disappear on the far side of the settlement. Tog ran up the slope, his breath coming deep and light. He felt as if he could have flown over the fields around the village and no one could have caught him but a terrible cry tore through the still air and stopped him dead. Then a voice called: 'Got him!'

More screams, more shouting. Tog crouched, turned and found the girl beside him, although he'd not seen or heard her approach. She wriggled forwards, all shoulders and hips, until she could see down into the dip and he followed.

There was a space in the middle of the settlement and the slavers had made the boy kneel there while the younger one pulled his hair. The boy looked so large and useless that Tog felt a burning hatred for him.

The girl hissed and said something in a language Tog didn't understand. Her lips were pulled back from her little white teeth and she looked like a rodent preparing to attack. She mimed taking a sword out of a scabbard, then pointed at the two men.

Tog shook his head. 'Too dangerous,' he whispered.

'Two men. Never used a sword.'

The girl made a little chattering noise in the top of her throat, took Tog's left earlobe between two fingers and pinched it with her nails. Tog bit off a cry and while he was distracted, the girl took the sword, kissed it, pointed to her eyes, pointed to his, then worked her way round the dip. She moved like a pool of darkness and Tog could only tell where she was by the glimmer of her bare feet.

The younger slaver called out: 'Right, anyone up there! Are you listening to me? Witch girl and the other fellow, we've got your big pal and we're going to make him scream. The only way to stop this is to give yourselves up. Both of yous.'

The silence rushed into stillness when he stopped talking. Then the boy's scream tore through the quiet evening.

'We've hardly got started!' the man called out.

Tog forced himself to keep looking and thought he could see a little shimmer in the darkness behind the men. If he could lure them away, maybe the girl could cut the boy free.

He stood up and called out: 'Let the boy go,' trying to make his voice deep.

'Who was that?'

'Over there.' Faces glimmered in the twilight as they lifted and turned to him. Good.

'What did you say?' one of the slavers called.

'Let the boy go!' Tog repeated.

'It's another kid.'

'You stay there or we'll put your friend's eye out with this little stick,' the younger man shouted while the other started to make his way towards him. 'Let me have a look at you. That's right. Come down from there slowly.'

'You don't want me to come any closer, not if you want to live,' Tog said desperately. The men laughed a lot. Tog wondered where the girl could be and what on earth he had been thinking of. He could have been away by now, and safe. She probably was, along with his sword.

'I'm armed,' he said.

'Oh are you, my sweet?' It was the older one that spoke. 'Then we'll have your weapon as well. What is it? A toy sword?'

A sudden rasping grunt behind him was followed by a slippery gurgle.

'See what happens?' the man said. 'That was your big friend being punished.'

'Er, I don't think it was my friend,' Tog said. 'I think it was yours.' He felt lightheaded.

The man stopped. 'Eh?' he said. He held a hand out as if to keep Tog where he was and looked back. The giant boy was standing and there was a dark shape at his feet.

'What have you done?' he called out. 'What's happened?' To Tog: 'You, boy, stop there.' In the other direction: 'Bryn! What the devil's going on? What's that?'

Tog saw the girl slide into the dark space behind him, kneel and pass the blade across the back of his knees. The man shifted, as if something uncomfortable had happened, then fell on his face, his hamstrings cut.

The girl jumped on his back and pulled his head back. 'Who is it?' the man asked, looking up at Tog.

'The girl,' Tog said.

The man closed his eyes. 'I never wanted to touch her. She's different.' A second mouth followed the metal across his throat.

Next, the big boy was sick.

II

Waning Gibbous

Tog felt shaky and sat down close to the giant boy. The girl squatted a distance away, cleaning the sword. She gave it back to Tog, handle first. He couldn't get it back into the scabbard and didn't know if it was because his hand was shaking or the sword was trembling, like a hound after a hunt.

The girl didn't seem bothered. She sat on her haunches and looked at him with her head slightly tilted on one side. At last Tog managed to sheath the sword. Took a deep breath. Couldn't look at the dead men. Wanted something normal to do.

'So what do we do now?' the giant said in a shaky voice. 'We've killed two people. Their friends will be after us.' He spoke the same language as Tog but with a different accent. He began to cry. The girl imitated him ruthlessly and he stopped.

'We'd better go,' Tog said. 'But we should get their bag. It's got food in it.'

The girl knelt by the body of the older slaver. Bled dry, the scars on his face stood up as if the skin had been ploughed. She felt under his blood-soaked tunic and took out a necklace of wolf teeth and bear claws threaded on to gold wire. It rattled solidly as she shook it.

'He was a warrior,' the giant said.

'Or he stole it,' Tog answered.

The girl bit through the soft metal of the wire as if it were a grass stem, let the teeth and claws run into her hand then scattered them on the ground, apart from a single bear claw that she rethreaded, then passed the necklace round Tog's neck. He blushed as her fingers pressed into his skin when she was twisting the ends of the gold together. Her face was so close that he could feel the warmth of her skin on his.

'I didn't do anything,' he said.

'You did more than me,' the giant answered. 'All I did was get caught and then sick up.'

Tog fingered the black claw. It had weight and carried a sheen that seemed to go deep under its surface. The end was sharp and he wondered if the bear it belonged to had actually mauled anyone with it. As far as he knew, there were no bears in Cornwall.

They crossed fields of dried bracken and about a mile inland found a dip in the ground to take them out of the wind. Tog took the first watch under the big white moon, but was shocked to see how time was paring it down.

Three nights gone, he thought. Three fewer nights to find an orchard.

The girl curled up like a cat. The boy started to sob again. After a while, Tog asked him his name.

'Allanza,' he snuffled.

'I'm Tog. How did you get here?'

'In a boat for two days.'

'Are you from Brittany?'

'Of course,' he said as if it were the most obvious thing in the world.

'I'm from Cornwall.'

'That's miles away.'

'Not quite,' Tog said. 'It's where we are.'

'What? I'm nowhere near home?' the boy said, his voice trembling. 'I thought we were going down the coast. I never realized we were going across the sea.'

The girl shuffled over to Allanza, curled up and arranged his arms and legs around her. When he made a sound, she reached behind her head and stopped his mouth with a thin hand. When Allanza went on watch and Tog took his place against her, it was the first time he remembered ever holding someone.

He woke to see the girl and Allanza crouching in the bracken looking back at where they had come from. A thin column of dark smoke was rising against the dark, dawn sky. The smell, carried to them faintly, reminded Tog of his burning home. The slavers had been back in the night to burn the ruined village down. He shivered and hugged himself.

Tog woke later with the girl's neck in front of his nose.

He looked closely at the tattoos, and saw there were two types: swirls and spirals that twisted in complex patterns and little pictures. On her bare shoulder was a circle with a smaller circle in the middle of it. Around her wrist was a dotted bracelet and on the back of her hand a pattern like a pair of crossed scythes. He wondered what they meant.

The picture people, he'd heard people say, were from a long way off – a really long way. Everyone was frightened of them: the northern tribes spoke of their terrifying weapons and the Romans had found it necessary to build an enormous stone wall right across the country to keep them out. Recently he had heard rumours that they were trying to invade. Could the girl be part of a raiding party? She certainly knew what to do with a sword. Would she slit his and Allanza's throats while they were sleeping? Or was she a witch? And if so, what did witches actually do?

Take the queen. She was a witch and could make her enemies' stomachs explode, apparently, but apart from that she didn't do any good. Didn't stop murderers killing woodcutters, for example, and blaming it on their blameless wards. He felt a lump grow in his throat and his eyes grow hot.

The girl had rolled away and was staring at him. To cover his embarrassment, he said, 'I'm trying to plan. We can't just sit here and freeze.'

'What do you suggest?' Allanza asked.

'All right,' Tog said. 'I've been given a mission. I'm carrying out a dying man's last wishes. He almost took his secret to his grave but just managed to get out a few dying words. You two are welcome to come along if you want.'

The words made him feel stronger and the idea that he had something to do was like a warm rock held to his belly on a cold night. He was suddenly full of love for the woodcutter who had protected him from evil, even if he had been a bad tempered, drunken old thief.

'What is it?' Allanza asked.

'I've got to get . . . somewhere . . . by full moon,' Tog said.

Allanza said, 'That's Easter. Think we'll make it?'

'We should.'

'Right. Where's this place?'

'Look for an orchard and we'll be getting somewhere. Can't say more than that.'

He nodded up the coast but the girl, who seemed to have picked up the gist of what they were saying, shook her head. She pointed at the waves and crossed her wrists in front of her.

The message was clear: go in that direction and get tied up.

'OK,' Tog said. 'We'll track inland then, um, make our way from there.'

After they had eaten, they had nothing to do but walk. Up hills and down hills, the further they went, the more anxious Tog became. The others accepted he was leading but right now he wished someone else would take a turn. The leaden sky squeezed the colour from everything and a vicious wind ripped what was left away so that everything was grey.

The fields they walked through had been worked once but were now stubbled with shrubs and last year's thistles.

The drystone walls were collapsing. Tog thought it might snow soon. Now they were climbing steadily up a long, wet, grassy slope. As they climbed, the wind in their faces grew stronger and was laced with sleet. Instinctively they got in line behind Allanza; Tog, then the girl. Tog reached his hands behind him to help drag her up. He could hear her teeth chattering.

'We can't carry on,' Tog shouted. The wind seemed to be growing even stronger. He was soaked through. 'We'll have to turn back,' he called, thinking he should have said this before they were half dead.

Allanza turned, his face running with melted sleet, his eyes as dull as the sky.

'Higher. Shelter,' he said. 'Saw it.'

Tog narrowed his eyes but all he could see was fog. They walked through a bog, feet crunching wafers of ice. The sleet was beginning to settle. Tog's world contracted to the sight of his feet splashing through mud. He had long since stopped feeling them. Behind him, he felt the girl collapse.

He helped her up and she fell over again. Her face was white and her lips were blue.

Tog tried to lift her but the bog was gripping hard. When he looked up, Allanza had disappeared in the bitter grey mist.

He knelt by her side and slid his arm under her belly. He

managed to haul her on to all fours but every time he let go, she collapsed again.

'You've got to try. I can't lift you.' But then he thought that maybe he could. Next time he got her on to all fours, he slid one shoulder underneath her and managed to work one of her arms over his other shoulder. He pushed himself up, tilting her to shift her centre of gravity until she was lying across his shoulders like a sheep.

His legs sank into the bog halfway up his shins. He was stuck.

There didn't seem much he could do. If he dropped her, he'd never get her up again. But as long as she was on his shoulders, he couldn't move. The dilemma was too hard to solve. Better to stay there, feeling like a tree in a gale. After a while, the weight of the girl lifted from his shoulders and he felt free and weightless but he couldn't unfix his legs.

The next time he felt anything, he was choking and could see the glow of a fire through his eyelids. He was so cold that the entire surface of his skin felt flayed and all he wanted to do was crawl inside himself and disappear. Then it got colder still, so cold he convinced himself that he would lose heat if he opened his eyes. When he did, he found himself lying on an earth floor in front of a dung fire that had almost gone out. His head was lying close to the girl's feet whose head was lying on Allanza's feet. The walls of the hut were stone, well plugged with earth, and the roof was turf.

Tog blew on the fire carefully to redden the glow, then carefully crumbled more of the sheep dung that was lying around on to it. He still felt chilled all the way through and his fingers barely worked, but with painstaking care he coaxed more life into the fire. He put his hands and feet close to it until the agony of returning circulation started, then he found a flat stone propped up against the wall, laid it down by the fire, and encouraged the flames to spread on to the stone, before adding more fuel. The smoke started to build and he felt strong enough to stick his head outside.

He guessed they were in a shepherd's shelter. That would explain the dung on the floor and the baffle on the door – a single large flat rock that forced any human, animal or wind to make a sharp turn before getting inside the hut. Tog wriggled round it to enter a grey world. The wind had dropped and the fog felt greasy. He wrapped his arms around himself, walked ten paces and looked behind him. The hut had disappeared. He turned carefully, placing his feet in his wet footprints, but even so, he was at the door before he saw it. How would he find water?

As he was stooping to go in, he heard a cry that was so close and so sad and sudden it raised the hair on the back of his head and tightened the skin around his heart.

The cry pierced him again. Tog took a step towards it, then another, and found the lamb caught on thorns. Somewhere nearby its mother's call blared out through the mist.

He took out his sword, moved behind the lamb but just as he was about to pull the blade across its throat, he felt a hand on his arm.

The girl pulled Tog away and motioned for him to squat. They waited. The girl listened then nodded off to her right where a patch of fog was thickening into a sheep. When the mother got close to the lamb, the girl leapt on to it and wrestled it on to its side. Tog kept it pinned down, while she went back into the shelter and came back with the bowl and Allanza. They held the sheep while she milked it, half filling the bowl. Then they freed the lamb and watched the mother and child run off.

The girl made a gesture with her arms, holding them out and spreading them wide and at that moment, a blue patch of sky appeared in front of them and the fog seemed to dance away. A few paces up the hill was a little spring, not too muddy.

They drank warm milk, cooked oatcakes, shared the last of Tog's bacon and some turnip. They had oats left for six more cakes, Allanza said sadly. Six small ones and then they were on to the fish.

Tog looked at the girl who killed people but would not kill a lamb and wondered what he had got himself into.

Smoke rising from the coast had put them in mind of the pirates again and so they headed deeper inland. Then the wind got up and the cloud dropped down and they were forced to huddle in the lee of a lonely stone circle.

Tog put all thoughts of pushing on to one side. There was no way they could survive a night in the open, which meant they had to find shelter – and fast.

Low cloud drifted around them bringing with it cold drifts of rain. What could they do? Which way to go? And then suddenly the curtains of cloud opened and he saw a long dark line snaking though the valley below them.

'There's a road down there,' he said through chattering teeth.

Allanza looked at him blankly.

'Someone might pass. They might be able to help us. It's all I can think of.'

They staggered down the rocky hillside and close to the road found a hollow under a budding thorn tree. The wind dropped; the clouds parted; nothing moved on the road. To kill time, Tog began to scratch letters in the earth. Allanza asked him what he was doing.

'Letters,' Tog said. 'They make words and the words are writing. Those are T, O and G. Spells Tog. And I'll tell you something odd. My real name's Artognu but you pronounce it Arthnu, so the Tog is sort of hidden in it, like a secret. Unless you know how to spell.'

Allanza shook his head. 'Why do that?' he asked.

Tog had never really thought about it, and shrugged. 'For fun. I'll write your name.'

'Not sure about that,' Allanza said. The girl came and knelt by them. She inspected the letters Tog had scratched. 'Do her,' Allanza suggested.

Tog pointed at his chest and said 'Tog', then at Allanza and said 'Allanza', then at the girl and shrugged. After laughing at his expression, the girl pointed at her chest and made a succession of soft sneezing noises.

'What?' said Allanza.

'She said something like Shennatennasten.'

The girl repeated the noises.

'Chenna?' Tog asked.

The girl rolled her eyes and said, 'Jenna.'

'Shenna?' Allanza tried.

'Jenna. Jenna, Jenna,' the girl said emphatically.

'Just what I said: Shenna.' Allanza sounded triumphant.

'Jenna,' Tog said but as he prepared to write, it hit him that he had only ever written in Latin before. He had no way of knowing whether it was even possible to do it in his own language.

Sweat froze on his forehead. Allanza watched him with growing respect as he fought to control a sense of panic that rose out of nowhere. Even the girl was still. Eventually he remembered that he had to break the word down in his head into little sounds, and then find a letter that matched the sound. Trouble was, the letters in his head didn't match sounds. The last bit was like 'enna' – he could manage that, but the first sound was somewhere between a T and an S with a sort of soft, comforting windy noise blended in.

He tried to go through every Latin word he had ever heard but where to start? He had a memory of starting Latin when every day involved standing in front of the woodcutter, hand outstretched to be whacked if he made a mistake.

Farmer. Table. Soldier. Citizen. Countryside. *Veni, vidi, vici.* I came, I saw, I won.

Wait a minute, Tog thought. I can do what I want! There's no one to whack me.

Tog scratched TSHENNA on the rock and stood back proudly.

Allanza put his ear to it. 'What do you do now?' he asked.

'You say it now.' Tog spelled out the letters. 'Of course, the real magic is when I write something down and then go

66

away. It means that if you come along later, you can see what I want to tell you without me being there,' Tog said.

'Why can't someone else tell me?'

'There is no one else,' Tog said, not really ready for the objection.

'There might be,' Allanza said warily.

'Yes, but suppose there isn't.'

'What would you tell me?'

'A message like: "I ate all the pies." '

'But that's not a name.'

'Writing can be anything you like. A while back I found this stone slab with writing on it that must have been done years before. It was Latin. *Rex quondam rexque futurus.*'

Tog went through it again, word by word, then tried to get Allanza to repeat the first two.

'Rexquodfute . . .' he began. His face went red.

'*Rex quondam rexque futurus,*' the girl chanted. She had a memorable, husky voice. '*Rexquondamrexquefuturusrequon dam – Rexque.*'

Tog stared at her, aware that his mouth was open, but not inclined to close it. Could she speak Latin too?

'I thought that was my spell,' Allanza protested.

Tog ignored him. '*Ne linguam romanorum loquitur?*' he asked the girl. Do you speak the language of the Romans?

'Neling urmromitus,' the girl said.

67

'Oh well,' Tog said, and sighed. She was just a mimic.

'Ohwell,' the girl said and sighed. She squatted on the ground and looked at the word, her head tilted to one side like a bird.

'Jenna,' she said. She pointed at the word and then at her chest.

'And she's got a name as well!' Allanza said. 'This isn't fair.'

He stood up, looking furious, then he turned to them with a new expression on his face. 'I think I can see people coming,' he said.

Tog counted them as they came down the hill, fifteen in all, led by a hooded man on a muddy white horse, its head low and loose. Half a dozen men and women walking on foot followed. In the middle of the procession came two heavy four-wheeled carts each pulled by two oxen. Behind the cart walked a group of four men and behind them a bearded man in a bright red cloak, accompanied by a burly fair-haired man who walked with a huge, shoulder-swinging stride. A polished helmet on a strap bounced halfway down his back and you could see the hilt of his sword poking up from behind his shoulder. Walking each side of the procession were guards who shouldered short spears.

Tog grew more and more annoyed as his polite greetings were ignored. By the time the last person had passed, he had grown sarcastic and was very rude in Latin.

To his horror, the man in the red cloak stopped and turned.

'*Num Cicero ipse nos adloquitar? Tanta est illi ars, tanta facundia, tanta eloquentia!?*' he called out, bright eyes darting between them.

'What did he say?' hissed Allanza.

'Surely that's not Cicero himself talking to us? He has such skill, such something, such eloquence,' Tog said miserably.

'And what did you call out?'

'I called them a pack of whoreson bitches that smelled of dead gazelles' bottoms. I didn't think they'd speak Latin.'

'What's a gazelle?'

'Never mind. We're in trouble.'

'No, you're in trouble,' Allanza corrected him reasonably.

The man in the red cloak approached them. He was small and wore a strange beard around his mouth and chin. He had bushy eyebrows that moved up and down like caterpillars and a thick, bulbous nose. He had hairy nostrils, hairy ears, and hairy cheekbones. More hair fountained up from the collar of his cloak and poured down his arms on to the back of his hands and fingers as far as the second knuckle.

He got close to Tog and squinted at him. They were more or less the same height. He looked Allanza up and down, making a good show of being surprised, and tilted his head on one side while scrutinizing Jenna.

'They don't look like pirates, do they?' the hairy man said to the big fair-haired man. His accent was oddly musical.

'Sneak-thieves if you ask me.' The big man's accent, in contrast, was harsh and gutteral.

'I quite agree. But one of them's a thief that speaks Latin like a bishop crossed with a Karduchi docker. Which one of you called out?' His head darted at each of them in turn, like a grass snake striking at frogs. 'You? No. A wild girl. Pictish, I'd say. You? Hard to believe that a boy who can't be bothered to close his mouth could have such a nimble tongue. Which leaves you.' He walked around Tog, sniffing. 'What do you think, Borth? Under the filth, could there be a brain?'

'Hate kids,' the big man said. 'Might make something of this one, if he wasn't British of course,' he said, looking Allanza up and down with small grey eyes pushed apart by a flattened nose.

'I'm sorry, Lord,' Tog said. 'It was an accident. I didn't know what the words meant. I was just trying to catch someone's attention.'

'Well, you certainly caught mine. Are you begging?'

'We're cold and hungry and need help.'

'So, you're begging. Be honest. At times we all beg, eh, Borth?'

'You're wasting your time, Melanius.' The way the big man said it suggested he had said it many times before. Tog felt his senses sharpen. They were friends, but competitive. And the hairy man liked being interested in things.

'I've got money,' Tog said, reaching inside his tunic.

'What would a brat like you be doing with money?'

As Tog took a step backwards, the hairy man took a step towards him, shadowed by the brute.

'Nothing. I'm just . . . Get back! I've got a sword!'

But before Tog could get his hand anywhere near it, Borth's blade pressed down into his throat while Melanius's pointed up into Allanza's midriff.

'Three children, armed and dangerous, with money. Interesting blade by the way,' he said to Tog. 'And you—' Without moving his eyes away from Tog, he reached out and yanked the neck of Jenna's dress down to reveal the raw marks the slavers' ropes had left. 'You, at any rate, are a slave. So the question is not so much *who* as *whose* are you?'

The action had attracted attention further up the convoy. There was a shout and the guards with the short spears started running back towards them.

'Tell us who you are quickly, if you want help,' Melanius

snapped. 'Those men would as soon kill you as look at you.'

'Why should we trust you?' Tog demanded.

'Oh, I don't recommend trusting me, but I generally hold to my bargains. Now, who are you?'

'I found them,' Tog said. 'They'd been captured by pirates. I rescued them.'

'And the pirates?'

'We killed them.'

'Hid the bodies?'

'No. Their friends found them.'

The eyebrows crawled halfway up Melanius's forehead. 'Just as well they didn't find you. Keep your secrets for now,' he said. His eyes lingered on them one by one before he turned to the guards.

'Late as usual. If they were pirates we'd be spitted, skinned and our ears sold as trinkets by now, but never mind. These are lost children and it amuses me to walk with them awhile.'

The taller guard said, 'We don't care what you feel. Crotus wants to see them.'

'And why would the great Crotus want to do that?' Melanius asked.

'None of your business, foreigner,' the smaller one answered. He looked at Allanza and prodded him with his spear tip. 'If you want trouble, I'm your man.'

* * *

Crotus had grey hair, yellow eyes and yellow skin with cheeks so sunken it looked as if he were sucking them in. His teeth were long and yellow and his strong, ridged fingernails were blue-brown, like flint. Wrapped in a thick blue robe clasped at the neck by an ornate golden brooch, he still could not stop an envious look at Melanius's cloak of startling red. Just a quick glance up and down, but it was enough.

'Do I really need you here, merchant?' he asked in a phlegmy voice. 'And your Jutland attack dog?'

'English attack dog, My Lord. Much superior. Just wanted to see if I could help My Lord,' Melanius answered easily.

'To spy, you mean. And snoop. To scavenge for tittle-tattle to sell to the highest bidder. You're a crow with a purse who has hijacked my sacred pilgrimage. Or perhaps you have caught wind of more important matters.'

'What matters would those be, My Lord? The fine weather has brought out the comedian in you. You are reminding us all that it was my purse that bought these guards after the last lot ran off with the bulk of your supplies.'

Crotus expelled a pellet of grey spittle. A well-dressed attendant with eyes as flat as skin wiped his lips and beard.

'What do you think, Pyrs?' The king flicked his eyes sideways and up.

73

'Search the brats, My Lord.'

The soldiers did this with brutal efficiency. The slavers' sack was emptied; Tog's sword and even the half coin were found.

'What do you think?' Crotus asked Pyrs.

'The bowl is black oak – the sort of thing Irish pirates like.' He squinted at the disc. 'This is a coin that's been cut in half. It's old. From a gravehoard, I'd say.'

'And the sword?'

'Bronze. Older than the coin.'

The old man's eyes floated from Allanza to Jenna to Tog, where they settled and hardened. 'So, we have grave-robbing pirate spies. Did you find out that, merchant?' he sneered at Melanius. 'Did you know that pirates send children to scout along the road for victims?'

'But we're—' Tog began but was silenced by a spear jab in his back. Crotus ignored him and looked at Pyrs. 'Shall we kill them now or in the morning?'

'Now, My Lord. Less trouble,' Pyrs said.

'True, but their bodies might attract dogs.'

'But we're not spies,' Tog said desperately. 'We took the bowl off slavers who we killed with the sword. Look! We took this off them too.'

He held up the bear claw. Crotus favoured him with a glance, then looked at Melanius. 'Well, trader?'

'If it's of any interest, Lord, that tallies with my investigations,' Melanius answered. 'The girl and the tall boy have rope burns from halters. The other one says he rescued them. At least question them to find out what they know.'

'I see,' the old man said to Tog. 'So you took the bowl and bear claw off the pirate but say the sword is yours?'

'Yes. I . . . found it.'

'Where?'

'I don't know the place. Near the . . .' He wanted to lie but could not think of what to say.

'Yes? Near the . . .' In his closed hand, the half coin rattled against a ring. 'A better lie would have been to say that you found them in the sack with the bowl, the turnips and oats. Then you could have blamed the grave-theft on the pirate. Wouldn't you say, Pyrs?'

'Yes, Lord.'

'Perhaps the merchant could help us?' Crotus opened his hand to show the coin against his soft, grey palms. Although Melanius was pretending not to care, Tog thought he was thrumming like a taut string. He took the gold disc and scrutinized it. 'It's from my neck of the woods,' he said. 'And here, it's hard to read in this light, you can just see some letters: CONSTA. Then the cut. Still, that must be the Emperor Constantine.'

75

'And why would the Emperor Constantine send his coin here, merchant?'

'The Emperor would know nothing of such things, having been dead these last one hundred and twenty years.'

'I know that!' the old man snapped. 'How did you get it, boy? Tell the truth. I would not kill my worst enemy for gold but I would spit a child that lied to me.'

'I told you all I know, Lord.'

Tog closed his eyes and braced himself. Nothing happened. When he opened them, he found that Crotus was balancing his sword on his outstretched finger.

'We'll talk more about these matters,' Crotus said. 'And meanwhile I'll look after this.' His hand closed over the sword's hilt. 'And the gold, merchant?'

'I—' Tog said but Melanius's hand clamped down on his wrist and squeezed the nerve.

'Looks like I'll have to feed them for nothing,' Melanius said. He shook the half coin in his fist so it rattled against his rings, then handed it over.

'And they'll rob you,' Pyrs said.

'My friend Borth would never let that happen. Being English, he never sleeps,' Melanius answered easily.

'That's right,' Borth said. 'On account of all the babies I eat. Their little bones are hard to digest.'

* * *

76

Melanius's meal was prepared by the cart driver, Glyn, and his wife Ula. He was small and wiry; she was large and motherly. She made a great show of being appalled by Tog, Allanza and Jenna's skinniness and told Jenna repeatedly how sorry she was for her, being foreign and all that. When she thought no one was looking, she popped bits of the stew straight into the girl's mouth and called her my little grass stem, twig, frond, pine needle – anything small and thin, in fact.

After they had eaten, Melanius sat Tog down by the fire. In spite of the food, better than anything the woodcutter had ever cooked, Tog felt sick at the loss of his sword. It represented his last link with the past and now it was gone, casually stolen by a bully.

'So, mystery boy. Your friend seems interested in Borth,' Melanius nodded at Allanza, who was following every movement the Englishman made as he checked the cart. 'Ever seen an Englishman before?'

'I can't speak for Allanza but I'd never have anything to do with an Englishman,' Tog said haughtily. 'They're the most violent, sacrilegious, stupid, cruel and barbaric people on earth – everyone knows that – but they always get their way because of their low animal cunning and brutish determination.'

'It may interest you to know that particular Englishman

has just saved your life. You think you'd be sitting here with me if Borth hadn't been looming in the background? Pyrs would have hung you by the thumbs from the nearest tree, if he could find one.'

'I'm quite capable of looking after myself,' Tog said. 'Six people have tried to kill me in . . .' he counted on his fingers, '. . . five nights. I'm still alive.'

'Six?' Melanius said. 'You're either very lucky or very clever. I know about Crotus. Who would the rest be?'

'Well, Pyrs,' Tog said. 'Then the pirates. Then two cavalrymen from the castle . . .'

'You got away from two horsemen? That was lucky.'

'Luck didn't come into it,' Tog said. 'First I hid in dead ground – a dip in the road where they couldn't see me. When they found me there I made for broken ground to slow the horses down and cut their advantage. But all the time I was working towards a nemeton – a sacred wood. You see, they didn't believe I'd dare go into it so they didn't really try to cut me off.'

'And you planned that?' Melanius said.

'You don't plan,' Tog said. 'You just use whatever you've got. When the stranger attacked I was lucky to find the knife but I knew how to use it.'

Melanius was counting on his fingers. 'Hold on,' he said. 'That makes seven people.'

Tog had decided to leave out the stranger in case people somehow found out he was wanted for murder, but now his tongue had run away from him and he had been caught out.

'Did I say six? I must have been getting confused.'

'And this stranger?'

'Did I say stranger?'

'And six, but it's none of my business really. Come on. It's too late for silence now. Anyway, I'm your protector – you have to suck up to me. Now, who taught you all these tricks?'

'My guardian. A woodcutter. Well, he was probably an ex-monk.'

'Some monk,' Melanius reflected. 'Fascinating. You see right now, I could be lounging on the terrace of my villa in Constantinople, a gentle breeze ruffling my hair, sipping wine, nibbling cheese, waiting for slaves to bring me the first course of a banquet involving obscene quantities of rare birds, but here I am instead: being fascinated by an urchin with hair like a hedgerow and a face like . . . hmmm. Where are you from?'

'The castle. It's a royal palace.'

'I know many palaces,' the trader said simply. 'But let's assume you mean the high queen's heap of stones down the coast. Here's another thing. Did you ever wonder why a Pict girl has ended up here, for goodness' sake, as far away from Pictland as it's possible to get? Or why the Cornish kings are too proud to band together against the pirates? Or why . . . ? Oh never mind. Your turn. What interests you? Amaze me.'

Tog flushed. 'I know Crotus and Pyrs don't like you because they think you're a spy. I know Crotus is ill from the way he looks.'

'Do you know where he's going and why?'

'He said something about a . . . pilgrimage?' Tog hesitated over the new word.

'That's right. He's on his way to the Island – Ynis Avalon to give it its correct name. It sticks up from the middle of a big marsh about a week's journey north of here. You must have heard of it.'

Tog shrugged.

'They say it's guarded by creatures that are half men, half fish. The Island's got this peak in the middle and under it there's a glass door which is the only place you can see the underworld from without actually having to visit.'

'Is that what Crotus wants to do? On his pilgrimage?'

'He uses the word loosely. Pilgrimages are Christian and he's a pagan through and through. The idea is, if you're sick, you visit a church or a shrine that has got something holy in it: a fragment of the true cross, a saint's head or knuckle bone. Of course, you can't get a bit of the Christ himself because all of him went up to heaven, even his fingernails and hair cuttings, according to the experts. But on the Island you've got monks who look after a holy spring created by the Christ himself when he visited Britain exactly four hundred and eighty-eight years ago. Or so the monks say. Right now, the high king's there, hoping the spring water will cure him. He's called the tribes together to sort out a successor. That's the real reason Crotus is dragging himself away from his hovel.'

'Will it work?' Tog asked.

'The assembly? I doubt it. The tribes might agree on a new leader, a Dux Britanniorum, but it won't hold. There's too much history between them and whoever's chosen will have fought or betrayed someone else in the past. It's a shame. Right now they need someone more than ever.'

'I meant the spring,' Tog said.

Melanius raised an eyebrow. 'If only the young would get interested in politics. In my opinion, the spring won't work. The high king would be better off sitting in an orchard and watching the apples ripen. An apple a day—'

'Orchards?' Tog interrupted. 'Are there orchards on the Island?'

'Now he's interested in orchards! Only the most famous orchards in the country.'

'Ah. The, er, assembly sounds really interesting,' Tog said earnestly. 'And all the . . . er, other stuff.'

Melanius smiled fondly. 'Liar. You're learning. You see, unlike Crotus, I like that in a person.'

Well fed and warm, Tog, Allanza and Jenna slept in a corner of the cart, under the cover. In the night, Tog went over what Melanius said about the Island – Ynis Avalon.

Point One: there were orchards on it, the most famous in the country

Point Two: orchards had been one of the last things the woodcutter had thought of

Point Three: there were monks on the Island

Point Four: monks knew Latin and so did the woodcutter

Why he had to go there was another question altogether, but that was just typical of the woodcutter. It was always do this, do that and a cuff round the ear if he asked too many questions, as if, as if . . . everything was a secret. Now he was on his own, Tog had a chance to find answers.

In Tog's dream that night, Jenna was cutting the throats of pirates, one after the other, but instead of bleeding blood, bright green apples rolled out of the slits in their throats. 'Bloody apples everywhere,' Allanza said, holding their wooden bowl that was brimming with blood. 'What we need is a lamb for the slaughter.'

Tog tried to say something but suddenly realized that he was covered in white lamb's wool. Jenna and Allanza saw him, and chased him all round an island until he was caught by the stranger who was really a woodwose in disguise. He grabbed Tog's head, pulled it back and said to Jenna: 'Once a lamb, always a lamb.' He took the bronze sword and . . .

Tog woke up shouting. The air in the back of the cart was close and stifling. Next to him, Allanza rolled over and muttered sleepily. Tog was so wide awake he might have been dreaming and pushed himself out from under the cover and drank in the cold night air.

Frost glittered under the starlight. The camp was in darkness apart from a glow coming from Crotus's tent. The stiff grass creaked under Tog's feet as he tiptoed towards the light, curious to see why the old king was still up.

He heard voices. 'That's it. Gently does it. I think . . . I think. It is, you know. It is!' Crotus's voice crackled with excitement. 'Give it to me! Give it to me. I knew it. As soon as I saw it, I knew.'

'And the boy?'

'He knows nothing. An urchin.'

'But he was carrying it.'

'He carried it to me! It's fate. You know the rhyme.'

The entrance to the tent was tightly laced. Tog worked his way round to the back where light leaked from a loose seam and pressed his eye to the gap. In the smoky torchlight he saw Crotus and Pyrs, bent over something, peering at it.

'Do you see the man deep down there in the blade? The shining man! Look at him move. Look at him dance.'

Crotus lifted Tog's sword into the light and turned it. The sword had been polished and Tog could not believe how it had changed. It was beautiful and deadly like a tongue of pale flame and on the blade, traced in silver, a shape that Tog could not quite make out but that made the skin across his forehead tighten. He shifted closer, lost his balance, brushed against the tent.

'What's that?'

'I'll see, My Lord.'

Already Pyrs was fumbling with the tent's laces.

'Cut them, man. Cut them.'

Tog sped across the grass, heading for the comforting black bulk of the cart. Crashed into something big and solid that shouldn't have been there.

'Get behind me. Into the cart.' Borth growled like a dog.

Tog dodged round the back, pushed his way under

84

the covers and lay in the darkness, panting and shivering. He heard voices, quiet at first and then raised louder. He lifted the cart cover and peered out.

Pyrs was confronting Borth, waving the torch in his face, making his shadow move though the man himself was immobile. Guards ran up. Borth shrugged, turned his back and walked away. The king's servant reached into his tunic for a knife but Borth, in a movement that Tog did not quite understand, was not where he had been and was grasping Pyrs, turning him and bending his arm so the knife was suddenly pointing up at Pyrs's neck.

A twist and it had fallen.

Borth stalked back to the cart. As he passed Tog he muttered, 'Only idiots leave tracks in the frost. Remember that for next time, British boy.'

Tog looked down at the ground to a mess of criss-crossing black trails in the frost and realized that the Englishman had walked in his footprints to cover them.

They set off the next day under a hard blue sky. The air was so pure and clean you could drink it, though Tog's thoughts were cloudy. The sword was magic: no doubt about it. It had a shining man – possibly the little man the woodcutter had mentioned – trapped inside it and the thought made Tog's head swim. Why hadn't the woodcutter told him? If he had known, he would have been much more careful with it. And the way Pyrs and Crotus had been looking at it left him in no doubt that this was the treasure that the stranger was after. Should he tell Melanius? That was a big question. On the one hand, he didn't know if he could really trust him, but on the other there was a chance he might help.

Glyn kept twisting round on the ox cart seat and looking over his shoulder until Ula asked him snappily what the matter was.

'First thing this morning I thought I saw a rider behind us.'

'So?'

'He should have overtaken us by now.'

'So he's taking his time.'

'But I can't think what he's doing.'

'Minding his own business is what he's doing.'

'Boy,' Glyn called. 'You tell Borth, all right?'

Tog nodded, hiding his panic. If the stranger caught up with them, he'd accuse Tog of murder and that would be the final straw. No one would believe Tog's side of the story now. It was obvious that he should have told them that he was being chased by a murderer from the outset.

Then someone called out and he saw that every spare person was gathering round the carts. They had stopped on the top of a steep, downward slope. Ropes were looped round the axles and everyone had to lean back hard on them to stop the carts from running away down hill.

Then the road began to sink between high walls of green and Tog saw Melanius looking anxiously around. As soon as the ground levelled out, Tog followed him to the front of the procession and caught him saying to Crotus, 'It's a perfect place for an ambush. Look ahead! There's a bend in the road. We can't even see what's coming.'

Crotus favoured him with a bleak smile. 'Be still. What will be, will be. I know this place and what it brings, even if you don't. There, you see? I sent word ahead. My friends are waiting for me.'

Sure enough, as they turned the corner, two horsemen blocked the way. They sat on black horses, wrapped in black cloaks and had black scarves wrapped around their heads. Tog caught the glimmer of jet on the pommel of a sword.

Crotus kept his horse walking at the same steady pace, only raising his hand as he approached the two men.

'Pilgrims,' he said. 'Asking free passage.'

One of the men unwound his black scarf from his mouth. 'I see pilgrims,' he said. 'And others, unless pilgrims wear red cloaks or disguise themselves as Englishmen.'

'My name is Melanius of Constantinople and all I

ask is for safe passage through these lands,' Melanius said smoothly.

'My name is Dilwin of wherever you bloody well want,' the rider said. 'What about the Englishman?'

'My bodyguard, Borthweald. He poses no threat.'

'I never said he did,' the rider replied. 'It would take more than a foreign mercenary to worry me. We just like to know who's moving where and why.'

'I'm a simple merchant on his way to Aquae Sulis and beyond.'

'What about the children?'

'Them?' Melanius said. 'Oh, just my party. I may have some use for them along the way.'

'You'll have to be escorted through Govannnon's country and that'll cost you.'

'And if we don't want to pay?' Borth asked.

Tog heard a pebble fall and looked up to a skyline hedged with archers, bows drawn, arrows pointing down. Melanius inclined his head.

'We are grateful and happy to pay for such protection,' he said.

They set off, closely flanked by the archers. Tog could see they were all wearing something black, even if it was just a rag tied around their wrist. Many of the men had shaved their heads apart from a long, heavily greased ponytail with black feathers stuck into it. They were restless and jittery and reminded Tog of a pack of dogs with not quite enough to do.

Govannon did not have a castle or anything like one. His big roundhouse sat like a topknot on the summit of a small, fortified hill. Halfway up the slope, a deep, steep-sided trench was topped by a line of sharpened stakes, dotted with rotting heads. Then another trench and then a wall. The entrance snaked to the left and the right between the fortifications.

They rumbled slowly past it. Ahead, a ragbag band of soldiers approached, some with the familiar black scarves and turbans, others wearing plaid tunics and their long beards plaited into two long forks. Tog's heart started to pound.

'There you are, brother Poraig.' Dilwin addressed one of the men wearing a plaid tunic. He held up a hand and the convoy stopped. 'How's business?'

'Nothing today. Nothing yesterday,' the man called Poraig called back. 'And we're off tomorrow.' Tog felt a big cold hand squeeze his heart. Poraig's accent was exactly the same as the slavers' they had killed.

The party moved to the side of the road to let the carts pass and Tog felt their eyes flick over them. He glanced back. Allanza was stooping down to disguise his height but in so doing had attracted the attention of Ula, who asked him loudly if he was all right.

Tog jumped up on to the side of the cart and ran along its edge, relieved to see that Jenna was hidden from sight behind a wheel. He knelt by Ula. 'Leave him be,' he whispered. 'He's fine.'

'Fine?' Ula replied. 'Fine? I only asked if he had a blister.' She tossed her hair in a silly way and Tog realized that she was putting on a sort of misjudged show for the soldiers and slavers.

'Leave it. Please,' Tog pleaded in her ear. He risked a look. They had passed the party now and none of them was looking interested.

Ula pouted in a hurt sort of way. 'I'll explain later,' Tog said.

They were past now. In the clear. Space was opening up between them and the other men.

'Hey!'

The voice rang out loud and clear. Ula began to pull on the reins. 'Keep going,' Tog hissed. 'Keep going.'

'I can't, dearie, not with everyone else stopped. What's got into you anyway?'

Then the man called Poraig called out. 'Just for the record: I don't suppose any of you have seen a few child slaves on the run?'

At that point, Allanza broke cover and ran.

It was hopeless. The archers surrounded the convoy to stop any of them helping him and the man with the plaited beard set off at an easy lope. He overtook Allanza before he was halfway across the next field, tripped him, slipped the halter round his neck and led him back as if he were a cow. Meanwhile, one of the others found Jenna under the cart and pulled her out by the feet.

'So,' the slaver said. 'Whose are these?'

'Mine, if anyone's,' Melanius said in measured voice. 'They joined us a few days back. I was going to sell them in my own good time.'

'They're ours. Two of our party who were looking after them got separated from us. We found them hamstrung and their throats slit. Horrible to think that kids could do a thing like that. We've got some of his lot back at the holding pen, if you want more proof.'

He poked Allanza in the stomach with his sword.

'So you say,' Melanius protested. 'I don't mind you taking back what's yours but I'm reluctant to give you what isn't. I've fed them for three days now and want something out of it. What about the girl?'

'We found her living rough on the coast. As for payment,

you must be joking. You've been sheltering them which makes you guilty. If you want to die with them, so be it.'

'When did a freeman of Constantinople have to accept a pirate's justice?' Melanius asked.

'A pirate? I'm a trader, like you. I just deal in livestock.'

'Which you've stolen in the first place. You can hardly complain if you lose something that wasn't yours.'

'Two of my men . . .'

'Gentlemen, gentlemen, please,' Dilwin broke in. 'Fun though this is, we're getting nowhere. Are these children murderers? Escaped slaves? Both? I don't care. But if you can't sort out your differences, I know someone who can. You.' He pointed to Melanius. 'And you, Poraig.' He pointed to the slaver. 'Argue your case in front of Govannon. Now turn that cart round and let's get moving.'

III

Last Quarter

Tog was tied down over a rock, facing upwards and bent backwards. If he rolled his eyes to the top of his head, he could just see the wavy line of the horizon and he hurt more than he had ever hurt in his life. The sky was cold and white and burned his eyes. Tears gathered under his eyebrows before running down his forehead. Snot dribbled over his cheeks and he could feel the damn necklace against his skin. One of the slavers had somehow seen it and recognized the bear claw. That was enough to get Tog captured as well. He should never have accepted it. He should have torn it off. Now he had failed the woodcutter.

A crow sometimes circled overhead and he knew it was only a matter of time before it landed on his chest and pecked his eyes out. If he strained to look to his left, he could just see Jenna and Allanza tied to a thick wooden post by their necks.

The rock and the post stood on a raised hummock in the middle of the slave pen. There were countless slaves in it, all with their hands tied and all wearing huge, heavy wooden boards around their necks. The boards, two bits of wood joined together with a neck-sized hole in the middle, made it impossible to do much. Even lying down was torture as the edge cut into your neck. Because of these precautions and the stockade of sharpened stakes around the pen, the slaves didn't have that many guards.

Tog could hear the sea and feel its cold breath. It got dark and he got colder and colder. When the moon rose, it grew colder still. He couldn't believe how unfair life was.

The trial had taken place in Govannon's hall. The walls and roof of the hall were smoked black and the sun that slanted down through the smoke hole was a golden blade. Tog watched Govannon through the light. Black hair, clean white skin, a flashing smile, but there was something blurred about his outline. His face was puffy, his eyes bloodshot and he lounged in his throne of old black wood and gold inlay as if he wished it were a bed. Tog, Allanza and Jenna were told to stand in front of the throne. Melanius was on their right, the slaver on their left.

'Now, what's going on?' Govannon's voice was surprisingly

light and slightly jokey. 'I really can't see how this concerns me. I know we lease facilities to Irish businessmen but we've made it clear that our responsibility ends there. Security, maintenance and upkeep are their concern, not ours.'

'I thought there might be violence, Lord,' Dilwin said stoutly. 'I thought it best you adjuc—'

'Adjudicate?' the king asked with an innocent lift of the eyebrows. The group of men clustered around him and behind him laughed creepily. 'Very well. Yes. I hate violence as all good-thinking men do. But let's be quick about it. You, merchant. You have a foreign look about you.' Govannon moved his head to show a thick gold chain around his neck.

'Melanius of Constantinople, Lord. A humble Greek merchant who is a long way from home and seeking only safe passage through your magnificent country.'

'And a fair price for everything.'

'Quite so,' Melanius said, smiling humbly. 'My only concern is that having looked after these children, not only preventing them from starving but actually building them up, I am reluctant to hand them over to a man who will be able to sell them on at a higher price than otherwise he would have been able to, as a result of my care and attention, not to mention the wages I pay the cook, the price of barley, fodder for the oxen and so on.'

'I see. And friend Poraig. What have you to say to Melanius?'

'Simply this. If you feed another man's cow in the hope of keeping it, you should be grateful when he just asks for it back and doesn't take your head with it. He knew what he was doing and, My Lord, he knew they were murderers. They killed two good men with wives and children who will now go hungry.'

'Some would say your two good men couldn't have been up to much if they were killed by these brats.'

'Witchcraft, My Lord. When Picts think of killing, they go invisible. It's well known. And it's me that's got to answer to their widows back home.'

'She looks like she wants to kill us all,' Govannon said. 'But I can still see her. At least I *think* I can.' Hoots of laughter. 'However, I agree. Such things are not to be taken lightly and justice must be done.' Govannon stood and raised his arms above his head. 'Very well. I have decided. Poraig to pay the merchant eight handfuls of barley, two armfuls of fodder and give him hearty thanks for his trouble. The merchant to give up the brats to Poraig and I give him the Cornish boy as a goodwill gesture. Is that fair?'

Melanius and Poraig both answered in the affirmative and everyone clapped. Govannon called for a beaker of mead while Tog, Jenna and Allanza were led off.

'I'm going to kill Melanius when I get out of this,' Allanza muttered. 'Why didn't anyone stand up for us?' Then he started to cry.

When Tog saw the holding pen, he wanted to cry too. It lay about a mile from Govannon's hall, down a valley that led to the sea. A stream ran through the middle of it and the swampy ground had been churned into mud deep enough to drown in. A few prisoners stood. Most sat or knelt. They made Tog feel almost clean.

Poraig had taken against Tog in particular. 'The brother of one of the men you killed is sailing in tomorrow and we'll see what he wants to do to you. Maybe he'll kill you here. Maybe he'll take you home to the widow and see what she wants to do.'

Tog couldn't talk because he had a leather gag in his mouth. Allanza was looking around, trying to spot his relatives. But no one called out. All around, they saw defeated eyes staring out of staring, filthy faces.

Poraig cast his eyes at the horizon and said, 'This place is really giving me the creeps. The boats should be here tomorrow to take this sorry lot to God's own country.'

A vole, smaller than Tog's finger, scurried upside down across the roof of the earth, jerking him out of his lethargy.

The creature paused above his head and started nosing in the mud for some invisible scrap of food. It was sleek with wet, splattered with mud and had a pronounced limp but it still carried on doing its voley thing.

Drawn backwards like a bow, and with lumps of stone digging into his back, Tog started to shift to ease the pain and found that by bracing his heels against the rock, he could push forwards and take the strain off his wrists. With the strain off his wrists, he found that the thongs tying him down were loose – as if the guards were used to tying them on to thicker wrists than his. By forcing one shoulder up, he could create even more slack on the other wrist and discovered that the straps were partly being held on him by tension. In other words, the less the tension, the more chance he had of forcing the bonds over the heel of his palm. The problem was, pushing down with his heels against the rock gave him cramp in his legs, so that slowed him down, and holding one shoulder up made his muscles scream if he did it for more than a second or two, so that that slowed him down even more. Still, by dint of ignoring the cramp and screaming pain, he did manage to get the leather loop over the heel of his palm, and by wriggling and tugging, he felt it scrape its dry, leathery way over his hand. He twisted sideways, worked the other strap free then forced his stretched muscles to pull him upright. The absence of pain was as shocking as the pain itself. He could hardly get his fingers to fumble the ankle ties free and the only way he could reach Jenna and Allanza was by rowing on his side through the mud.

Jenna and Allanza were tied to a pole by a single rope so that if one of them moved, the other got strangled. It took a while for Tog to work this out and then even longer to unpick the knot with his numb fingers. They both collapsed, coughing.

'We've got to move qu-qu-quick.' Now Tog was free, his body was trying to shake itself apart. 'They'll 'spect us go th-tha-that way. Go th'other.'

They began to crawl through the scattered mass of slaves. At first, it looked as if they were sleeping but when Tog looked more closely, he saw the moon pool in the whites of watching eyes. Allanza stopped and stared into the face of a sleeping girl.

'Wwwhat is it?' Tog asked.

'M-my family m-might be here,' Allanza whispered back, his voice shuddering with him. 'You h-heard the man earlier.'

'They've prob-bably gone,' Tog said. 'It looks lll-like they're emptying the camp.' Now he was free, he felt an urgent sense of selfishness. All he wanted to do was get out as quickly as possible from this hell.

'You don't know that. You go if you have to. I'm staying.'

Tog sighed and looked around. There was no sign of the guards and provided they kept low, he guessed that they would not be too visible. He groaned inwardly and followed Allanza.

They passed from huddle to huddle. Sometimes people were asleep and Allanza would be cursed as he lifted a chin or turned a face towards him. Sometimes the whole group would be awake and people would beg them to untie them. They started off untying everyone they saw but this took too long and so they left the freed slaves to free their companions.

On and on they went. Tog was used to the stinking mud by now and no longer gagged when they passed shallow graves where dead slaves were buried. There were a lot of them and the smell hung over some areas of the camp like a mist.

Tog was sure they had covered the whole area and started to urge Allanza towards the perimeter fence, as far away from the entrance as they could get. One good thing: the moon was down so they were less likely to be spotted. One bad thing: it would be hard to escape in the total darkness and it would be light before they could get far away.

Ahead, Jenna was hissing at them and pointing at

the fence but Allanza was like a dog that didn't want to leave a bone.

'Come on,' Tog pleaded. 'We're running out of time.'

'We haven't looked in that corner.'

'There isn't—'

'I've got to check. You go if you want; I don't care. Just let me be.'

Tog was about to tell him how useless it would be when a voice called out from a pile of bodies huddled against the wooden uprights of the fence.

'Someone said my name!' Allanza said. 'Someone knows me!'

He broke away from Tog and splashed through the mud in the direction of the sound, calling out, 'It's me, Allanza! It's me!'

Tog followed, appalled at the noise he was making, but unable to call out for fear of attracting more attention. Allanza was swallowed by an indistinct mound of bodies and when Tog found him, he was on his knees, rocking back and forth, holding the hand of an old man who was lying on his back in the mud.

'It's our neighbour,' he said. 'He's from my village. He's alive.'

The old man's eyes flickered open and his mouth twitched.

'Don't worry. I'll get you out of here. I'll get you home.' Allanza patted his hand, touched his face, smoothed his hair.

Sounds rattled in the old man's throat as he spoke. Allanza bent his head to listen.

'They took my family away from this place to Ireland two days ago, he just told me. They were here. All the people from my village were here and they took them two days ago in boats. My mother. My father. My sisters. I've only just missed them.'

Then Tog heard the sound he was dreading. In the middle of the field, someone shouted. The shout was picked up from further away.

'That's it,' Tog said. 'Now we've got to go. They'll start searching the camp and find us!'

'Go!' The old man echoed him hoarsely. 'I'm dying and I'll die on you if you take me. Go and it'll make my going easier. Towards the sea the fence is lower. Go, Allanza. Live so you can find your family.'

Reluctantly Allanza allowed Tog to lead him away. Under a greying sky they found a place where the ground rose and the fence stakes had been blunted to make climbing easier. In their complacency, the guards had not bothered to repair them.

Allanza went down on all fours, Tog stood on his back so

that Jenna could climb up Tog and pull herself on to the top of the fence. Next Allanza cupped his hands to make a stirrup for Tog, then hoisted him up on to his shoulders.

That's when they hit the snag. Neither Jenna nor Tog was strong enough to pull Allanza up. Each time, the weight of the giant boy threatened to pull them over.

There was only one thing to do. Tog jumped down and told Allanza to climb up on to his shoulders.

'Are you sure you can support me?' Allanza asked.

''Course I am,' Tog answered. He braced his back against the fence, and bent his knee. Allanza stepped on to it, then put one foot on to Tog's shoulder. The pressure down was enormous and Tog thought his shoulder was going to break. He felt a scrabbling above his head, then Allanza's second enormous foot landed on his other shoulder. Tog nearly buckled. The pressure ran right down his spine into his hip and to his bent knees. He felt them trying to give and jammed his back harder against the fence, fighting against the slipping mud.

'Almost there. Almost there,' Allanza muttered. 'Give me another push.'

Above them, Jenna gave a warning whistle.

Tog tried to jam his feet into the mud and strained to straighten his legs.

Jenna whistled again.

Tog forced his eyes open.

Two men were walking towards them, Poraig and the stranger. They were not even hurrying and the slaves flinched from them. The freed slaves were nowhere to be seen.

Then Tog felt a slight lightening of his load as Allanza's scrabbling fingers hooked over the edge of the fence. He pushed up and the weight was suddenly gone. Poraig and the stranger were closer now. He turned. Allanza and Jenna were astride the fence, reaching down. He jumped but couldn't get the muscles in his legs to do much. He'd have to take a run at it but would only have time for one go.

'Now, now,' Poraig said. 'What's going on here, then? Just when I brought someone to meet you.' Ominously, he wasn't running.

'Jump!' Allanza shouted. Tog stepped back and took a running jump at the wall, trying to run up it. His fingers slapped the wood, touched skin. He felt a hand close on his, then he fell back.

'Get away,' he hissed. 'Come back for me.'

'But . . .' Allanza began.

'Go on. Get away,' Tog said. 'GO!'

As he turned, he heard the thump as they landed on the other side of the fence.

'That's him,' the stranger said.

'Well, well,' Poraig said. 'If I'd known you were a famous murderer, I'd have kept better care of you. You've built up quite a reputation for one so young. This lot are so hopeless, I must have grown complacent.' He aimed a kick at a slave that was lying close to his feet.

'It's good to see him face to face,' the stranger said. The wounds on either cheek were still raw and dragged one side of his face down and the other up.

Poraig unsheathed his sword with a leathery sound.

'Now then,' he said. 'How little trouble are you going to give me? Thing is, my friend here would like to buy you but if you give us any more trouble, I'm afraid we can't let it go unpunished. You see, it would be a terrible example to the rest of the prisoners and we can't allow that to happen.'

'What does he want me for?'

'Why does anyone want a slave? Although in your case it might have something to do with sticking a knife through his face. What else did he do?'

The stranger smiled. 'Murder. Tomb breaking. Theft.' He counted the crimes off on his fingers.

'Theft, eh?' Poraig said. 'And what did he steal, exactly?'

'Oh, nothing of importance. Just—'

'Nothing of importance?' Tog interrupted, making himself sound indignant. 'Nothing of importance? Why do you think he's been after me for six days and nights, on his own and in mortal agony? He wants what I've got!'

'Which is?' Poraig asked.

'Something shining,' Tog said.

Poraig registered the way the stranger started. 'Treasure?' he said. 'Now that's a good one.'

'Didn't he tell you?' Tog asked. 'Ask him. We're both after the same thing, same as you. That's why he wants me alive rather than dead.'

The way Poraig looked at him was different now. It was as if he wanted to see inside him.

The stranger's voice was measured and controlled. 'Desperate people say desperate things. Careful, young man, or he might just believe you. You don't know what he'll do to get the truth.'

'You won't have to do anything to me,' Tog said, looking straight at Poraig. 'I'll share it with you. I'll give it all to you. Just let me live.'

'Pathetic!' the stranger said. 'Can you believe it?'

'You don't know who to believe, but you've got nothing to lose by believing me,' Tog said. 'If I'm telling the truth, you'll be rich. If I'm lying, you can still do what you want.'

'You believe this little bastard?' the stranger said. 'I've a mind to run him through right now.'

Poraig's eyes narrowed. 'Why don't you?' he asked.

'What?'

'Why don't you run him through?'

'I want to have my fun first.'

'He wants me alive,' Tog said. 'He knows I haven't got what he wants on me.'

'You little . . .'

The stranger drew his sword, swung it at Tog but at the last moment, the blade slashed past him and towards Poraig's chest.

But Poraig was ready. He swayed back on his heels, his sword drawn and stabbed at the stranger. The stranger parried, feinted, drew Poraig into a wild blow and slashed him across the side. The bloom of blood was sudden and shocking. Poraig staggered back, his sword drooping. The two men stood facing each other, breathing heavily, in the grey dawn light.

Tog got behind the slaver and began to back away.

'He's escaping,' the stranger said.

'Think I care?' Poraig said. Holding his wound together with one hand, he lifted his sword. Blood ran fast between his fingers. He swore and toppled forwards, grabbing at the stranger who stepped easily out of the way and clubbed him on the back of his head with his sword hilt.

'You next,' he said to Tog. 'You're coming with me.' But then his eyes slid sideways, narrowed in surprise and he backed away. Tog turned and saw Borth forging his way through the crowd of prisoners, followed by an out of breath Allanza. When he turned back, the stranger was gone.

'You all right?' Borth asked. 'Who was that? And what's he doing?' He prodded Poraig with his toe. 'Never mind. Melanius sent me back. I was breaking into the compound when I found your two friends breaking out. The girl's by the fence. This one made me bring him. Better run before someone raises the alarm.'

'But what about the slaves?' Tog asked.

'Did any of them help you?' Borth asked. 'Let them look after themselves.'

'Some of them come from Allanza's village. What are you going to do?'

Allanza looked away. 'I don't know. I just don't know.'

'I've got to push on,' Tog said, 'and if you stay, you'll just be captured. Come with me. We . . . won't forget and one day we'll be able to do something.'

The giant nodded. 'That's right,' he said. 'We'll do something one day.'

He was the first to leave and did not look back.

Dawn saw them back on the road, skirting Govannon's sleeping settlement. They caught up with the convoy before Ula had even got water boiling for porridge. Her shrieks woke the camp and soon they were surrounded by people who couldn't believe they had escaped. Crotus kept to his tent.

Melanius stood back and waited until they had eaten. Then he drew Tog off to one side and walked him to the top of a small rise where a fallen stone pointed at the rising sun. Borth followed at a distance and stood between them and the camp, facing away.

Melanius looked around. The wind caught his hair so that it stood in a wiry crescent above his forehead. When he spoke, his voice was low and intense, very different from his normal light tone. 'This is a good place to talk. As I understand it, we're more or less on the edge of Cornwall. From now on, things will be different. Now listen to me, boy. You were set up – I'm sure Crotus sent word ahead to Govannon. He wanted you out of the way but didn't want anyone to know about it. That's the first thing. The second is this: you need help and the only place you're going to get it is from me. But my price is to know what is going on. Now, the big question. Who are you?'

'I'm – I'm just a woodcutter's boy,' Tog said. 'That's all. I'm nothing.'

Melanius blew air through his lips. 'Woodcutters' boys don't speak Latin. Woodcutters' boys don't get away from mounted cavalry. Woodcutters' boys don't escape from slave camps. You've been trained and you've been trained quite well. What I want to know is what you've been trained for.'

'You're just picking on me because I've survived. That's not fair,' Tog protested. Part of him wanted to get away from this scrutiny but it was as if a little flame had been lit inside him and he stayed.

'And woodcutters' boys don't know about fair. By now that should have been beaten out of you. Now get this through your dense skull. I am not picking on you. That night when you were spying on Crotus, and Borth saved your bacon: what did you see?' When Tog paused, he added, 'Remember. You owe me.'

'They were looking at the sword,' Tog said carefully. It was true: he did owe Melanius but he still didn't trust him. At the same time, he knew he needed help and right now there wasn't much of that around. 'They polished it, then it got really weird. Crotus started talking about a man inside the sword. A little shining man. *The* little shining man.'

'The what?' Melanius seemed honestly taken aback.

'That's what they said. It's a line from a nursery rhyme.' And he recited:

Oh little shining thing
My little tinny thing
Make me a king.

Oh little shining man
As your start was stone
Water is your end.

'Whoa there. Right. Let's go back to the beginning. Where did you find it?'

'In an old tomb in a sacred wood – a nemeton. There was the skeleton of a child in it, the sword and the coin that you saw. They were laid out on a stone table. The woodcutter told me to go there but he was dying so it wasn't very clear. He could just get a few words out: full moon, little man, shine, stone, orchards. I sat down and worked out what they were. The stone was the gravestone on top of the tomb. Full moon – well, that must be the next one. Little man – I've found out that must mean the sword or have something to do with it. Orchards – I'm betting they're the ones on the Island. I think the woodcutter might have come from there or known something about it. He was always going on about apples, you see. And he knew Latin and writing and the only people who know Latin and writing are monks and there are monks—'

'And I told you there were monks on the Island,' Melanius said. 'Now, this dead child. Who was it?'

'The queen and high king's,' Tog said. 'He left her

after it died and she turned to drink.'

'And do they normally bury little babies in big tombs in sacred woods?'

Tog said he honestly didn't know but he could feel an idea growing.

The woodcutter had always respected the old religions: why had he specifically taught Tog never to be afraid of nemetons?

Unless . . .

'It was planned,' he said suddenly. The words took him by surprise but the idea was suddenly in his mind, as bright and complete as the full moon. 'I was meant to go to the wood. I was meant to find the tomb. I was meant to read the writing.'

'You can read?' The merchant's face was frozen in a sort of blank surprise, but Tog was too excited to notice.

'And write. Latin and a smattering of Pictish,' he said airily. 'Well, I wrote Jenna's name. But I've got to warn you. What I'm telling you is dangerous – at least that's what the hogman said.'

The merchant smacked himself on the back of his head. 'A hogman? And I suppose he's an expert in gnostic heresiology and Pythagorean philosophy?'

'What?' said Tog.

'Don't ask,' the merchant answered. 'So, the sword is

important and you were asked, trained might be a better word, to find it.'

'And take it somewhere.'

'A mission. You've been trained for a mission but you don't know what it is. How does that make you feel?'

'It's better than being trained to chop wood,' Tog said. 'Except I've failed. I haven't got it. That old man took my sword and I gave it up like it meant nothing.'

'There's plenty of time,' Melanius said. 'Look at it this way. That little sword bought you passage and is taking you where you want. You almost got killed but you didn't and you'll be all the stronger for the experience. I don't believe in fate but it almost seems that you were meant to survive.'

'If you don't believe in fate, what do you believe in?' Tog asked.

'Fate helps people make sense of the world when they feel things are out of their control. I prefer to find ways of taking control. It's not something you can force. Suppose you're rafting down a fast river. You can't stop it, you can't even slow it, but you can take steps to avoid the rocks that other people get smashed on. They're the ones that believe in fate, but it's not much comfort when you're drowning.'

Tog, Jenna and Allanza were allowed to recover in the cart. They slept most of that day and through the night, so that when Tog awoke before dawn on the second morning after their escape, he was beginning to feel better.

He brushed dew off the driver's seat, looked up at a sky that was the colour of mackerel flesh and breathed in earthy air that almost smelled of spring. Jenna joined him and pointed to the shrinking moon and started talking excitedly, her finger describing arc after arc in the sky. Tog thought she might be talking about lunar cycles, months in other words, but lost count. He saw how the blue spirals on her cheeks followed the line of the bone and accentuated the slant of her eyes. Whoever had put the paint into her skin had loved her face.

She saw him looking and blushed, stretching her hands out in front of her and gestured for Tog to do the same. She pointed a finger. He copied her. She frowned, looked at his finger, then brought it closer to her face to examine it. Suddenly she bit it incredibly hard.

Tog yelped and yanked his hand away.

'You're mad!' he said. 'Completely mad!'

Allanza's head appeared from under the canvas. 'What's going on?' he asked sleepily.

'She bit me,' Tog said. 'We were getting on fine and she bit my finger.'

'Oho,' Allanza said annoyingly. 'That means she wants you. Oh yes.'

'You can't possibly know that,' he said.

'Isn't it obvious?' Allanza said.

Jenna jumped down from the cart and started dancing sarcastically on the dewy turf.

'No,' Tog said. 'Not at all.'

'If you don't know I can't explain,' Allanza said.

'I hate you both,' Tog answered.

All through the day, the weather worsened. There had been discussion about when to stop for the night and Crotus had decided that they should push on until they found shelter. Now, as dusk was falling, the road was climbing the side of an endless, stony slope. A steady, cold wind blew hail into their faces. Tog tried to crouch lower behind the cart for shelter, forcing himself to keep thinking. If you didn't worry, he thought, things went wrong. The night before, he had noticed how Melanius had checked the wheels of his cart, then checked them again. In the morning, he checked the ties holding the leather cover over the cart before breakfast and before setting out. He had made Glyn check that his tinder was dry and the kindling under cover.

Tog now remembered the woodcutter had done a lot of checking without letting him know. Every night it was the same: where have you been? What have you seen? How many? What kind?

And yet he had let the stranger in. Had he been expecting someone else?

Behind him, Jenna sneezed. As the weather had got colder, she retreated further into herself. Now she had her hands hooked into the rope securing the cart's hide cover, allowing it to pull her along. The wind blew her wet tunic against her body, reminding Tog how skinny she was. He could see her hipbones under the thin fabric and her tattoos stood out starkly against the white skin of her neck and shoulders. Her face and feet were blue. When he asked Melanius if he thought she was all right, he barely glanced at her before replying carelessly that Picts were tough. Tog lowered his head and trudged on.

The weather grew fouler and fouler. The road levelled out on a high moor of rock and bog. Grey stone outcrops loomed through shifting mist like giants. Tog, head bent, walking next to Jenna, watched his feet turn from blue to white and his knees from white to angry red. His ears were so cold they were screaming.

They found shelter in the lee of a big grey rock that was howling in the gale. Tog stood and shivered until Melanius shouted at him to join Jenna and Allanza who were standing between the oxen to warm up. Before Tog was anything like warm enough, he saw Pyrs approach Melanius. When he had finished, Melanius caught Tog's eye and beckoned.

'This is your chance,' he said.

Tog's brain felt frozen. 'For what?'

'They need my help. We can bargain with them.'

'But if they need help . . .' Tog began.

'Idiot Briton! Crotus wanted you dead, boy, so he could steal what was yours. Don't you forget it!'

Crotus was bent almost in half, propped against the big grey rock. There was snow in his hair and ice in his beard. He had to move his lips a few times before sound came out.

'We are dying,' were the first words he said. He gestured towards his followers, huddles of grey, wailing in the mud. One of them was lying still and no one was helping. 'My guards haven't been replacing our wood and the rest of them think God will provide so long as they sing those damn psalms all day. We need your wood and anything else you can spare.'

'Your people are not dying yet,' Melanius said, 'but I can see that they cannot last much longer. However, my wood is my insurance against a real disaster and everything else is my livelihood.'

'We need your blankets.'

'You want to buy my rugs and my fire? My Lord, the rugs are not thrown up on a handloom by some village lout. In some the threads are so fine that only the eyes of children can see them and they go blind after a few years from the strain. Emperors—'

'Silence!' Crotus could not shout. The word came out in a harsh croak. 'I *will* buy your blankets. As for your claims, who would venture into the wilds of Britain, carrying a king's ransom with just an Englishman to guard him? A man who values his goods as poorly as you deserves to lose them.'

'I won't say try and take them,' Melanius said, 'because I don't believe in tempting fate, but let's just say that I have faith in my arrangements.'

Anger brightened Crotus's eyes for a brief instant. He made as if to loosen the sword in his belt, but as he did so, he was wracked by a violent spasm of coughing that twisted him sideways, so that he slid even further down the rock.

Melanius looked down at him and said: 'But let us suppose I was prepared to sell, three factors influence this: the thing itself, the depth of the buyer's need and the level of the seller's indifference. At present, your need to buy is greater than my need to sell. It follows, therefore, that the price will be high.'

'Foreign pig. What were your real reasons for coming here in the middle of winter?' Crotus managed to spit out.

'Ever tried to sell rugs in summer?' Melanius said sharply.

'Money grubbing, tramping, hustling . . . tradesman.'

'My Lord.' Melanius gave a deep bow.

'You can't just stand here arguing,' Tog blurted out. His teeth were cold stone; his bones creaking ice. 'At least we could light a fire.'

Melanius silenced him with a gesture but kept his eyes on Crotus. 'How badly do you want to be the king who froze to death for want of a faggot? What do you have to bargain with?'

'Enough gold to buy food.'

'What else?'

'In my domain, fifty head of cattle and one hundred sheep.'

'Your domain, as you call it, consists of a couple of fields and a hovel on a hill. And in my experience a British fifty is more like twenty. And anyway, what would I do with sheep?'

'You could sell them.'

'To whom? And what would he pay me with? Goats? I'm afraid your wealth is worthless to me, a mere humble trader, a money-grubbing foreigner unworthy to tread Cornish soil.'

His words seemed to knock the old king further down the rock in little jerks.

'Name your price,' Crotus said. 'Anything.'

'What does the boy say?' Melanius asked contemptuously.

Crotus's eyes slid over to him, suddenly sharp and calculating. He wanted me dead, Tog reminded himself.

'We'll do it for the sword. My sword. That's the bargain.'

Crotus's eyes narrowed and flicked from Melanius to Tog and back again.

'I can't. It's important. It's not mine to give.'

'You're telling me.'

'You would hand it over to this . . . thing?' Crotus asked Melanius.

'This *thing* has obviously chosen wisely. You'd have surrendered your kingdom but want to keep a funny little bit of old metal.'

'Old metal? Have you . . .' He breathed in, bringing himself under control. 'Call Pyrs.'

Tog found him striking sparks into wet tinder.

'The king wants you to fetch the old sword,' he said.

Pyrs spat, but oddly, went straight to the tent, brought it out and handed it to the king. As Tog stepped up to take it, Crotus leaned over, gripped his wrist and pulled him down.

'So, the little brat wants to shine, does he?'

'I don't know,' Tog said.

Crotus looked at him, then hooded his eyes. 'You'll find out what it means sooner or later.'

He started to laugh but it was too much for his lungs and he started coughing again, great wracking shudders that threatened to shake his frame apart.

'We haven't finished yet,' Melanius said. Crotus didn't even answer. Just looked up at him, sideways. 'We need an oath from you. After all, you've tried to take the sword once. Who's to say you won't do it again?'

'I . . . won't . . . take . . . it . . . again.'

'And you'll help protect the bearer.'

The old man hissed.

'Swear it.'

'I . . .'

'Do it.'

'Swear.'

'Kiss the sword. Tog. Hold it in front of him.'

The king kissed the flat of the blade, then tilted his head like a lizard and ran his tongue up the sword's edge. The sword drew a line of blood that quickly dripped down the old king's chin.

'The deed is done,' Crotus said. 'When he is out, he wants blood.'

'You mean the sword? Why do you call it "he"?' Tog asked.

'It was always the way.'

And as he spoke, he gripped Tog by the arm. Tog tried to pull away from the darkness that pooled in the old king's eyes, that dripped from his gaping mouth and hovered around him in a sour cloud. 'It was always the way and the way must be honoured.'

And the old king pressed the cold sword hilt hard into his belly – hard enough to make him gasp with pain. At last he pulled away and took the sword. 'That was . . . interesting,' Melanius said, as they walked away. 'I mean, the way Crotus came round. By the end he almost seemed to be enjoying himself.'

'What's it to you?' Tog snapped. He was upset by the whole episode.

'Just a Cornish kingdom,' Melanius said. 'But hey, what's that between friends?'

'Sorry,' Tog said. 'But did you have to be so horrid to him?'

'This is what I think of Crotus,' Melanius said. 'He's failed and leaders can't fail. That's the way of the world. I despise him and this miserable country where every cattle thief with a hut calls himself a king in a castle, and where the real kings in real castles sulk like dogs in a manger. It makes me sick that I've helped spin out that miserable creature's last days so he doesn't feel quite so bad when he finally dies . . . Anyway, ask Borth to make a belt for your sword – best keep it close. I don't trust Crotus at all.'

'But what is it?' Tog asked. 'Those things he said . . .'

Melanius looked fastidious. 'British things,' he said. 'What is it, Glyn?'

Glyn looked cowed. 'Really sorry, boss, but water's leaked into the tinder box. I've been trying to get a spark to take but it's just too damp.'

'What? Is everyone here incompetent?' Melanius barked. 'Here, if you don't mind.' He pushed Tog to one side and started unhooking the cart's cover at the end nearest the driver's seat – and the corner where he or Borth always walked, Tog noted. He started pushing rolls of fabric to one side, eventually revealing a small chest, snug in the corner of the cart, but it was held so tightly in place that he couldn't open it. He ordered Tog to clear a space around it, and Tog began to lift out tightly wrapped rolls of fabric, some heavy, stoppered jars, some of which slopped greasily, others which smelled of smells he didn't think existed. At last, there was enough space to push the chest out from the sides of the cart and open it.

In a specially fashioned tray lay a row of small, glazed phials. Melanius chose one and bustled towards Glyn who was still trying to strike sparks into the damp tinder. He pushed the cart driver to one side, took the tinder from him, then carefully poured a tiny amount of grey powder on to it from the phial.

'Now try,' he ordered. Once, twice the sparks showered

down, then there was a whoosh, a puff of white smoke and the tinder was alight. A cry went up from the pilgrims gathered around. Some fell to their knees. Others held their arms in front of them in a cross shape. Ignoring them, Melanius handed the phial back to Tog.

'No use saying it's not magic, I suppose?' he said, his eyebrows arched.

Tog shook his head.

'Just remember, it isn't,' Melanius said emphatically. 'It's natural science.'

Tog replaced the phial in the chest as if it were alive, and slammed the lid shut.

He found he was breathing heavily and his hand was trembling. But when he tried to push the chest back into the corner of the cart, it wouldn't go. He peered down behind it. One of the planks making the bottom of the cart was raised slightly. It wouldn't flatten easily so Tog lifted it to try and lay it flat but as he did so, his fingers touched something underneath.

He lifted the plank right out. Under it was a hidden compartment where a row of leather pouches nestled like plump squabs. Tog pulled one out, loving its heaviness. He untied the neck and pulled out a golden disc – a coin – with a head on one side and a winged figure on the other, very similar to the one he had found in the tomb. They were all like that.

Tog had no idea that there were so many coins in the world. He plunged his hand into the purse and felt the gold around it. Then he was overcome with panic. This was another secret worth fighting for and killing for. He closed the bag, put things back the way they had been and joined Allanza by the fire.

When the pilgrims had gone to bed, he drew the sword and held it up in the fire glow. A pattern that seemed to float beneath the surface of the metal emerged.

It could be a man, Tog thought. Or a sword. Or . . .

It reminded him of something else but he was too tired to work out what it was.

IV

Waning Crescent

All morning the road had been climbing a series of low, relentless hills but now it was running along a high ridge that commanded the surrounding countryside. To the left, the sea glowed between hills. To the right, sparse woods. Straight ahead, it snaked down over a succession of undulations before disappearing into a forest. But what really caught Tog's eye was a mass on the far horizon like a low storm cloud. Too wide to be called a hill, it looked like another country rising out of the earth: browny purple, with the land hammocked between rough peaks.

'That's the country of the little people, if you believe our friends,' Borth said, nodding to the front of the convoy where Crotus's pilgrims were keeping up a constant wailing of psalms.

'You should listen, even if he is an Englishman,' Glyn said from the cart. 'That's where we're heading. The place is crawling with pigseys and spriggans – tommyknockers too, I reckon.'

'And that makes a difference?' Melanius asked.

''Course it makes a difference. Tommyknockers, they lives in caves. Small, they are, with great big eyes that glow in the dark. You ask any miner about them, and they'll tell you about footsteps in the blackness, whispers in the shadows, sounds of working in worked-out holes, tools getting blunter overnight. They like gifts – fruit's best – and if you don't leave 'em stuff, you'll get bad luck and bad luck down a mine means death, like as not.'

'I've no intention of going down caves or mines, you superstitious idiot,' Melanius said.

'Well then, you'd best keep away from ruins or high places too 'cos that's where the spriggans live. They'll suck out your eyes if they come across you at dusk. You look up there,' and he pointed to the landmass in the far distance. 'People live in terror on account of them.'

'Well, then we'll keep away from the high places too.'

'And the forests,' Ula chipped in. 'We've been lucky up until now but all up ahead is pigsey country. They live in the woods and they hunt with magic arrows. I saw one once and the shock nearly killed me. I was looking for puffin burrows on the cliff when suddenly this rock turns into a pigsey and runs off laughing. It was a tiny little thing, but I was that scared.'

Allanza had been listening closely. 'In my village we've got corrigans. A girl was taken by them one night and nine months later had a baby. But do you know what? When it came out everyone said it looked like her neighbour. Imagine that.'

'A blessing for all concerned,' Borth said. 'Good for the baby. Good for the mother.'

'The neighbour was none too pleased. He had to give the corrigans a sheep in case they made any more mischief and the corrigans only went and gave the sheep to the girl's father. Ha! You just don't know what they're going to get up to next.'

'No, indeed,' said Borth politely. 'Have you had dealings with them?' he asked Tog.

'Not personally, though I know they steal babies,' Tog said carefully. 'And the night before Beltain the woodcutter always left a sack of whisky in a certain tree in the woods and in the morning the sack would be empty. Do you have pigseys in the English lands?'

'It's all goblins and gods for us,' the Englishman said. 'What about you, Melanius?'

'Oh, we have djinns and angels. Djinns bad, angels

good, with one notable exception. But angels are complicated. They have three hundred and sixty-five different ranks in all and if you want to go to heaven, you have to remember them in the right order. That's civilization for you.'

On the outskirts of the forest one of the oxen started hobbling and, after poking around in its hoof, Glyn found a small piece of flint. It was passed around the travellers with a great deal of head-shaking. For once, Melanius did not know what was going on.

'It's a pigsey's arrowhead,' Allanza explained. 'They wanted to make the ox lame but Glyn thinks he found it in time.'

'An ox goes lame from a piece of stone and you blame it on the little people?' Melanius asked. 'What do you think the ox has been walking on for hundreds of miles, if not earth with bits of stone in it?'

'Not flint, though,' Allanza said with certainty. 'This isn't flint country. And this one's been shaped.' He spat on the sliver of stone and rubbed it between his finger and thumb. 'See how it's been worked at the end to give it that point?'

'And what does it mean for us, flint expert?'

'That the pigseys are with us.'

They all looked ahead. The grey army of trees closed

around the road like a dry sea swallowing a causeway.

'We'll be all right,' Melanius said. 'I've been on this road before when the leaves were so thick you couldn't see more than an arm's span into the forest.'

'But that was in the summer, Master, when the road was crowded with travellers. See anyone else?' Glyn asked.

'No, but we're armed,' Melanius said. 'We'll set a watch and nothing will happen. You wait and see.'

Towards evening they found a partially overgrown clearing and started to gather enough wood to make a fire that would last the night. While foraging, Tog found the skull of a dog in the cleft of a tree trunk, its eye sockets plugged with stones. When he touched the delicate roughness of the bone, he thought he heard a rustle in the trees behind him. Touch, rustle. Touch, rustle. It was as if the two were connected and he wondered if the dog's spirit was somehow tethered to its skull. He stroked it and walked the clearing's perimeter, finding three more skulls, and feeling the prickle of fear on his neck and back.

'Hmm. I haven't had much experience of this sort of thing,' Melanius said, when he told him. 'Of course we can't go back . . .' He chewed a nail. 'Go, tell Crotus. See if he can prove his worth. And if he's difficult, wave the sword at him.'

Crotus listened to Tog with a small, tight smile on his purple lips.

'And what would you do?' he asked.

'Melanius is right: going back would be begging for an ambush so that means we're stuck here,' Tog said. 'We should make sure we have enough timber for a decent blaze all night and double the watch. And have the guards patrol with their weapons showing. Pigseys hate metal.'

Crotus nodded. 'None of us will sleep tonight as it is,' he said. 'The pilgrims have decided to chant until dawn – they're frightened the pigseys will swap one of them for a changeling. Pyrs!'

The servant approached and bowed. 'The boy would have us double the watch and keep a fire going all night. Tell the men he won't have them sleeping. See to it, will you?' Crotus watched Tog go red with embarrassment as the older man bowed and moved away again.

'You just asked me for my opinion. I thought you . . .' Tog stammered.

'You thought I would value the opinion of a brat like you?' the old man's voice was low and shook. 'Just because you have . . .'

'The sword? Say it. You can't stand to see me have it.'

Crotus opened his mouth to show his grey tongue and made a dry laughing sound. 'I made an oath but there was no mention of helping you. However I will. I will give you some valuable advice. The little man is bigger than you. He has his own destiny and he's got a job to do. Ask yourself: why does he travel to the Island? And what will he do when he gets there?'

Tog found it hard to sleep. The air in the forest was close and cold. The crackle of the fire, the uneven wailing of the pilgrims stopped him settling. Jenna was excused watch duties – no one expected her to – and she was snoring softly beside him in the cart. Allanza had opted to watch with Borth and Melanius.

Tog had his hand resting lightly on the sword to see if he could feel its life. *He's got a job to do*. It was no use pretending he didn't know what that meant. Swords killed – that was their job – and although the sword had killed the pirates, that was when Jenna had it. His turn next. Was there really nothing he could do about it?

He must have dozed. He dreamed that the little man in the sword had woken up and had started going through Melanius's flagons because he was thirsty. He was thin as rope, pale as pus and very determined; nothing could stop him and now he was calling.

Tog woke up with a hand clamped across his mouth. 'Tog. Tog.' The voice was in his ear, low and insistent.

'Something in the cart. Keep quiet.'

Jenna was lying half across him and it was her hand on his mouth. He moved his head under her hand to show he understood.

'Listen.'

Her voice just mouthed the word in her ear. Tog heard a tiny little rustling sound that shouldn't be there. It came from the other end of the cart where Melanius kept the jars of oil and wine. He touched the sword, thought he felt it twitch but somehow kept hold of it. Cold terror sat in his belly like a toad. He stood up and all hell broke loose.

On the far side of the camp, sparks flared as something fell into the fire. There were shouts, people running. Tog saw an arrow sprout from a pilgrim's eye.

With a roar, Borth ran towards Crotus's tent, sword out, and helmet on, Allanza following. The whole camp was up now but thick white smoke was billowing from the fire, making it hard to see what was going on.

The cart jerked stealthily, hard enough to throw Tog and Jenna off balance and hold each other. Tog looked for the oxen but they were picketed a distance away, undisturbed by the commotion. So how come the cart was moving towards the forest?

Tog ran to the front. Ropes had been looped over the yokes. Even as he looked, the ropes stretched, tightened and jerked the cart a few feet nearer the trees.

He waited until they tightened then slashed through them and backed away. Jenna was dealing with a lump under the cart covers, pouncing on it like a fox, trying to pin it down.

Then the wind changed and Tog saw the pigseys.

They were standing under the shelter of the trees, as if unwilling to venture further out. Small, not much bigger than children, and slight. They had long lank hair and all of them wore long grey tunics. Some of them carried stone hammers while others had short bows slung over their shoulders by the string.

He pulled out his sword and brandished it. The pigseys seemed to peer at it from under their heavy fringes before shuffling back slowly. He thrust the sword at them again and as he stepped forwards, they melted back into the woods.

The attack was over.

As a reward for saving the cart, Tog and Jenna were allowed to lie in and he had the luxury of hearing the others strike camp. He waited until the oxen had been hitched before sitting up.

They were moving through thick wood, the convoy bunched up now for safety, Borth walking by the wheel, looking watchful.

'We were lucky,' he said. 'A pilgrim lost an eye, a guard's arm was broken by a pigsey axe and there's the hostage you caught.'

The thing that had crept into the cart had been a pigsey, a girl they thought. The guards had taken her and right now she was bound by the wrists to the cart, and hobbled so she could not help falling over. She was guarded by the same rat-faced man Tog had met on the first day – Kirric was his name – and when he saw that he had Tog's attention, he leered and prodded the pigsey with his spear. The pigsey's hair had fallen over her face but Tog was sure she was looking at him.

'Don't get soft,' Borth said. 'We need her as protection.'

'But we're hurting her,' Tog said. 'Kirric jabs his spear in whenever he feels like it.'

'Just be grateful they didn't carry you and Jenna off into the forest. And don't feel bad just because it was you that caught her.'

'I can't help it,' Tog said.

Ula had been listening. 'I don't like it either,' she said over her shoulder. 'We should be shot of her and pressing on, not stopping, not even for meals. I can feel them all around us in the woods, staring at us right now. What will become of us? She knows,' she added suddenly, nodding at

Jenna, who was staring out at the forest. 'She may be foreign and she may be a witch but she's a deep one. Oh yes. My little picture girl's a deep one.'

A deep one. As Tog looked at Jenna, a strange memory from the night before rose up and burst in his head like a bubble.

He pointed to her. 'You . . .'

Jenna shot him a look, eyes wide and pleading.

'But you spoke!'

Jenna's hand slapped down over his mouth and then she was on top of him like a wildcat, one hand at his throat, the other hooked over his eyes like claws. Her head was bent over his, with her mouth close to his ear. 'Don't say anything, please,' she whispered. Tog tried to kick her off and to his amazement, sent her crashing backwards.

Borth chuckled appreciatively. Ula was outraged. 'What's going on back there? What are you doing to that poor dumb creature? She knows you're teasing her, oh yes she does, and don't think she doesn't feel terrible being a foreigner and all and unable to speak, and all you do is make it worse for her. Poor lamb, so far from home, though why anyone would want to live there is another question altogether. Come here, my pet.'

Tog knelt in front of Jenna. 'When?' he hissed.

'Soon.'

He watched her feign tears, scramble to the front of the cart and nestle against Ula who fed her piece after piece of dried apple from the depths of her apron.

Just after midday they stopped in a patch of cleared land that dark gorse bushes were trying to reclaim. Melanius was checking the contents of the cart again with Glyn and a clash of metal told Tog that Borth was teaching Allanza sword fighting. Most of the men were gathered round in a circle. He walked across the clearing and looked between them. The pigsey was a dirty heap on the floor and they were poking her with sticks.

Feeling sick, he tried to talk to Jenna again, but Ula was still feeling protective and threw sticks at him until he went away. In the end, he wandered back up the track to see if he could spot any signs of being followed. Beyond the clearing stood a cramped army of grey trees, grey branches and grey twigs clawing at a grey sky. When he moved, the whole perspective shifted and it was all too easy to imagine the forest was alive.

A squirrel ran along a branch. A blackbird spurted through the gorse. A crow called from far away. Nothing to report.

But he still ran back to the convoy.

* * *

'A week's travelling north of Constantinople, where the wild lands start, there are stories about little people,' Melanius said. 'I have heard them called the-ones-that-were-left-behind, but perhaps they should be called the-ones-that-were-left-alone.'

They had stopped for the evening by a river. Half the camp was on watch, the rest huddled around fires. Everyone's back felt exposed.

'By who?'

'In the case of the pigseys, by the British, when they came to this island.'

'We've always been here,' Tog said. 'This is our land.'

'I cannot prove you weren't and you cannot prove you were,' Melanius said. 'But just as the Romans came and conquered you, so your people, the British, came and drove the little people into the woods. As sure as eggs is eggs, as Ula would say.'

'All right. Perhaps they deserved it,' Tog countered.

'What? Because they're weaker than you? And suppose the English come and drive you into the deep valleys and high mountains? Will you have deserved it?'

'That will never happen,' Tog said. 'This country will never be English.'

'Why not?'

'No disrespect to Borth, but we're more civilized

138

than them. Everyone knows that.'

'Tell that to the pigsey girl. And even if it were true, who brought you writing, reading, roads and running water, you dolt? The Romans! Your conquerors. Look: I admit it's complicated – just don't go believing that you're right because of who you are or where you're from. As a Greek resident of the Eastern Roman Empire with a Jewish grandfather and Phoenician mother, I know what I'm talking about.'

'You sound rather confusing to me.'

'Confusing maybe, confused never. Listen, fool. Civilization has its points but a lot of so-called civilized living is nothing more than luxury bought with blood. Have you heard about the Dacians?'

'No,' said Tog sullenly. 'Because I'm a fool.'

'Not your fault. This is your first history lesson, but not your last, I sincerely hope. The Dacians were a people who were unlucky enough to have gold mines, to be independent and to be rather too close to Rome at a time when the good Emperor Trajan was busy building roads and baths and harbours – all the things that make a country civilized. The Dacians were only too happy to sell him the gold but Trajan didn't think that was quite enough. No. He marched his army to Dacia, stole their gold mines and then set about killing every single Dacian there ever was. A whole people, a whole race, a whole country wiped out for gold. Call that civilized?'

'No but . . .'

'And take Crotus.'

'What's it got to do with Crotus?'

'With Crotus you don't even get the roads,' Melanius said. 'He thinks he's more civilized than the English but he's just a small-time crook who hates anything that isn't Cornish. He thinks Cornishmen are the only true born Britons, but that's all he thinks. Does he really think that Cornishmen can throw the enemy back into the sea? He doesn't even know who the enemy is.'

'The English, of course.'

'Maybe. In that case, perhaps you could explain why some of the British tribes want to join forces with the English against the Picts? You really don't know any of this?'

'No.'

'But you do know what lesson to take from this little lecture? I'll tell you. If Britain is going to fight off the Picts, English, Jutes, Saxons, Goths, Visigoths, Vandals, Huns, Scythians, Sarmations, Ethiopians or even the godforsaken pigseys, the kingdoms have got to unite or they'll be picked off one by one. In other words, you won't be a country worth fighting for.'

Up ahead, the pigsey started screaming again and Tog

went to see why. The river, racing over big grey stones, bent close to the road up ahead and a guard was plunging the pigsey up and down in the water.

'What's going on?' he asked.

'Baptizing her. Making her a Christian,' one of the pilgrims said. 'Now get lost.'

'They're baptizing her,' Tog said to Melanius. 'It's OK.'

'Excellent. So when they murder her, she can go to heaven. Civilization's a fine thing, isn't it?'

For security, the cart was now in the middle of the convoy, and Kirric was experimenting with new ways to make the pigsey's life even more awful than it was. This involved tripping her up with his spear haft and laughing as she bumped and twisted along the ground, pulled by the cart. Tog told Glyn who shouted at Kirric that every time the pigsey dragged, the cart slowed and lengthened the time they would have to spend in the wood. Kirric lifted the pigsey's lank hair and spat full in her face.

Ahead they heard a cry. 'Clear ahead. Clear land ahead!' Tog felt Jenna beside him. Without looking at him she said, 'Bad man. I hate him.'

Without looking at her, he said, 'Let's free her.' His heart accelerated and gave his voice a bumpy ride.

'And kill him,' Jenna said curtly.

'Jenna, why didn't you talk before? Why didn't you tell us?' Tog asked.

'I was scared, then I didn't know how . . . or when.' Her voice was clipped and musical.

'Why were you scared? I mean, I understand that you were scared of the slavers but after that . . .'

Jenna pursed her lips and shook her head.

'You don't trust me,' Tog said unfairly.

Jenna shot him a look that made him feel guilty.

'What then?'

'It is hard to explain . . . and if I explain, then . . .'

'What?'

But before Jenna could answer, from the head of the procession came a dull crash and a warning shout that turned into a sudden cry of pain. The convoy came to a stop and a guard came running back, his face white and strained.

'Man down. Man down. They've dug a hole in the road. The first cart's gone into it. Move your cart round. Keep moving!'

'Wait!' The voice of Melanius rang out above the confused shouting. 'Don't do anything. How do we know the ground all around isn't set with traps? Tie the prisoner to a wheel and everyone to the sides, facing outwards. Spear carriers – use your weapons to test the ground for more traps. GO!'

Tog backed up against the cart and scanned the wood. Nothing moved. Not even a bird.

'I go,' Jenna hissed.

'No. Me.'

A hand gripped Tog's wrist.

'What's your game?' Kirric had slipped behind them.

'Leave us alone,' Tog said.

'I would, but I don't trust you. Don't like the way you look at me when I'm going about my business with the girl. You wouldn't be planning anything, would you?'

Kirric's hand found the nerves in the side of Tog's wrist and started to crush them. Tog jabbed his free hand into Kirric's throat. The guard let go of his wrist and grabbed him by the front of his jerkin, so Tog broke the grip by sweeping his arms up and out. Then he grabbed the front of Kirric's tunic, swivelled, pulled him off balance, threw him over his hip and landed on him, driving his knee into his solar plexus. It was a move he had practised a thousand times with the woodcutter but it was the first time he had done it in earnest. Breathing hard he leaned over Kirric and said, 'Leave the girl alone.'

Glyn had noticed the fight and hurried over. 'What's going on?'

'Nothing,' Tog said. 'He fell.'

Kirric got to his feet, winded, doubled up with pain and

red with embarrassment. 'I'm going to kill you and that foreign bitch,' he hissed as he walked past Tog. 'I mean it.'

The pigseys didn't follow up with an attack and the travellers moved on. The woods started to fall away: low moorland ahead and to the left, to the right the steep slopes of fairyland. Tog noticed something strange. From the top of a small rise, over to the right, the ground disappeared into a steep tree-lined rift, steeper than any valley Tog had even seen.

'Have you seen that?' Tog asked Allanza who was walking with him – one of the few occasions when he wasn't with Borth.

'The guards were talking about it,' Allanza said. 'It's a gorge with a sacred river at the bottom with this pool where you can hear the gods deciding your destiny. Once you fall in, you can never get out and if the pigseys catch you anywhere near, they kill you.'

'Why aren't we doubling the guard?'

'After the last attack failed they all think the pigseys have given up.'

Tog dropped back and fell in step next to Jenna. 'They think we're out of danger. That means they don't need the pigsey girl as a hostage and I'm sure they're going to kill her. We're going to have to free her soon.'

'Where will she go?' Jenna said. 'Not strong.'

'There are still pigseys in the woods over there.'

'Give me the sword.'

'I can't,' Tog said. 'It's . . . dangerous. I'll go.' He wanted to tell her that he had changed since she had slipped away to kill the slavers; how he needed to prove himself somehow.

'No.' Jenna's voice was low but intense. 'Girl not scared of me. But need time.' She mimed untying the ropes.

Tog realized she was right. 'I'll try and arrange something. Maybe they'll relax a bit and not keep her under guard.'

But of course, Kirric made sure she was guarded. When he went off with a party to forage for food, he instructed one of the guards to watch her.

Jenna nodded at him. Tog said, 'He's called Slone. He's all right really. Please don't think about killing him.'

They waited. And waited. And waited.

Jenna looked up at the sky. 'Dark soon,' she said. 'Soldiers come back. I go.'

Before Tog could argue, she slipped away, making a wide circuit of the camp, then dropped out of sight. The next thing he saw of her, she was about ten paces from the pigsey girl, flat on the ground, almost merging with the tussocks of wet, brown grass, waiting for the next chance to get closer.

Tog looked around for inspiration. The pilgrims were knocking earth off turnips, ready for their evening meal. Melanius was asleep. Allanza was cleaning Borth's sword.

Tog squatted next to him. 'Could you pick a fight with Borth?' he asked. 'Quick.'

'Are you mad?' Allanza asked.

'Not a real fight. Something more like an argument that would get everyone running over to look. It's got to be quick.'

'Why?' Allanza asked.

'I just need to do something and I can't say what at the moment.'

'It's the pigsey, isn't it?' Allanza said. 'I've been watching you. And I watched Jenna. You want to free her.'

'That's right.'

'Why didn't you tell me?'

'I . . . I don't know,' Tog said. 'You seemed so caught up with Borth.'

'You stopped talking to me.'

'Did I? I suppose I've had a lot to think about.'

'But you want me to help.' Allanza's eyes slid to one side. 'I've seen her talking. I knew she understood more than she was letting on but you never asked me about it. I know I seem slow but the Englishman's teaching me how to fight so I'll be more use. I asked him specially.'

'You're not slow and you saved our lives – that night in the snow when you dragged us out of the bog and found the shelter.'

'A donkey could have done it,' Allanza said flatly. 'But I'll help you again. You don't even have to tell me what it's for.'

He stood up and wandered over to where Borth was stretched out by the side of the cart, whittling a stick. Allanza dropped his sword carelessly, so the hilt struck the Englishman on the knee.

'Careful,' Borth growled.

'Take your stupid sword,' Allanza said. 'You know where to shove it.'

He gave it a small kick.

'What's up with you? A touch of moonmadness, perhaps?'

'I don't think so,' Allanza said. 'I've done enough for you.'

'Done enough for me? You've been begging to clean my sword since the first night when you turned up and started following me around like a little seal pup.' Borth spoke loudly enough for people to sniff an argument, raising their heads like dogs catching scent of a fox.

'Well, I'm not doing it any more!' Allanza shouted and

kicked out at the Englishman's leg, catching the sword, which jumped, twisted and nicked Borth's leg.

'RIGHT!' he roared, grabbing the sword and rearing up. 'YOU!'

'That's right!' Allanza shouted. 'You're brave enough with a sword in your hand. But can you fight like a Briton?'

And he dropped into a wrestling crouch.

People brushed past Tog to get closer to the argument. At last Slone stood, craning his neck to see what was going on. He moved away from the pigsey, a smile growing on his face as he caught sight of the fight.

Now, Jenna, now! Tog urged. At last she moved up behind the pigsey and started to work at the bonds. The pigsey struggled, then suddenly went still again. How long could it take to untie two knots? The fight could not possibly last long; already he had heard some groans from the crowd, a sure sign that Allanza was getting mashed.

There! The pigsey was getting up into a crouch now. She tried to stand and promptly fell over. Jenna helped her up on to all fours and began to crawl off. The wood seemed very distant but darkness was falling and they were using the scattered gorse bushes as cover. Then the pigsey stopped again. Jenna put an arm round her waist and tried to urge her on.

No good.

Jenna knelt and managed to drape the pigsey over one shoulder. She staggered, made a few weaving steps, seemed to pick up a bit of speed. Now they were halfway to the wood but Tog could see the pigsey was slipping and Jenna had to stop, put her down again, lift her. It was all taking too much time.

And then Tog heard a shout. The hunting party had returned and they had seen the prisoner escaping.

He didn't have time to think. He just sprinted as fast as he could to get between Jenna and the hunters.

Now Jenna had heard their shouts and tried to run. Her feet caught in a tussock. She almost fell. No! She was still upright, though weaving even more, and rowing the air with her free arm.

The guards were overhauling them quickly – there was no way Jenna could win the race – but fortunately the men had other ideas. They stopped, one of them took a stance and the next thing Tog saw, a spear was arcing through the air. It landed two feet away from Jenna on her left. She veered right but the movement was too sudden and the pigsey fell, taking her down with it. Fortunately the next spear was badly thrown and landed short, but the pigsey had fallen again and Jenna was trying to pull her towards the trees, which were almost close enough to touch. As he ran, Tog willed her to leave the pigsey and save herself but she wouldn't. Foot after foot she half dragged, half lifted her.

Tog could hear the men now. 'Steady, Kirric, steady,' one said. So it was Kirric with the spear. Tog saw there was no way he could reach Jenna before Kirric threw, so he swerved towards him, keeping low and trying to stay as quiet as possible. So far, no one had noticed him.

'Now, mate now!' the other guards urged. 'She's getting away!'

But Kirric was unhurried. He steadied his stance again, pulled the spear back, bent his back – but just was he was about to launch the weapon, Tog reached them. He slashed down with his sword, opening Kirric's arm from the shoulder to the elbow, jinked right and hared off after Jenna and the pigsey, invisible now against the wood.

Where were they? Had they got there in time? He thought he saw movement off to his left and adjusted his course. Then branches whipped his face and clawed at his clothes. The ground began to slip away and draw him downwards. He ran until he stumbled and fell heavily against a tree. Winded and bruised he was forced to stop and take stock of the situation.

He was in a very strange place. Immediately in front of him, the ground sloped away almost vertically. Thin trees with inordinately long trunks strained for the sky.

Some had tried to fall and were slanted at crazy angles. Under his feet, the ground crawled with roots struggling to fix the trees to the thin, sloping soil. Through an intricate web of bare branches he could see how steeply the ground fell in front of him: the tops of trees further down the slope seemed no distance away. Below him the darkness roared dimly.

He listened hard for sounds of pursuit.

Nothing.

He shifted his weight from one foot to the other and forced himself to think.

First job, don't get caught. Second job, find Jenna. He was on his own and must have come further into the wood than them.

He hauled himself up the hill from tree trunk to tree trunk, crabbing sideways to head in their general direction.

A soft white flake landed on the back of his hand.

He looked up. Wet white flakes were falling in such numbers that he could hear their catspaw patter all around him. He pushed on up the slope with new urgency, trying to see and hear but feeling stifled. While wiping snowy sweat from his eyes, he stumbled over the body.

Kirric was still warm. His wounded arm was hastily bound and his free hand was frozen in the act of plucking a little arrow that was stuck in his throat. His eyes were wide open and his tongue was sticking out.

Off to Tog's right a crow sounded. Was it Jenna or Kirric's killer that had disturbed it? Tog drew his sword. Over the loose roar of his breathing, he thought he heard the squeaky crunch of a footfall.

He whirled round.

Heard one behind him again and whirled round again. Heard a little chinking sound that could only be two flints knocking against each other. Chink-chink. Chink. That was certainly coming from up the hill, so he backed down it.

A patch of darkness that he had taken for a bulge in a tree trunk moved. Tog heard a sudden crashing off to his right, then the choked scream of a fox. A lump of snow wet his head. He caught a whiff of woodsmoke and rancid meat, saw a shape in the trees above him move. His nerve broke completely and he ran.

It was too dark to see where he was going. He flailed with his arms to keep his balance and crashed into trees. Branches tore at his face and stabbed him; roots wriggled underfoot and tripped him. It was inevitable that he was going to fall and when he did, it was a relief because he was cocooned in air and nothing was hurting him.

For a split second.

Then he slammed into the earth and raced on his belly down mud, through leaf, over stone. He rolled once for the last time, his head full of roaring whiteness and as he fell, saw towering above him a great white ghost. He screamed, reached out with both hands and scrabbled for whatever came to hand. Ground ivy tore loose with a long crackle, gave and gave and gave then suddenly jerked him to a hanging stop, nearly wrenching his arms from his shoulder sockets, trying to slice through his fingers. It held his weight but momentum slammed his head against the rock face.

Stars flared.

He dangled.

He wondered why he couldn't hear and how the snow had turned to rain so quickly. When he opened his eyes he saw why. He was hanging over a small cliff, just a few feet from the ground, and above him the biggest waterfall in the world was roaring out of the darkness. The waterfall fell into a pool and the pool merged with a fast flowing river. Downstream, the ground opened out on either side but Tog thought that would take him in the wrong direction. Upstream the river narrowed, and the gorge sides grew steeper and more rocky.

Thick and soft, the snow blued the air. Tog shivered, hopped, stuck his tongue out to catch flakes. He set off upstream and very quickly realized that he could not see enough to move safely.

It was one thing to fall through the darkness, another to arrive relatively unscathed in the darkness. But when you were trying to find your way along the stony banks of a fast-flowing river, with everything slick with water, weeds or snow, you needed to be able to see more than half an arm's length in front of you. If he managed, for example, to climb over a rock, the chances were that he couldn't get past the next one and had to backtrack – which was really hard in the darkness – and begin again.

Then he realized that he didn't have a plan.

Then he realized that his head was throbbing and he had been knocked a bit silly.

He began to shiver in earnest. He was at the bottom of the pigsey gorge in the middle of the pigsey wood and paddling through the pigsey's sacred river that was death just to see.

And it was night. And it was snowing.

His mood suddenly changed from elation to complete despair. He found a sort of hollow in a bank where the earth had fallen below the roots of a tree, squatted in it and hugged himself. Right then, he thought he was probably going to die and did not care at all.

He dozed. He dreamed of little dark shapes growing out

of the snow. He dreamed that they approached him with little bent spears and little bent bows. In his dream he was angry they were bothering him because he was so cold and tired. He got up to shoo them away but they snagged him round the ankles with a weighted rope, wrapped him in a net, took his sword, hoisted him on to their shoulders and carried him off.

Then he woke up and of course, that was what was happening. He was being carried away by the pigseys and the man leading the procession was holding his sword flat above his head, with ceremony, and all the others were holding back although occasionally one would steal forward and try to touch it. Tog was so scared he couldn't make a noise.

The woodcutter had told Tog that in his youth he had seen a wolf pack bring down a deer. In the end, he said, it wasn't the savagery that made the impression, but the deer's resignation. As the teeth were tearing into its side, the deer had looked over its shoulder as if to reprove the wolves for making such a crude growling noise.

That was how Tog felt as he was carted along the side of the sacred river. If he was going to go, he wanted it to be quick and easy. He minded the jolting more than the prospect of death. His mind wandered – where were there wolves in Britain? In the north or the west? What had the woodcutter been doing there? He had never talked about his past. Now all those memories were gone, snuffed out like a small flame.

And soon his would be too. He started to struggle.

The party was moving upstream alongside, and occasionally in, the rushing river that squeezed between narrow rock walls. The gorge was so narrow in places that the fallen trees could span it.

Tog was carried on shoulders most of the time, except when the pigseys had to negotiate a steep rock, when they would simply drag him up and over it, scraping and bruising him. Once, where the path narrowed and wound around an overhang, they simply tied a rope around his waist, carried it past the overhang, pushed him off the side and then pulled him along through the numbing, battering current. Where the gorge widened into a flat glade, there was a cave overhung with dead ferns and dripping with water. They threw him down on the floor and left, closing a door of woven branches behind him.

He groaned. The floor was piled high with animal skins that were soft but stank. He was face down and struggled to roll over. Then he froze.

He had heard a rustling. There was something else in the cavern with him and it was making a dreadful, thick, greedy snuffling sound as if its snout were testing the air, patiently seeking out its prey. It stopped. Tog went still.

'Hello?' Allanza's voice said. 'Tog. It's you, isn't it?'

'It's me. What are you doing here?'

'I followed you into the woods. It seemed the obvious thing to do. Then they caught me.'

'Have you seen Jenna?'

'No. I thought I could see where she went but by the time I got into the woods, she'd disappeared. Then I thought I could see her ahead – running – so I followed but it was too dark to see properly. I didn't want to shout because I knew the guards would be after me. Anyway, I followed the slope down until I got to a river. That's when they got me. They just appeared – a lot of them. They had spears. There was nothing I could do.'

'I didn't do any better,' Tog said. 'They might not be very strong but when there're enough of them . . . Why didn't they all attack the carts? They could have taken us easily.'

'I don't know,' Allanza said. 'I get the impression they're not very good at anything apart from hiding.'

'Still,' Tog answered. 'They gave it a go. You can't take that away from them.'

And this struck them as so funny that they both started to laugh. Allanza told Tog that mostly he was running from

Borth. At first the Englishman had thought there was something wrong with Allanza and had not taken his challenge seriously. They had boxed for a while and Allanza had been able to cope as long as he kept Borth at arm's length. Luckily, as soon as Borth had managed to get him on the ground, they had heard people shouting about the pigsey girl's escape. Borth asked him in a whisper if the fight had anything to do with the escape. Allanza whispered back that it was a diversion. He waited for Borth to slacken his grip and when he did, kicked him really hard in the balls. He didn't know why he had done it: it was like he was getting his own back for all the times he had been beaten, kicked, or punched by an adult when he was growing up. Anyway, he could see that Borth was really angry and that had made him run.

'At least they won't suspect you of helping plan anything,' Tog said. 'Not if you really did hurt him.'

'He'll be in the cart for a couple of days,' Allanza said and they both laughed again, but a bit less heartily.

'What do you think is going to happen to us?' Allanza asked.

'I don't know,' Tog said.

'If they've got the girl Jenna rescued, do you think she'll get us out of this?'

'Sure. Of course. She's probably just sorting things out.'

'And she'll be with Jenna?'

'Sure.'

It was light when the pigseys came for them. Allanza refused to come out and the pigseys were nervous about coming in so there was a stalemate. Then the first rock came sailing in, and then another until Tog and Allanza surrendered.

Outside the cave, the gorge opened into a glade, hemmed in by almost vertical wooded slopes. The bare branches of trees drooped with white snow but the air in the glade was grey. Crowding the valley floor were the pigseys, all various shades of grey. Allanza's face looked grey and Tog felt grey.

In the middle of the glade, on the banks of the river, was a huge rock, almost the same size as Tog's old home. On it sat three figures, their heads bowed. One was Jenna, the other two were pigseys.

'It's their bloodstone,' Allanza said. 'I'm sure of it. I feel sick.'

At the slow clap of a small, flat sounding drum, Tog looked up at the sky, rosy with dawn, but veiled by the cobweb of branches. He and Allanza would be tied, dragged up to the top of the stone and as soon as the first of the sun's rays shone on to them, they'd be killed.

That was just the way it was.

He wanted to find something to say but couldn't. A spear prodded his back and pushed him forwards. The silver chuckle of the river grew in his head until it was roaring like a winter storm. When they reached the bloodstone, he saw that a rough ladder had been propped up against it. It struck him as the greatest cruelty that he would have to climb to his own death, but he did so, hand over cold hand.

Terror sucked all the joy from being reunited with Jenna and tears blurred her so he couldn't see her anyway. She seemed to be talking but her voice was just a thin, distant noise.

Allanza said something. Tog straightened his shoulders, lifted his chin and glanced down at him. The idiot seemed to be smiling.

'Sit down then,' Allanza said.

'I'd rather stand,' Tog replied.

'You're being asked to sit,' Allanza said. 'I think it would be rude not to.'

'Hah,' Tog said bitterly.

The sound of the drum was getting louder and louder. The pigseys started stamping together on the soggy ground. The rock trembled. The river seemed to be pouring through his brain. He half closed his eyes as the figure in front of him rose, pointing the sword at his belly.

'Take it,' Allanza said. 'Take it, you idiot.'

Top opened his eyes. The sword was being offered to him hilt first.

'They're thanking us,' Allanza said. 'They're giving your sword back.'

The horror burst like a bubble.

'Thanking us?' Suddenly he could see and hear clearly.

'For saving the girl.'

'What's Jenna saying?'

'I don't know. It's in her language, I think.'

Jenna was talking intently to a tiny ancient man with thin white hair and an incredible, collapsed face. He had four lines tattooed on each cheek and was wrapped in a sheepskin that still seemed to have a lot of sheep inside it.

Jenna sat opposite him with her head bowed as he talked to her in a soft, musical language.

'She's crying,' Allanza whispered. 'Look.'

'What's wrong?' Tog asked her, when the old man stopped talking. 'What did he say to you?'

'He's telling me things about my people.' She inhaled marshily. The tip of her nose was red.

'How does he know about your people?'

Jenna laughed, a quick, bitter sound. 'He knows everything. Ask him something. Go on. Anything.'

Tog looked at the sword lying across his lap. 'All right,' he said, forcing himself to look into the old man's watery eyes. 'Can you tell me about the sword?'

The old man nodded to the younger pigsey who translated the question, and listened to the answer from the older man with his head bowed. Then he turned to Tog.

'Ssword iss of tin and copper made. We do not love metal. We ssay it iss wrong to draw metal from rock. Metal iss angry, set hard in his wayss. Wantss to kill. Always wants *to get inside*. Sseven hundred ssuns have died while it has lived. Iss . . .' He stopped and asked the old man a question in his own language, listened to the answer, then nodded. 'Once wass known to men-who-love-metal but now iss not respected.'

He stopped as suddenly as he started.

'This sword? This actual sword?' Tog asked.

'Thiss ssword. He hass killed many kingss.'

'But it's so . . . small. Not much use in a fight.'

'Not when men fight. When the king musst die, he iss the ssacred ssword that killss the king. It iss what he doess.'

Tog felt Jenna grip his arm and dig her nails into his flesh. The words seemed to suck the air away from around him. Sound and colour faded.

'And who does the actual killing?'

'He doess.'

'Do you mean the sword or the person who . . . has it?'

The pigseys conferred, the younger seeming to ask a number of questions, but each time, the old man gave the same answer. The younger man bowed his head.

'You asked: who does the killing. The answer is always the same: He doess.'

'The sword?' Tog asked.

'He doess.'

'The person carrying the sword?'

'He doess.' He waited while the old man spoke some more, then continued. 'Not for many sunss hass thiss happened. When the men who-love-metal came to our land, they chosse a king who ruled for a year and then wass killed by the new king. Later, when kingss were sstronger, they said the ssword give them power. If they held the ssword, he would protect them.'

'When you attacked us, did you want the sword?'

'The sword musst reach the king. We wanted to make ssure. Now. We think it you are chossen and musst carry it. We think you know. We think you know sstone as well as ssword. We know sstone. It is here in you.'

And he cupped his hand on his belly. As clearly as if thought had been plucked out of the air and placed in his mind, Tog saw the Bloodstone, saw his fingers trace the whorls, felt the smoothness against his fingers and felt the

163

stone grow inside him. He felt sick and suffocated. 'No one told me. It must be a mistake.'

'All iss one. Ssword comes from sstone. Sstone is in man. Man is in ssword. Sword is in man. He is the blade.'

There was a long pause. The river chattered and a breeze rattled the branches of the trees in the still valley.

'Good,' the young man said. 'Now you musst go to see the god in the water.'

They were hustled down from the rock and forced to the end of the glen by gentle crowd pressure. Tog had an impression of blank faces looking up at him and small hands clutching at his sleeves. When he turned to take one last look at the glen, the old man was being passed down from the top of the rock with a certain amount of ceremony.

A single pigsey led them on up the gorge. The path climbed, narrowed to a rocky ledge and they had to turn sideways and hug the wall to feel safe. On and on. Where the river gushed down into a cleft an arm's breadth wide and a fine spray drifted above it like smoke, the pigsey pointed and indicated that he would leave them there.

Around a shoulder of dripping rock, the river roared towards them. The ledge widened and led them into a chamber in the rock. Black water swirled smoothly at their feet, lapping at the stone ledge. At the far end of the cavern, the river tumbled down the rock face into a round pool.

The three looked at the sight, stunned by the noise of the waterfall, soothed by the smooth flow of the water as it left the cavern and the dark mystery of the pool.

'Throw it,' Jenna said.

Tog shivered. He had never felt less significant. Surely something would happen: a voice in his head would boom something important, the waters would grow still, a shaft of sunlight would dance with significance. Nothing.

'Throw it. Here. Into the water. Now. Now! NOW!'

The waterfall thundered. A little fern clinging to the walls of the cavern trembled in the spray. Tog pulled the sword from the scabbard and watched its blade mist over. When he held it up, the tiny droplets gathered and ran down the metal in twisting streams.

'I don't think I can,' he said. 'I think . . . I think we're connected. If it goes in, I go in.'

'No! What it does is not . . . it is not for you. Listen!'

Spray from the waterfall lay on Jenna's face in bright beads but under her eyes two drops suddenly tracked down her cheeks. He thought of his fingers tracing the grooves in the stone. How did they know which way to go? Did they tell the stone or did the stone tell them? The water roared and drowned out any other thoughts.

'I've tried,' Tog said. 'I was asked to carry the sword. It's the only thing I was ever asked to do. I have to.'

'You aren't a killer,' Jenna said. 'Sword is to kill. You . . . are different.'

'I don't know,' Tog said. 'I just don't know. I just think I've got to press on.'

At the fork in the path, the pigsey had left them a leather pouch containing smoked pigeon breasts wrapped in leaves, rough cakes made from ground chestnuts, six rabbit skins and best of all, two flints, a handful of tinder and a large, flat, dried fungus that made Allanza excited because he said it would hold fire for a week if they were careful.

They followed the track up out of the valley and through the wood. After a while it petered out but they carried on heading uphill. The going was hard – sometimes they had to wade through freezing streams – and the longer they walked, the darker the sky grew.

The trees thinned but at the same time, the ground became boggier. They carried on in a sort of stumbling daze, unwilling to stop because it would mean they had to take stock of where they were and what they were doing. Eventually Allanza said, 'We've got to stop. It's getting colder.'

'There's nowhere to shelter,' Tog said.

'We need wood otherwise we'll freeze whatever happens. We should go back into the woods and build something before it gets completely dark.'

'We don't have time,' Tog said. 'It would take a whole day to build a shelter.'

The wind shifted and blew, damp and freezing, right down the valley into their faces. Tog stuck his fingers under his armpits and hopped from foot to foot. There was so much they should have done: gathering firewood, wrapping their feet in the rabbit skins . . . Allanza's nose had gone blue and there was a red streak between it and his mouth where the snot had chapped him. Jenna looked like a drowned rat and was sniffing the air like one. Then she kicked at the ground, clearing an area with her foot. She knelt and held up loose shale, turned around again, sniffing, then began to walk up the valley side, following a little stream whose course was like a black scar in the blanketing whiteness.

'Where are you going?' Tog shouted.

She pointed up the streambed. 'Track,' she said.

They found the hut in a dimple in the land, sheltered from the wind. The door was fastened with a simple hasp on the outside so they knew it was empty but the hearthstones still held a memory of warmth and there was enough stacked peat to burn for weeks.

Allanza got a fire going with a flint and iron that sat by the hearth, Jenna laid out the food the pigseys had given them and Tog forced himself to take the cooking pot down to the stream for water. It was easier now he knew they had somewhere to go back to. Around him there was nothing to see but weather: swirling snow, driving snow, dark sky.

Suddenly the snow seemed to fold into a shape right at the edge of his vision. He had a glimpse, no more than that, of a hunched shape driving forwards that could have been a man, followed by a bigger shape that could have been a horse.

He dropped to a crouch. Could it have been the stranger? Was it possible that he was still on their trail? He looked around. There! Another shape! There! Another. No, he was going mad: seeing snow ghosts. Anything was better than being chased.

They slept the rest of the day, straight through the night and well into the next morning. The storm was still raging and because there was nothing else to do, they slept for much of the next day too.

Tog woke up with his mind racing. Dull winter light crept under the door – it must be late afternoon or evening, he thought. The sword lay by the bed. He didn't want to touch it but he couldn't stop himself thinking about it.

The sword killed the king. He had the sword. He would kill the king. The woodcutter had told him where to find it. The woodcutter had trained him to be a killer. No, worse than that: to be *the* killer? It was brilliant of course. No one would suspect that a little skinny brat was going to kill the king. But why? What was the reason? Was he part of some militant Cornish plot or something bigger and less understandable than that? Perhaps it was just his destiny.

But I'm not prepared, he thought. In his mind, there seemed to be two of him: Tog the woodcutter's boy and Tog the king killer. Which was he?

He thought of all the times he had been cuffed, the woodcutter's appalling drinking sessions, the poverty, the isolation . . . Could he have been normal? Had the woodcutter deliberately deprived him of friends, of useful skills, of a life, of any future but this?

As he tossed and turned in the fug, he became aware that Allanza and Jenna, who had been talking to each other in low voices, were in the middle of a full-scale row.

'All right,' Allanza shouted. 'If picture people aren't sneaky, how come you never told us you could talk? When the pirates took me, they already had you. You could have talked to me, but you never. You just made out you were dumb. Well, as far as I'm concerned, dumb is what you are: a dumb girl with pictures all over herself. They look like spiders' webs to me. Dirty spider's webs. Perhaps the old man Crotus is right. You know what he calls you? A spy.'

'He calls everyone a spy.' Tog tried to break up the argument.

'Ask her! Ask her what she's doing down here! Go on.'

'Perhaps she doesn't want to tell us.'

'Tell you, not stupid crying boy,' Jenna said. The nostrils in her thin nose were flared and her skin was very white. 'I was with my family.'

'And where are they?' Allanza sneered.

She shook her head.

'All right. What happened?'

'I was coming here in boat. The boat . . . went down?'

'Sank,' Tog said.

'The boat sank. Then the pirates.'

'Hah!' Allanza shouted. 'That's a lie. Caught you out. Stupid boy's not so stupid, maybe. The pirates said they found you living rough. I heard them.'

'The boat sank, I swim . . . swam to land. Pirates found me.'

'That's a new story.'

'New story, true story.'

'All right,' Allanza ploughed on. 'Suppose it is true. Why

were you coming here with your family?'

'Family of spies,' Jenna said sarcastically. 'Crying boy knows.'

'If the boat went down, did your family die?' Tog asked. 'Is that why you don't want to talk?'

'My family die?' she repeated. But her eyes moved from side to side, as if she were looking for a way out of a trap.

'You must have swum to shore. Did they drown?'

'She's lying,' Allanza said. 'Look at her. She can't pretend her family drowned and can't think up another story. Looks like thicko's caught her out again!'

'What is it with you?' Tog rounded on him. 'If she's hiding something, maybe it's for a reason.'

'That's right. You stick up for her. I know there's stuff you don't want to tell and all. That's fine. We'll just—'

Jenna interrupted him. 'I ran away from family,' she said.

'You ran away from them and then were caught by the pirates?'

Jenna nodded.

'Why?'

'Can't say.'

'How long were you alone for?' Tog changed the subject.

Jenna held up both hands with fingers spread. 'Ten days.'

'Why did your family bring you all the way down here?'

But Jenna just shook her head and her eyes filled with tears.

'That's right—' Allanza started. But Tog interrupted him.

'That's enough. She's upset. And if you want the truth, I haven't been honest with you either. The truth is, I'm being followed by someone who wants to kill me and because you're with me, he'll probably want to kill you too. He killed my guardian, he had a go at me in the slave camp and he's been after me ever since.'

There was a pause. A gust of wind made the house shake and a sprinkling of snow spurted through a gap under the eaves. The peat smoke eddied.

'We know that,' Allanza said. 'You'd have to be an idiot not to. Borth told me about the man in the slave camp and then there's all that looking back over your shoulder. Anyway, maybe the pigseys got him.'

'Maybe the snow,' Jenna said.

'You know too?' Tog asked. He felt shocked but overwhelmingly relieved.

'If the stupid boy knows, for certain I do. The man wants the sword too.'

'Maybe I should leave it somewhere,' Tog said. 'Bury it. Maybe I should have chucked it in the pool.'

'What good would that do?' Allanza asked. 'That stranger wouldn't know and would still be after us.'

'Maybe I should give the sword to him. Hand it over. Here you are mate: it's up to you now.'

Jenna shook her head. 'Time has passed. Now . . . it would be bad for you. Make you smaller.' She paused. 'At the pool, you throw the sword, then it makes you bigger. Now smaller.'

Without really understanding why, Tog recognized the truth of what she said.

'Then maybe I should just go on my own.'

'No,' Allanza said urgently. 'You can't leave me with her.'

'With my dirty spider pictures, big crying boy,' Jenna said and yawned delicately.

Tog meant to stay awake and guard the door as a sort of penance but in the peat fug he managed about ten heartbeats before he fell asleep.

The snow fell for a day and a night and the rain fell for a day. When the rain was followed by sunshine warm enough to make the ground steam, they knew it was time to go. There was nothing they could give the hut's owner as a parting gift so on Jenna's insistence, Tog found a piece of stone and scratched the words *Tog Allanza Jenna Tibi Gratias Agant* on it. *Tog, Allanza and Jenna give you thanks.*

V

New

At close quarters, the high brown plateau they had seen from the road turned out to be a mixture of rough grazing and bog. On the first day, they passed an old stone circle in the grass with little white bones piled by the foot of each stone, so they knew the little people were around. But Ula's land of the little people was a peat desert, the monotony broken only by a few scattered trees and ancient drystone walls that marched up hills and down to little rivers. On their left, the ground dropped to low hills and thick woodland. To their right, the high moor stretched out like a still sea, waves of brown land topped with breakers of grey granite. Winds darkened the grass, sun dappled the distance with bright pools of light.

They kept to the edge of the moor and learned its

ways. They might find a patch of bog on the summit of a hill while the valley below was firm soil. Equally, the bottom and top of a valley could be a quagmire, while its sides were springy turf. The first night they slept in the shelter of a wall, having made a point of collecting bracken for bedding and dead gorse wood and broom for burning. They didn't sleep. They had saved the food the pigseys had given them, but it turned their guts to gruel and kept them up. They rose in the freezing dawn and moved on. Halfway through the morning of the second day, Tog saw the stranger.

Ahead, the ground was rising over scree to a watchtower of weathered granite. Behind them on a shoulder of land, he saw something, as small and purposeful as an ant, tracking across a patch of unmelted snow.

'You think it's this man that's after you?' Allanza asked. His face was yellow.

'I know it. And now he's got a horse.'

'Well, if we can't go back, we'll have to go forward,' Allanza said. 'First thing to do is throw this person off our trail. Look – he's hidden in that fold in the hillside. The way we're heading, it looks like we're planning to drop down off the moor just ahead of us. Right?'

Tog nodded.

'So instead, we climb straight up and over the top of the hill, then drop down the other side. He'll be rootling around for us down there while we'll be over there.' He pointed straight ahead and Tog was too tired to argue.

It was a hard, punishing slope that went on and on without ever getting to the end or offering a place to hide. Tog felt a bitter heat grow under his tongue and looked behind him. Jenna was on her hands and knees, hair falling over her face. He held out his hand to her, hissed encouragement at Allanza, promised them that the end of the hill would be soon, but it wasn't. The bare slope, ridged by sheep trails, unrolled relentlessly above them.

'Sorry, can't go,' Allanza panted. 'Got to rest.' His head was rocking from side to side.

Tog looked past him, expecting the stranger's head to emerge behind them any second. He wouldn't be tired. Ahead, the horizon was bent like a bow. Only a small outcrop broke the smooth arc.

'Make it to the rock,' he panted. He and Jenna managed to pull Allanza up the last fifty paces.

The wind had scoured a dip behind the rock and they felt safer in it, although it was horribly wet. Allanza was on all fours and retched. Jenna fell sideways and then crawled forwards so she could look back down the slope.

'We've got to move on, Allanza,' Tog said. 'Anyone

coming up the slope will make a beeline for this rock.'

'We're fine. My legs won't work any more.'

'It'll be downhill soon.'

'I'll fall. Leave me. Want to die.'

'Shh!'

Jenna flapped her hands at them. Tog joined her. She pointed to her ear, then down the hill to the left. Tog wished Allanza would stop wheezing. He closed his eyes and listened.

He heard: the rough soughing of wind in grass; the bubbling prickle of the bog; the muffled gurgle of underground streams; the sawing call of a rook. His sweat froze. He heard Jenna swallow, his own hand move on the rough rock, then the silver chink of a horse's tackle, the sucking thud of hoof on wet peat.

Someone whistling a psalm.

Jenna's arm came across him and lay on his shoulders. She moved herself close to him. Allanza wriggled up to them. The three of them watched the stranger's head sway into sight, then his body, then the fine black horse. He was heading diagonally up the hill on a course that would take him past the rock. What would he do when he came to the rock, so casual and calm?

Look behind it.

Tog pointed up the hill. They would have to crawl

keeping the stone between them and the stranger. If they couldn't see him, he couldn't see them. Right?

He scuffed out the dents in the mud they had made and scuttled backwards, joining Allanza and Jenna in a runnel the rain had cut into the peat. The heather met over the top of it and the water was only about a hand's breadth deep but so cold it felt harsh and grainy. Ever since leaving the pigsey valley, he had kept the sword next to his skin. Now it was digging into him, making it hard for him to get as flat as he wanted. It would be an interesting reversal if the sword ended up being the death of him, he thought, weirdly calm.

Here came the stranger, looking down, always down. He spied the rock and turned his horse's head to it. Slowly they padded up the hill towards the rock, the long horse head looking down for grass, the stranger's foxy nose questing for kids. Once round the rock, the stranger leaned right down over the black mane to investigate the scratchy marks Tog had made, then straightened up, sniffing the air and heading on the same course.

Tog felt Allanza try to get up and gripped him hard. Wait. Freeze. Drown. Wait. Good things come to those that . . .

Above them grey and white patterns formed and reformed in the grey dome of the sky.

Wait.

Tog began to shudder with the cold.

Wait.

There. He heard the horse behind them, so close he didn't dare look, followed by the aimless whistling of that psalm again that he could now identify as number one hundred and twenty-one.

Canticum graduum levavi oculos meos in montes unde veniet auxilium meum.

I raise my eyes to the mountains from where my help will come.

Tog lowered his head into the stream, praying that the heather had closed above them. Heard the slow, deliberate step of the hooves pass by on his left. Waited till he thought the stranger was out of earshot. Waited a bit longer, then rolled out of the ditch, too cold to be frightened or relieved.

'That tune he was whistling,' Allanza said between chattering teeth. 'It reminded me of something.'

'It was a psalm. You would have heard Crotus's pilgrims singing them. I was taught them.'

'Is he a pilgrim then?' Allanza asked.

Tog shook his head. 'You don't have to be a pilgrim to sing psalms. Just a Christian.'

'And now he is ahead of us,' Jenna said. 'This is a prroblem.'

* * *

They dropped down off the moor and came across the girl in a clearing on the edge of the forest. She was lying on the far side of a narrow, dark, swift flowing river with her arm in the water. As they passed her, she lifted her head and called weakly for help.

They crossed over a tree-trunk bridge but when Tog tried to help her up she called out in alarm. She had been filling her cooking pot with water but was too weak to pull it up. Jenna knelt by her but she couldn't budge it and it was only when Allanza joined them that they could lift it from the water.

'Thank you,' she said. 'I couldn't drop it. The water's high this time of year and we would have lost it.' Her pinched face was grey apart from an angry red flush on her cheekbones. Suddenly she was overcome by a violent fit of coughing that doubled her up.

'I think I'd have a job carrying that,' Tog said. 'Haven't you got anyone to help you?'

'Not any more,' the girl said faintly, then began to cough again. She slumped back against a tree. At that moment, a boy burst into the clearing, shouting, 'What are you doing to her? Get away!'

Tog and Jenna backed away while the boy knelt by her.

'She's wet!' the boy shouted.

'She couldn't lift the pot out of the water and obviously didn't want to lose it.'

'What are you doing here? You have no right! These are Ecta's lands. You are not welcome!'

The boy had thick, bright red hair that stood up in patches, a freckled face and light blue eyes.

'Who's Ecta?' Tog asked.

'You don't know who Ecta is?' He made a spitting noise. 'Who do you think you are?'

'Who do you think we are?' Tog asked.

'I think you're stupid! Ecta is the greatest bard in the world. He has been honoured by kings and emperors.'

'Well,' said Tog. 'We don't want to upset him. We'll head up hill again.'

'Wait. You can't do that. Your ignorance is an insult and the insult is taken even if it wasn't meant. I challenge you to a fight.'

'All of us?' Tog said.

'Just your champion.' He was bigger than Tog, and had just gone through the change so that his voice broke like a donkey's when he spoke.

'What?'

'Your best fighter. I'll take him on. Or wilt thou be forever branded a coward in the sight of your maiden?'

There was a moment's silence.

'He means Jenna,' Allanza said.

'I know he means Jenna.' Tog was irritated. 'I just want to find a way out of this. I mean, we were just trying to help.'

'We need to go straight on to head away from your stranger,' Allanza said. 'Let's humour him. I could beat him with one arm tied behind my back.'

Humouring the boy involved recrossing the river and waiting for him to take up a fighter's crouch in the middle of the bridge.

'What brings strangers to Ecta's lands?' the boy called out.

'We need to get to the other side,' Tog said. 'May we pass?'

'No.'

'Please,' Allanza said.

This made the boy furious. 'No. I say I'm going to challenge you and then you can say you're going to fight me.'

'Just get on with it,' Tog said.

'I challenge you to a fair fight for the glory of this land,' the boy called out.

Allanza stepped on to the bridge. The boy made a few grappling moves but Allanza held him at arm's length and used his weight to push him steadily back. Suddenly the boy flew under Allanza's guard and went for one of his legs. They rocked for a second in the middle of the bridge, hanging on to each other, then toppled into the water and were swept downstream. Tog and Jenna ran along the bank beside them and almost immediately it became clear the boy could not swim.

Eventually Allanza was able to get his footing where the river shallowed at a bend and pulled him out by the scruff of his neck. On dry land, the boy started sicking up water like a puppy, his hands digging in the ground. An instant too late, Tog saw that he had dug up a stone the size of an eagle's egg which he brought round in an arc and smashed into Allanza's forehead.

Allanza's eyes rolled up and he went down into the water.

'Hah! I said you will not pass. These are Ecta's lands!' the boy shouted, leaping to his feet. His arms were rigid by his side and the tendons on his neck stood out so far that his head looked as if it were balanced on spikes.

Tog and Jenna plunged back into the water and dragged Allanza half on to the bank. The stone had split the skin above his eye, and very dark blood was now spilling out and running into his eyebrow. Jenna tore a dock leaf from a clump and began to tease the red rivulet away from the eye. Tog was out of the river without even thinking. He felt light, tight and ready to fight.

The boy still had his stone; Tog had his sword but didn't want to use it because then they would be stuck with the dying sister.

The boy leapt at him. Tog sidestepped easily, trying to read him, as the woodcutter had taught him. Everyone has their own way of fighting, he'd say, like they have their own way of walking and talking. Get a handle on that and you're halfway to winning the battle. The boy dived in again, and again Tog sidestepped, but this time the boy's foot lashed out as he went down, catching Tog on the shin. It didn't hurt much but it showed him that the boy was learning, so he was watching the next time the boy launched himself, saw how he checked and, instead of aiming to grapple him round the waist, darted in low. Tog slid to one side and fell on the boy's back, knocking the wind out of him.

The boy squirmed like an eel and where Tog expected to find an arm so he could twist it behind his back he found nothing. He broke and leapt back. The boy turned, followed, fingers clawed and going for Tog's eyes. Tog ducked, grabbed him by the front of his tunic and swept his legs away. The boy landed with a thump and a cry but was up again quickly, blinking away his tears. Tog elbowed him in the throat and he broke off, choking. The next attack was weaker; the next weaker still and the boy's breath started coming in whooping grunts. The next time he closed, Tog grabbed his right arm, spun round the back of him, still holding his arm and jerked it brutally up behind his back. Jenna dropped a leather thong over his neck and tightened it, then they tied his hands behind his back.

Tog was panting. He was surprised at how many bruises and cuts he had, not to mention a ring of toothmarks on his forearm which he hadn't even noticed. Allanza was sitting up now, pressing a pad of dock leaves on the bruise above his right eye.

Jenna gave the leather thong a tug and the boy stopped crying and tried to headbutt her. She skipped out of the way, tripped him, then sat on his back, pulling on the tie until he started to choke.

'Stop it!' The weak cry came from the far bank where the girl was now standing. 'He doesn't mean any harm!'

'He bloody does!' Tog shouted back. 'Look at my friend! Look at me!'

'Don't hurt him. He's all I have.'

'Make him promise not to attack!' Tog said.

'Kai, promise,' the girl called faintly.

'I will never submit,' the boy shouted back.

'We don't want you to,' Tog said. 'She needs help and so does my friend, thanks to you. That's a really bad cut. Now will you just stop attacking us?'

The boy bowed his head and thought. 'I suppose I could bid you welcome to my hall,' he said.

'That would be good,' Tog said. 'And we'll take your lead off.'

A valley opened up, greened with lush grass and separated from the shaggy moorland by an old stone wall. Backed up against the woods was a compound of four round huts surrounded by a fence of sharpened stakes. 'Welcome to our home,' the boy said. But as he spoke, his back stiffened and the words seemed to be cut off in his throat. He pushed open a gate in the stockade, gappy and rotten, and led them across the compound. He shouted and clapped his hands. From behind one of the huts, three crows flapped into the air.

Something about the settlement made the tiny hairs on the back of Tog's neck stand up. It was silent, that was one thing, and after days living in the open, the smell of the midden was strong.

'There's food,' the boy said. 'Meat if you want it. Barley too. Fruit, even. We're particular about fruit. There will be feasting and tales told around the fire.'

I can't smell smoke, Tog thought. He looked around. Half a dozen thin chickens scratched in the dirt. A bare loom was propped against a smaller hut. Off to one side, between two of the huts, lay four long mounds of earth.

The girl saw where he was looking. 'Kai,' she said. 'If there's to be any feasting, we'll have to cook a meal. Go inside and light the fire.'

She watched as the boy trotted into the roundhouse, then said, 'He's been like this since mother and father died. And worse since the monster started coming in the night.'

Tog followed the boy into the roundhouse. In the middle of the room was a proper hearth surrounded by flat stones. A blackened cauldron hanging on a sooty metal tripod stood close by. Two semi-circular benches stood on either side of the fire.

The boy busied himself collecting wood from a pile by the door. Allanza blew on his fire fungus until it glowed and lit tinder, then kindling. The fire started to blaze and he turned in front of it, drying his clothes.

'Tell me about the monster,' Tog said to Kai.

'It is death,' Kai said. 'It comes in the night. We hear it, my sister and I, and I have tried to . . . tried to . . . I can't. It puts a spell on us, I suppose. I can hear it round the graves and it won't leave them alone – that's how I know it's death. Then it comes to the house and walks around the walls. You can hear its footsteps. It's huge and you can hear its breath. It scratches at the walls and door. It's . . . horrid!'

'But why did you want to fight us?' Tog asked. 'Your family's dead, you're being bothered by a monster . . . surely you could do with all the help you can get.'

The boy sucked in snot and straightened his back. 'We don't need help,' he said. 'We're Ecta's people. My father rode with the high king. He was much honoured. We are proud and stand alone.'

'You're going to fall alone if you're not careful,' Tog said.

But the boy just squared his thin shoulders and put his face close to the fire so that it would look as if the smoke were making his eyes water.

Tog left him to it and went to find Jenna.

'The girl is ill in here.' She punched Tog's chest. 'The sickness that killed the family wants her. All she says, "What happens to Kai when I'm dead?"'

'And the monster?'

'It comes in the night. They hear it breathing and trying to get into their hut. Sometimes it makes a noise like this.' She made a deep moaning. Tog could read the challenge in Jenna's eyes, and the curiosity behind the challenge. 'They're too scared to move. If we go, we feel bad.'

Tog knew what Jenna meant because he felt the same. At the same time, he felt she was challenging him and resented it. He thought out loud, to make his decision seem reasoned. 'If we move on we'll just think about them and feel guilty, and if we're going to meet the stranger, maybe this isn't such a bad place. There are three of us, four with Kai, and you're worth two. We must be able to defend ourselves.' He looked from Allanza to Jenna. 'By the way, neither of you really believe in this monster, do you?'

'Of course I do,' Jenna said.

'Of course too,' Allanza echoed.

They had eaten and were now in the roundhouse, sitting on the benches where Ecta the bard had held court in his glory days. Kai was telling them what had happened in a little voice. 'First it was my little brother. Then my mother. Then my father. Now my sister's ill. I couldn't help them. All the time it was like they were drowning; I had a little cough and nothing else.'

'You did what you could, I'm sure,' Tog said.

'There was nothing I could do against the monster. My father – maybe he could have fought it but he was old. He was a bard who rode with Utta, the Great Dragon, High King of Britain – and wrote songs about his battles afterwards. The Dragon was so pleased he gave him this land, gold, horses and cattle. But the horses and cattle are gone and the money and the Dragon of Britain is dead.'

'What now?' Tog asked. 'Who's high king now?'

'I don't know his name. He's useless. Everything's broken down and gone to hell. You only have to look around: disease . . . pirates . . . civil war. How come you don't know any of this? Where are you from?'

'Cornwall,' Tog said.

'The Cornish are worst,' Kai said. 'Where's he from?' Nodding at Allanza.

'Across the water. Brittany.'

'They're just as bad. Where's the girl from?'

Kai, Tog noticed, couldn't look at Jenna.

'She's a Pict.'

'I can see that. Why are you travelling with a girl?'

'We all just came together.'

'A warrior can't trust women, my father told me.'

'He might have told you how to fight fair,' Tog said. 'Did your father leave any weapons to help us take on this monster?'

'Follow me,' the boy said. It was almost dark and he carried a flaming branch across the compound to one of the smaller huts. On the wall half a dozen hunting spears lay on a rack. A long dark cloak hung from a peg below a metal war helmet with a Roman look to it.

'We buried him with his sword,' the boy said. 'Are you sure the spears will work against the monster?'

Tog took a spear from the rack and looked along it,

something he had seen the castle guards do when they were bored. As far as he could tell, the shaft was strong and straight. A necklace of feathers and bird skulls, tied round the base of the blade, rattled as he turned it in his hand.

'This will do,' Tog said. 'Now we'd better get back because Jenna says we've got to stand by the fire so the smoke covers our smell. When does it come?'

'In the darkest hour of the night,' Kai said.

'Then we'll have to watch and wait. Allanza and Jenna will sleep in one of the other huts, I'll sit outside. We'll need blankets and you'll need to tell us all you know about the beast.'

'Yes,' Kai said. 'Now you have eaten of my bread and taken up my spear and pledged your lives to my cause, I'll tell you. But I warn you, it'll scare you.'

He sat them down on benches and struck a pose by the fire, and although he looked absurd, he must have inherited some of his father's qualities because Tog, Jenna and Allanza were spellbound by his words.

The story concerned a warrior who one day came across a beautiful maiden sitting by a well in a forest, but before he could kiss her he was challenged to a fight by her husband, the King of the Greenwood, who had lived among the trees so long that he had turned green.

The warrior fought with the old king and after many a full blow and sore, the warrior chopped off the old king's head but as it rolled on the ground a strange and terrible thing happened. The jaws started to work and the tongue flopped around and then the head of the old king told the warrior that *whatever happened* he must remain pure and resist the temptations of the maiden or in exactly one year's time, he would get his head chopped off too.

The maiden, who seemed to grow more desirable by the minute in the warrior's eyes, took him to her cave where she crowned him King of the Greenwood and lay down beside him on her bed of green leaves and fragrant heather, but try as she might, she could not get the warrior to marry her and do all that being married involves.

For a whole year she brewed magic potions, got him drunk on whisky and honey, fed him on boars' testicles, bulls' blood, his favourite berries, nuts, mushrooms and so on, but the brave warrior resisted, even though his desire grew day by day. And as time passed, the new king turned green and exactly a year to the day when he had killed the old king, a warrior came by and found the maiden sitting by a well in the forest.

The Green King challenged him to a fight but because he was not knackered by loving, won the fight and sent the challenger packing. Feeling great, he turned to the queen thinking at last he could give in to her charms, but to his horror, he saw the beautiful maiden swell to the size of a hut, turn all hairy and become a hideous, snuffling, stinking old monster that shuffled off into the forest and was never seen again.

'Until now,' Kai said. 'The monster has returned. It won't be happy until it's killed every member of my family apart from me for whom it has reserved a fate worse than death. I am to be taken to its cave where it's going to marry me and turn me into the next Green King. Do you see now why I'm so scared?'

It was a cloudless night so Tog could see the monster quite clearly. He heard her long before she came through the barricade: the snapping of twigs and a sort of snuffling wheeze as she quested for her young husband and his sister's soul. Tog meant to call his friends as soon as he heard the first twig crack, but realized that his voice would give him away and then she might pick him up in her thick arms and waddle off with him instead.

So he had no choice but to wait as she started to squeeze through the stockade. She was bigger than the picture in his head, and denser, hairier, blacker and more real. Dear God, Tog thought, she was as big as a hut and although she moved on all fours for the most part, sometimes she would rise and try and stand like the person she once was, questing for the scent of a boy.

He watched the moonlight glint on her thick, wet snout and fervently wished he'd spent longer standing in the woodsmoke.

There! She ignored him and was padding on all fours across the beaten earth of the compound towards the roundhouse, pausing only to sniff at the graves. Round the house she went, just as Kai had said she would, scratching at the walls, sniffing the air at the door, making an occasional wet moaning sound.

Tog could not imagine what it must be like for Kai and his sister to live with that horror night after night. As for him, he felt as if all his sinews had been cut. He thought he was safe – he was in the shadow of a hut and the monster had shown no interest in his scent at all – but it didn't alter the inconvenient fact that he was too scared to move.

A movement next to him would have made him scream if the sides of his throat had not been stuck together.

'Bear,' Jenna breathed. 'I know this thing.'

He was acutely aware of her presence. To talk, she had to press her mouth in his ear and he could feel the warmth of her breath and her urgent pressure on his shoulder.

So, the witch of the wood had turned herself into a bear!

It made sense. Although Tog had never seen a bear before – as far as he knew there were none in Cornwall – the fact that she was something substantial, something real, made him feel better.

'How do you know?' he asked.

'Many bears in Pridhain – my home. All boys must kill a bear.'

That's why she's here, Tog thought. She wants to see how I measure up against the boys back home.

A bear. Just a bear . . .

Using the spear he pushed himself to his feet.

Jenna rose with him and gripped him by the arm, took a pinch of skin between her nails and pinched and twisted. The pain was like a little lightning strike and jerked Tog into another state. His muscles tightened even as the fear flooded him.

He took a grip on his spear and stepped into the faint moonlight.

The bear sensed Tog immediately and reared on to its back legs. Its arms were as thick as his chest and he didn't like the way the moonlight refused to catch in its little piggy eyes. It was built on a different scale from anything he had seen, apart from a horse: a horse with thick arms, claws, teeth.

It moaned again, a horrible sound, went down on all

fours and moved towards him with a quicker sort of purpose than he was ready for. He gripped the spear haft and shook it as he stepped back. The bird skulls rattled dryly. The bear sank back on his haunches and moaned again.

Tog circled round in a crouch, almost hoping the bear would make a move so he was spared the responsibility.

'Now,' Jenna said.

Tog took a step forward and rehearsed what he would have to do. A sudden quick thrust followed by a step so he could throw all his weight into the wicked spear tip. The bear turned to face him, its arms by its side, its chest exposed, reeking of casual violence. Then it reared into the air, and enfolded Tog in its dark, musty smell.

Tog lifted the spear. This was it . . .

The bear lifted a paw, very delicately hooked it over the spear point and drew the metal blade closer to its face where it sniffed it.

Tog felt the skinny moon lean in on him as if it were watching. The world drew itself around him. He raised his eyes above the bear, above the hut roofs and the scratchy branches of the trees to the night sky where seven stars made the bear in the sky.

The claw round his neck burned his skin.

He thought of the scars on the old dead slaver's chest and lowered the spear tip slowly and the bear followed it down until its head was on the ground.

There was a sudden sharp intake of breath from Jenna. Her eyes were wide and she was staring not at the bear but at Tog.

She said something quietly and intensely in her own language.

'It's just a bear,' Tog said. The bear lay on its side and snuffled. 'It's a big, smelly old bear.'

He felt immersed in calm as if he were up to his neck in a cold sea, and great, clear waves of joy and relief were rising inside him.

Let this moment last, he thought: the bear on the ground, the bear in the sky, me with a spear and Jenna to see it all happen.

Something crashed in the roundhouse. The spell was broken.

The bear lifted its head to look reproachfully at Tog, rolled over and shambled back into the woods. Jenna came up to him. She took the bear claw from under his shirt and drew it four times down each cheek, pressing in so hard it drew blood.

'Now you are monster brother,' she said and shot him a look.

'Bear brother sounds better,' Tog said.

'Monster.'

'Did you kill it?' Kai's shaky voice came from the other side of the door.

'No,' Tog said. 'But it's gone away.'

'Oh. The other thing is: I think my sister just died.' Pause. 'I feel rather sad about it as a matter of fact.'

Digging the hole for Kai's sister took most of the morning. After it was over, Kai asked them to stay again.

'We can't,' Tog said. 'We've got to get on.'

'You stay,' he said to Tog. 'I quite like you. Let the others go.'

'But it's me that got to go. They're really doing me a favour in coming along.'

'Go where then?'

Tog told him about the Island.

'I know all about the Island. Stay here,' Kai said. 'I've got food and we can trap things in the forest. You can set off when the weather gets better.'

'I need to get there by Easter and there's a bad man who wants to kill me.'

'I can lead you through the woods. I know all the roads and paths. It'll take half the time. And there are real Romans on the way.'

'Real Romans?' Tog said. His stomach felt jolted. 'Now you're just being silly.'

'North of here. There's a house – a real Roman house with real Romans living in it. My father talked about them. We might be able to stay there. He said I would be introduced if I kept myself pure. He said they were very particular. If I wanted to be the best warrior in the kingdom, I would have to keep myself pure and stay away from women. They've got stones that talk.'

'I'm sorry,' Tog said. 'Now I know you're just—'

'Stay for lunch,' Kai said. 'Please. Show me how to cook. I've – I've never been on my own before.'

Tog was carrying water from the stream and saw the black horse tethered to the compound fence before he saw the stranger. His head felt as empty as a bladder on a stick. He ducked to get out of sight and worked his way round to the perimeter fence. He followed Kai and the stranger round to the graves.

'No,' Kai was saying. 'It took me ages to dig the hole.'

'So it's just you, here on your own.'

'Yes.'

'No one else.'

All Tog could hear was the sound of his own breathing.

'Then you won't mind if I look around.'

'What for?'

'Children. Three of them. Two boys, one girl. You've gone red. You look shifty.'

'Miss my parents. That's all. Not used to talking to strangers. I don't like you here.'

'Oh, I bet you're more sociable than you look. Now, shall I start in this little hut?'

As the stranger put his head inside, Tog saw Allanza and Jenna appear in the doorway of another hut across the way, looking panicked. The stranger reappeared and they darted back inside.

'What are these?' The stranger came out holding Kai's father's helmet and carrying a broken spear.

'They were my father's.'

'He's here, isn't he? You're lying.' He swung the helmet at Kai and hit him on the side of the head. Kai went down and the stranger knelt on his back.

Tog simply could not understand where the violence was coming from. The stranger used it like an experienced craftsman used a tool to do a particular job. It was chilling.

'We buried him with his sword.' Kai's voice was muffled.

'Who's we?'

'Me and my sister.'

'And she is where?'

'Dead. Last night.'

'Oh yes. How very convenient. Tell me another.'

'Let me go!' Kai roared.

The stranger gave a little derisive laugh and let him stand. Kai leaned forwards, his neck braced and his arms and legs curiously rigid. Recognizing the signs, Tog braced himself.

'What is it? Lost your tongue?' the stranger said carelessly.

Kai launched himself head first at the stranger's belly, hitting him so hard and unexpectedly that Tog heard the ooof of air being expelled from his lungs. Kai shouted, 'Run!'

Allanza and Jenna appeared in the doorway but before Kai could move away, the stranger grabbed his hair and twisted it down and round, forcing him to his knees.

Jenna and Allanza stopped together.

'I thought for a minute this was my brat,' the stranger said, jerking Kai's head round so he was looking straight up at him. 'But he's too ugly. A giant and a picture girl. I heard about you two at the slave camp. Where's the thief? Hiding somewhere is he? I bet he is.'

'We dumped him,' Allanza said. 'Way back. Up on the moor. Didn't like him.'

'And where exactly did you leave him?'

'Up there. I don't know.'

'I see. So how come there are four sets of footprints by the grave?'

Tog willed Allanza to deny it. No one could tell how many people had been walking there after so quick a look.

'Ah,' Allanza said. 'That would be . . .' He dried up.

'My neighbour,' Kai said.

'Called what? Mr Big Man With A Club? Spare me. Now this is your last chance. Where is he?'

'Here,' Tog said. The stranger threw down Kai as Tog reached for the spear that had been propped up inside the door of the weapon hut and pointed it at the stranger's belly.

'Clever,' the stranger said. 'If I'd seen you had a spear, I would've kept hold of the brat as a hostage.'

'I know,' Tog lied.

'No you didn't. What do you want?'

The question threw Tog off balance. 'What do you mean?'

'For what you've got. For what you stole. For what's rightfully mine.'

'Does he mean the magic sword?' Allanza asked. Tog could have killed him.

'Magic. Sword,' the stranger said, as if he were savouring the two words. Tog was aware of a mind thinking very fast behind an impassive face. 'Magic sword. No, you can't. No one's seen that for years . . . But of course! Call me an

Englishman and make me eat mud. You don't mean that's . . . My God! I'd smile if I could.' He touched the wounds on his cheek. They were healing, though still painful looking. 'Now then, you know there's good magic and bad magic. Well, this sword is bad magic for you but good magic for me. Do you understand?'

'You know about it?' Tog asked.

The stranger snorted: 'Know about it? Of course I—Listen, this has all got off on the wrong foot. We can't do business at spear point. Can we drop weapons and talk?'

'No.'

The stranger sighed as if Tog were a rather rude child.

'All right. Can we at least do names?'

'Is this how you did business with the woodcutter?' Tog asked. 'Asked him his name, then killed him?'

'That was all a dreadful mistake.' The stranger sounded serious and earnest. 'Maybe I was a bit pushy. He lost his temper. It all went horribly wrong. But that's in the past. Let's just get down to business. I'm going to be honest with you and then it's your turn. I want that little sword and I'm prepared to pay you a great deal of money for it.'

'Have you got a great deal of money?'

'Not yet, but I will when I have the sword. Don't think it will do you any good because it won't. You see, I know how to—'

'No. Whatever you say, you can't have it.'

'What did that old fool the woodcutter tell you?' the stranger almost howled. He took a step towards Tog who made a trial jab with the spear.

'Don't move,' Tog said.

'You're not going to kill me,' the stranger said. 'Why are you doing this?'

'Because it was the last thing the woodcutter asked me to do.'

'Asked you. Asked you. Asked you. Yes, it's all coming together. You're taking it to the Island, aren't you? Call me an Englishman again! I should have got that. No, no, don't shake your head. I'm right! I'm brilliant! But tell me this: did you really know your precious woodcutter? I'm guessing you didn't. Did he tell you about the tomb? I'm guessing he didn't. You forget. I went into it. Ever wondered how the little baby in there died? Doesn't take much to kill a baby.'

Tog took a step backwards, shaking his head. 'That's not true. I mean, I don't know. He was good to me.'

'He kept you alive as cover. With you around, he didn't show up as a deserter. A murderer. A liar. A traitor. An outlaw. With you around he was just a poor old drunk struggling to keep body, soul and his brat alive. Any kindness he showed you was just to keep you loyal. You know it. I know it. Just admit it.'

'Stop it!' Tog made another thrust. His arms felt like twigs and he could feel his hands slip in sweat. 'He wasn't like that. I've got to take the sword to the Island. It's treasure. You just want the reward.'

'Oh please,' the stranger said. 'I've told you about your woodcutter. Why bother to do what he wants now? Look. It's make your mind up time. Kill me or give me the sword.'

He grabbed the spear just behind the blade and held it against his chest, over his heart.

'Go on. If you can't kill me, I am going to hound you to the ends of the earth. You'll never be able to rest. Never be able to sleep. And all for . . . what?'

Sweat stung Tog's eyes. Tension in his arms made them tremble. As if he felt the tremor, the stranger smiled. Tog pushed, felt the spear go through the stranger's jerkin, felt it press a rib . . . then stopped. He thought of the woodcutter dying in a ditch while his home burned. He tried to imagine the stranger was not there and he was pushing the spear into a side of pork, a tree, anything.

Still the spear would not shift.

'Give me,' Jenna said.

'NO! If I can't, no one else can,' Tog said, but he found himself pulling back, empty and wretched.

'You know I'm—' the stranger began, then he went down, collapsing like a sack of grain as Allanza hit him on the side of the head. He tossed a round, palm-sized stone in his hand and looked at Tog.

'Thank you,' Tog said.

'We'll tie him up. Then if he escapes, it was meant to be. If we get away now, he won't find us.'

'Is that the rock I hit you with?' Kai asked.

'It is,' Allanza answered.

'Why were you keeping it?'

Allanza gave Kai a long and level stare, then turned his back.

The stranger's horse had two saddle bags, one containing clothes, the other two loaves of stale bread, dried meat and cheese wrapped in leaves. With the last of Kai's stores, Tog thought it would keep the four of them for three, maybe four days, realistically. After that, he just hoped they were near the Island.

VI

Waxing Crescent

Kai really did know ways through the woods that kept them away from the roads. The paths he found were dry and invisible to the naked eye. Where they crossed streams, they crossed where the banks were firm. When they came to a river, a line of mossy stepping-stones showed just under the surface, lifting their backs like small green dolphins. They emerged from the wood above a bare shoulder of land, looking out over a softly rolling landscape of forest and clearing. By the sun, it was late afternoon.

'The Island's that way,' Kai said. He'd taken over the stranger's horse and had ridden ahead. Now he returned, manoeuvring the horse with an easy grace and making Tog feel insignificant. He gestured ahead but slightly to the left of the sun. 'In a day or so we'll be leaving the land of the

Dumnoni and passing into the Durotriges' land. It's all better than Cornwall, at any rate.'

'Why is he like this?' Allanza asked, waiting until Kai was just out of earshot.

Tog shook his head. 'He just thinks he's better than us. That's all.'

'But he's not. We rescued him.'

'The truth is, he knows where we're going and if it makes him happy to put everyone else down, we just have to put up with it,' Tog said.

'I don't understand . . .'

Tog exploded. 'I don't have an answer. I don't know everything. I may be on a fool's errand and you're even bigger fools for coming with me. I'm doing this because I thought the man who sent me on this mission was good, but maybe he wasn't. Maybe he was bad.'

'I don't think you're bad,' Allanza said. 'I'm sorry if I made you angry. All I was going to say was: I don't understand anything much except how to fight.'

'But if you don't know why . . .'

'You'll tell me,' Allanza said firmly. 'I trust you.'

'But that's my point! You shouldn't. I don't know what I'm doing.'

Allanza put his head down and looked mulish.

'How's that cut?' Tog asked to change the subject. The

wound on Allanza's forehead was not healing. The skin around it was puffy and red, and it constantly wept a thin stream of pinky, yellowy fluid.

'It hurts.'

'You should have said. Moss. That can help.'

Allanza's eyes slid past his shoulder and his face flushed. Tog turned his head and saw Kai on the horse, close enough to hear, his face set in an odd twist: stubborn, vulnerable.

'But I do trust you,' Allanza said. 'Even if you don't know what you're doing.'

An odd thing happened later. Tog had stayed behind with Kai to try and make a camp for the night while Allanza and Jenna went off to see if they had caught anything in Jenna's snares.

An hour later they came back in high spirits, just as Tog managed to coax a fire into life. For once the snares had worked, rewarding them with a rabbit.

Allanza held his hand out to Tog who unsheathed the sword and handed it to him.

'Do you know what you're doing, you oaf?' Kai suddenly asked.

Allanza chopped the rabbit's feet off, then slid the sword under the skin, careful not to puncture the belly or the guts.

'He knows what he's doing,' Tog said.

'And where would you be without me?' Kai asked. 'Lost in the woods.'

'Where would you be without us? Starving to death in your hut.' Allanza shouted.

'Oh really?' Kai shouted back. 'And who are you? Just because he found that sword you think you know everything. You have no idea, do you? That's what makes it worse.'

'No idea of what?'

'What you're doing. There are legends about the sword and you treat it like it's a butcher's knife.'

'You know about it?'

'Everyone knows about it – everyone who wasn't brought up in a hovel, that is. It was stolen and that's why the country's gone to the dogs.'

'When?'

Kai shrugged. 'I don't know *when*,' he said. 'It's not important *when*. What is important is that in the middle of the Island there's this hill they call the tor and top of the tor there's this stone. Long ago there was this king that pulled the sword from the stone – magicked it out – and even now if you go there you can see the hole the sword came out of. The king's meant to keep it safe but it was lost and now you've got it and you don't even realize.'

'Does that mean if I give it back to the king, everything will get better?' Tog asked.

'How should I know?' Kai said. 'Why should I tell you if I did?'

It didn't rain all night. When Tog woke just before dawn with the ecstatic yell of a blackbird echoing in his ear and a red dawn burning low on the eastern horizon, he thought he could smell spring. But it didn't dull the hunger or make them any less weak as they moved listlessly through the land. Kai found some moss and gave it to Allanza but it didn't take the swelling down around his wound. Tog tried to see the significance of what Kai had said about the sword but couldn't. If anything, it just made him seem even less important than before: just a single, tiny, unimportant element in the old sword's story.

The following night their snares stayed empty; the same in the morning. They went to bed hungry and woke up even more tired than the night before.

They fixed their sights on a clump of trees on top of a ridge over to the west. Kai thought they might even be able to see the gap in the hills from there. He stayed on his horse and tended to go ahead to scout out a route. It meant taking detours – for the horse's sake, he tried to avoid any sort of woodland that the others might have gone through

– but then he was good at spotting bogs and finding ways over streams and rivers that might have held them up.

Halfway through the morning, they saw smoke rising a couple of miles away to the east and guessed it came from a village.

'We could get food there,' said Allanza. 'Swap the horse for a pig. Even a leg of pig, roast it over an open fire, get hold of some bread, wrap the pork in the bread . . .'

'They'll just steal the horse,' Tog said.

'Then we could eat the horse,' Allanza said. 'I'm serious.'

Tog looked from Allanza to Jenna and from Jenna to Kai. Allanza's cut was yellow and purple, Jenna was like a wraith and Kai's skin was the colour of whey.

'The way I see it is this,' Allanza said. 'We're avoiding villages in case we get attacked or something but what's the point if we die of starvation?'

'What do you think Kai? Jenna?' Tog asked.

Kai shrugged. Jenna said, 'First beg. Hide the horse.'

'All right,' Tog said. 'Let's go.'

They were looking for a place to cross a deep, fast-flowing river when they heard angry shouting. The noise came closer and closer and a cart train consisting of a painted cart and a cage on wheels careered into sight down a sunken lane, pulled by straining mules and driven by a man wearing a yellow tunic and brown stockings. The cart plunged into the water in a cloud of spray, hit a rock, reared up and stopped dead. The driver was thrown loose, the mules started to rear and flounder and the cage fell over and started drifting downriver.

A group of men and women wearing a weird assembly of clothes – robes, hats, furs – appeared on the far bank. All of them, the women as well as the men, made for the cage, three of them trying to hold it back against the current, the others trying to right it.

Meanwhile villagers in hot pursuit arrived on the bank, where they waved farm tools and scrabbled about in the mud for stones to throw.

'Circus people!' Allanza said excitedly. 'Look!'

Tog looked at him worriedly. In the night, Allanza's wound seemed to have got worse and he had thrashed around, muttering and whimpering. His forehead felt papery and hot. 'You're not going to . . .' he called out, but it was too late. Allanza was splashing through the water. He hooked his hands under the cage. There were encouraging shouts. The cage rose further, further, then crashed back on to its wheels. The driver crawled back on to the cart, cracked his whip and the train creaked out of the water.

'We go now,' Jenna said. 'I don't like them.'

But the group had gathered around Allanza and were

making a huge fuss of him. One of them leapt on to the cart's wooden seat, stood on his hands and clapped his feet. There was a lot of whooping.

Allanza's face was split by a mad smile. 'Saxon players,' he called. 'A circus. I saw some at the midsummer fair back in my village. They were chased away from that as well.' He laughed again.

'My friend! I can't thank you enough.' The man who had been driving the cart approached them. His flat, slightly harsh accent, contrasted with his flamboyant manner. 'What would we have done? Stuck in that river with the brutes from that village pelting us with God knows what and waving those dreadful farm implements. I hate to think what might have happened after such a little thing, such a simple misunderstanding.'

'What was it?' Kai asked.

'Oh, just one of us in the wrong place at the wrong time. Lord, what a horse,' he said, running his hands expertly over its sides and legs. 'Whose is it?'

'We go,' Jenna said to Tog. 'We go now.'

'My word, the painted lady speaks. No, no, pay no attention. So must we, dear lady, so must we. Here today, gone tomorrow and try not to outstay your welcome: that's my motto. But at least let us repay your friend here for what he's done. That cut above the eye, for example, does not look good. My name is Penda and that good woman there is Hilda, my wife. She's skilled in medicine and will know what to do. You, my tall friend, are from Brittany, are you not? What brings four young people together in this cold old world?'

'We're not four,' Allanza said loudly. 'We're three. We just picked *him* up two days ago on the edge of the moor. I've seen people like you before at our village. You had jugglers, a sword swallower, dancers, singers and a man who danced with his bear.' Allanza hopped around clumsily.

'We have all that, or rather I should say we had all that. Alas, the climax of our little show, the sine qua non, as it were, is no more.' Penda opened his hands and looked at the dirty palms mournfully. 'Orson is absent. A voice in the night whispered in his furry ear, "Bruin begone," and off he went because some lazy little scum forgot to fasten his cage last thing at night.'

He directed a vicious look at one of his companions, a small, spidery man with sticking-out ears, sticking-out teeth and sticking-out hair.

'Sorry,' said Tog. 'I don't understand.'

'Our dancing bear escaped because that little toerag forgot to lock his cage about two weeks ago. All right?'

'Dancing bear? What does it look like?' Allanza asked.

'It looks like a bear. But instead of eating you, it does tricks like lying down and rolling over. Why?'

'But that's amazing!' Allanza had started shivering again and was hopping from foot to foot with excitement. 'We saw one do that! He was scared of it,' and he pointed triumphantly at Kai, 'but Tog sorted it out.'

'Where?' Penda said.

'No!' Tog hissed. 'Don't—'

'What?' Allanza imitated Kai's breaking voice. 'These are Ecta's lands. I'm just too scared to look after them.' He shrugged. 'We sorted it out.'

'It's miles back.' Tog tried to raise his voice above Allanza's. 'We got lost. We don't really know . . .'

But Allanza was describing exactly how the circus people could find Kai's old home and they were talking about short-cuts and slapping him on the back.

Tog collapsed against a tree trunk, where Jenna joined him.

'They'll find the stranger,' he said.

'Maybe he's dead.'

'I don't think so,' Tog said. 'As long as I'm alive and have the sword, he'll come after me. We'll have to get away from these people.'

At the sound of clapping from the side of the clearing, he took his eyes from Jenna's face. He saw Allanza standing stock still, his hands joined together and cupped in front of his belly. One of the circus girls faced him about ten feet away. She took two springing steps, checked, somersaulted with straight arms and back so she planted both feet in his cupped hands, flipped over again, with her hands on his shoulders and landed behind him. Then she somehow ran up Allanza's back as easily as a squirrel runs up a tree, planted her feet firmly on his shoulders, fanned her long skirts in a way that made her people cheer, and somersaulted off.

'And there's another thing,' Tog said. 'That bear. I thought I'd met a real bear, a wild one and had managed to tame it, but it was a just a circus bear doing its thing. Oh, don't look at me like that. You thought what I did was good. You said I had the bear inside me. Now all that's . . . it doesn't mean anything.'

Jenna shook her head, took Tog's hand and cradled it in her lap. 'I think you were brave, not magic.'

'Suppose I wanted to be magic?' Tog said. 'I thought maybe the sword was giving me special powers.'

'No magic,' Jenna said. 'Magic too easy. Only this.' And she thumped his heart. 'And this.' She tapped his head. 'And this.' She gripped his arm. 'Don't believe magic. When slave men took me . . . live, die, don't care. Then you . . .' She pinched his ear. 'Listen: Island close. Get there soon. Men not back for four days and they must follow. We leave now. Now.'

'You think so?' Tog asked.

'Yes.'

'And watch the sword.'

It was a good plan and might have worked but for one thing. Allanza, who was dancing with the circus girl, suddenly crumpled and fell. And he did not get up.

The circus people made plans quickly. They would ride on until they found a suitable camping place, then the cart would be unhitched. Sebbi, the bear keeper, and Alric, a blond man with a sleepy smile and huge sloping shoulders, would ride back with the cage to collect the bear while the others rested.

Allanza was lifted on to the cart and they set off, reaching a clearing by a stream before the sun had travelled much further towards the horizon.

As they set up camp, Penda explained that they had been forced out of the village because Helori had been found in a hut with one of the village girls – all a big misunderstanding but these peasants did tend to jump to conclusions. Helori was the good-looking man and it was his sister, Morvana, who had jumped on to Allanza's shoulders. She had oiled black hair that shone with blue

218

glints in the sunlight and very white teeth that she didn't mind showing in a smile.

'And that's the travelling life: welcomed one day, thrown out the next, but I suspect no one knows that better than you, my dear Tog,' Penda concluded, watching while Helori gave a final, tightening yank to the guyrope of a dun-coloured tent. 'We'll make good companions. I just know it.'

One day passed and then another and each night the cold moon grew fatter. By day, the stranger filled more and more of Tog's mind. He watched Allanza, paralysed by the knowledge that while they could not leave him, staying might get them all killed. Allanza knew it and kept on telling him to get lost, move on and leg it, while he'd sit tight, stick it out and stay strong. Behind the tired old words, Tog heard the harsh grate of fear and loved Allanza even more for stupid bravery, even though the prat had got them into this mess.

After growing hotter, Allanza started to cool down, thanks to Hilda and Morvana's care. By the third day, it looked as if they had drawn the pus from the wound and he was getting better. On the fourth, Tog woke up in a sweating panic with sunlight beating on the tent like a drum and Kai hissing in his ear.

'They're back with the bear! No sign of the stranger. No sign of your girlfriend either. If you ask me, she's done a bunk.'

They were standing by the cage. The bear was sitting back on its haunches, paws in its lap. 'Can't believe I was frightened by it,' Kai said. 'Sebbi says it's in good health, all things considered. And Allanza's making a complete idiot of himself with that Morvana so he must be recovering. God, it's so obvious that he fancies her.'

Allanza, on his feet but pale, gave Tog a wink. Morvana was juggling with pebbles near him, her hands weaving neat patterns in the air, the pebbles going click, clickety, click. The horse was gone, Jenna was gone.

'Girls! I told you. And she never even said she could ride. Must have been planning this for days,' Kai said.

Tog felt too sick even to hit him. Jenna running off was unbelievable but undeniable.

'She'll be back,' he said, without conviction. 'She's just . . . mucking around.'

'You don't really think that mate. Anyway, Sebbi might be able to throw some light on the subject. Go and ask him if you don't believe me.'

Tog approached Sebbi. He was smiling at the bear through the bars of its cage.

'Isn't he a beauty?' he asked. 'What a boy. Who's a good boy?'

The bear looked blearily back at him, flicked a glance at Tog, then licked its nose with an unexpectedly thin tongue.

'Have you seen Jenna?' Tog asked bluntly. 'She went out riding. I thought she'd be here by now.'

Sebbi turned slowly and scratched his head. 'Your bit? Ye-es. Ye-es. It was odd. We did see her when we were coming back, but she was in the distance.'

'When?' Tog asked. 'Please?'

'Worried about that horse, are you? Well, let's see. First light, or thereabouts. She was heading east, I'd say. Steady trot.'

Tog swallowed. He tried to control his voice and said, 'The bear. Where did you catch it?'

'In the main hut. Happy as a pig in mud, weren't you, my big bad boy.'

Tog tried to control his voice. 'And was there . . . anything else in there?' he asked.

'Anything else? Like what?'

'Anything odd. Like someone . . . hanging around.'

'Hanging?' Sebbi did a hangman mime. 'Apart from the bear? I think we'd have noticed. Something you want to share?'

'No, not really,' Tog said.

'Well, then. Breakfast for me and then we strike camp and it's the wide open road.'

The road became busier. In the course of the day, they passed twenty or thirty people, either in pairs or larger groups. Some greeted them and asked them for news of the road, others kept their heads down. Tog managed to rouse himself out of the fug of depression to ask directions to the Island from a travelling smith. He was told that the best way was at a crossroads below a huge old oak tree standing on its own on a hill. He hadn't seen a girl on a horse and said she'd be hanged for horse theft if she were caught.

The hills on either side of the narrow plain they were following came nearer, shrank away, came nearer again. Then the landscape really opened up as a flat plain melted into a misty sky of golden blue.

'We must turn off soon,' Tog said.

Penda clapped his arm round Tog's shoulders. 'Come to Aquae Sulis with us. There's nothing for you on the Island. Just a load of monks. What do you want with them, anyway?'

'I can't say,' Tog said. 'I'm sorry.'

Tog tried to notice anything different in Sebbi's behaviour but couldn't and, whenever he could, he looked to see if he could see another figure moving purposefully behind them on the road.

Alric caught him at it and asked what he was doing.

'I . . . we've come a long way,' Tog said. 'Sometimes I just like to remind myself.'

Alric gave a lopsided smile. 'As have we all, my friend. Never look back, that's my motto; otherwise all the bad things you did will come and get you. They follow us around like ghosts, you know: people we've hurt, people we've cheated, people we've stolen from. Ignore them for long enough and they go away.'

They reached the crossroads by the old oak tree in the middle of the afternoon. The sky was a uniform grey, heavy enough to squeeze out a light drizzle.

Morvana burst into tears. They were going to share a last meal, on Penda's insistence, before finally saying goodbye.

Allanza patted the girl clumsily. 'I don't understand why she's so upset. Someone tell her it's all right. It's me that should be upset.' He appealed to the circus people.

'It's all right,' Penda said. He took the girl by the shoulders and forced her to look into his eyes. 'Remember what we said last night? You must be brave.'

But the thought of it only seemed to make the girl cry harder.

Penda clapped his hands and raised his voice. 'Now, if you're sure I can't change your mind, at least let us perform one of our circus tricks for you. Good. It's a simple little game but one that we find very, very rewarding. To make it work, you two boys and three girls all have to stand in a line. What, Allanza too? All right, my fine fellow. You too, Morvana. No slacking. And Hilda. That's right. Positions please.'

Morvana tried to put a brave face on it and squeezed into the line between Tog and Allanza. Hilda stood the other side of Allanza between him Kai.

Alric stood in front of them, eyebrows raised in encouragement. 'OK,' he said. 'Right. There's a be-oo-ti-ful woman between each of you.' Tog felt Hilda's unfamiliar hand give his wrist a warm squeeze. 'Isn't there? I said, "isn't there?"'

'Yes,' Allanza said. 'Yes,' Tog said. 'Yes,' Kai said.

'You sound like three men on the way to a funeral. Let's begin again. Right. There's a bee-oo-ti-ful woman between each of you, isn't there?'

'YES,' they shouted.

'No man *could* turn down, no man *would* turn down women such as these, could they?'

'NO.' Allanza shouted the loudest,

'He knows,' Alric said to general amusement. 'He

224

knows. But how can just two women serve three men? Can you guess?'

'NO.'

'Really?'

'REALLY.'

'Good, good. Here's what I do. It's a sort of test to find out who is the cleverest and who is the strongest out of you all. Agreed?'

'YES.'

'ALL right. Everyone lift their hands to find out who is the clever one to get the bee-oo-ti-ful woman.'

With a great whoop, Hilda and Morvana raised their arms so that they were straight out in front of them. Sebbi skipped along the line with a thin leather strap, tying it around each of their wrists in a complex knot.

Alric started a countdown: 'Five. Four. Three. Two. ONE!'

On 'one', Hilda and Morvana gave a quick jerk of their wrists and were free. Tog, Kai and Allanza tried to do the same but remained tied. Morvana ran away, her head in her hands. Hilda stood back and looked at them, one hand on her hip.

Penda said, ''Fraid you've all failed. Right. Alric, search the bag. You three – kneel down or Sebbi will cut off your feet. Put your hands behind your backs and let us tie you up properly. And remember, you're worth more to us alive than dead, but not if you give us any trouble. I'll have that sword off you for a start.'

Tog gave the leather tie a yank but it just tightened the knot. Allanza was looking stunned.

'Got them!' Penda shouted over his shoulder and the stranger appeared from behind the oak tree and walked down the hill towards them.

Then Tog heard a cry and turned. He had a dim impression of a horse rearing up, Sebbi staggering back and then it was on them, a concentration of pure fury: pumping hooves, white teeth, and a high-pitched, terrifying screaming. Penda collapsed beneath the hooves. The horse turned and Tog saw that Jenna was riding it, no, powering it in a way he could not ever have imagined. She was one with it, now urging it on, now leaning over and slashing down with the little brass sword that she had somehow snatched from Penda's hand, wheeling, rearing, perfectly balanced.

Hilda made a lunge for Jenna's leg, fell back with a cry and blood across her face. The horse reared again and its hooves paddled the sides of the bear cage, smashing them to kindling. The mules roared and set off.

Someone cried, 'The bear!'

Jenna threw the sword so it stuck in the ground in front

of Tog. The stranger leapt for it but Allanza blocked his way, knocked him down and kicked him hard in the ribs. While the stranger writhed on the ground, Tog held the sword out so Kai could cut his ties, then waiting impatiently while Kai sawed through his and Allanza's. They crashed through a hedgerow just as Jenna leapt over it, pointing to the top of the hill. Then she wheeled and headed off parallel to the road to draw the pursuit away.

VII

First Quarter

Tog found he was making frantic calculations. Sebbi would hold the bear; Penda, if he were still standing, would check that Hilda was all right before giving chase. Alric would go after the mules and the cart. Morvana could run but might not be too inclined. Helori was the problem. He looked fast and he would be vicious. Kai was ahead of him, Allanza slightly behind. They heard the sound of pursuit and jagged off to the right, crashing through another ragged hedge plunging straight into a shin-deep bog.

Allanza fell once and Tog helped him up, pleased to note that Kai had stopped too and was checking behind them. Jenna had jumped a drystone wall and was galloping to the left, hunched low over the horse's neck.

Tog felt his strength draining away as they forced themselves to run up the sparsely wooded hill. His breath stormed in his ears. Sweat and mist ran down his face. A low wall loomed ahead. He tumbled over it and collapsed on the other side, chest heaving, Kai sprawled on one side, Allanza on the other.

'Was anyone following?' he gasped.

'Don't think so,' Allanza spat. He was breathing fast and light.

'They'll be after us,' Tog said. 'Maybe even track us. Helori's got woodcraft. We've got to push on.'

They crawled along behind the wall, partly to keep out of sight, partly because Tog felt that if they stood, they'd be obliged to run and he didn't think he could run any further.

They heard shouts and he risked a look over the wall. He counted four pursuers below them, fanned out and climbing the hill, and thought he could make them out as Helori, the stranger, Alric and Sebbi but even as he looked the figures grew dimmer. He blinked and rubbed his eyes. It was as if a film had come down in front of his eyes. Blinked again.

'Fog,' Kai said. 'We're in luck.'

Seconds later, the figures below were swallowed up.

'We'd better carry on uphill,' Tog said.

* * *

Jenna was waiting for them over the brow of the hill, holding the horse by its bridle and brushing foam from its flanks with a handful of grass. Tog's heart lifted. Her hair was plastered back from her face and she had colour in her cheeks.

'What happened? Are you all right?' he asked. 'When did you learn to ride like that?'

'Go further,' she said. 'Talk later.'

A path of flagstones, worn smooth and slippery underfoot, followed a ridge. Overhanging winter ferns soaked them; thorn bushes sent them on small detours but they were able to cast around until they found it again. The track wound past an old quarry with dripping, mossy walls of stone. Where it crossed boggy ground, wooden poles, now black and rotten, had been driven into the ground to make a solid surface. It was, they recognized, a serious path.

And Jenna told them where she had been.

She hadn't planned it, she said looking defiant. She had just woken up in the night, seen that everyone was asleep for once, and known what she had to do. Her first thought was that she could take the horse, overtake the cart and kill the stranger, if he was still in the hut, but she got lost and was still heading in the direction of Kai's old home when she saw Sebbi returning with the bear. She detoured round them, hoping that if they saw her, they would assume she was running away, then doubled back on them when it got dark. It wasn't too hard: she knew she was downwind of them and pushed on until she smelled their woodsmoke, and then the bear.

She crept up to see Sebbi, Alric and the stranger sitting round the fire. They were talking about what they were going to do with the money – she gathered that the stranger had promised the circus people a massive reward if they could deliver the three of them to a certain person. She had tried to head back to warn them there and then, but had got lost again and been forced to track back to the road. As luck would have it, she came across them just after they were tied up.

'And instinct took over?' Kai asked lightly.

'Good instinct,' Tog said. 'We should be grateful.'

'Instinct didn't come into it,' Kai snapped back. 'The only people who can ride like that are horse thieves or cavalry. Which is she?'

Above them, out of sight, a flock of geese cried out to each other as they sped past.

'Jenna?' Tog asked. 'Thief or cavalry?'

Jenna looked delighted.

The mist thickened and wrapped them in soft grey sheets. They passed another quarry – deeper and with a dark pool at its foot – and then stopped dead.

The shape that loomed up skewered Tog with a sort of horrified awe. He had to blink and stare to understand it. Three flat squares, each made of smaller squares piled on top of each other with mind-numbing regularity, were joined to make a half-enclosed shape, open at one end but for three dreadful, bare trunks of stone, ridged like an old man's nails.

Across the gap, shaped lengths of wood had fallen in and lay at crazy angles. Tog stared, unwilling to believe that anything shaped so carefully could be so abandoned and so purposeless. He ran his hands over one of the squares, then round one of the trunks and the sense of the place seemed to float into his mind like a thought. Suppose the squares were walls, the bare trunks were pillars and the lengths of wood were roof beams . . . If that were the case, then this was an old building.

He shook his head. But how did men make stone so square or so round, and so smooth? It was beyond the wit of anyone he knew even to make wood regular. This ruin had the effect of making all the houses he knew seem crooked and malformed.

'Romans,' Jenna said. 'Holy place.'

'What would you know about it?' Kai asked.

'Romans were in our country. We have their houses

now,' Jenna answered simply.

They walked on. The land above and below the track opened up. Above them it had been cut into great rough steps, now overgrown. A sheep looked down from above before scooting away and bleating. Tog heard a stream, and then saw another ruined building, larger than the first one and less decrepit. Could this be the Roman's house?

No lights but it was hardly dark yet. He looked through an open door and took a step inside, his feet crunching on fallen shards of pottery. Roosting pigeons exploded in the gloom and sped past him out through gaping holes in the roof. Tog noted that the roof was made with tiles. Rough wooden partitions ran the length of the building, and at the end of each cubicle a metal basket full of hay was attached to the end wall. This palace was a stable?

Kai coaxed the horse under the roof and tethered it in one of the stalls where there was hay still in the manger. He took a handful of straw from the ground and began to rub the animal down, keeping his face close to the animal's flank and breathing strangely.

'What's wrong?' Tog asked.

'Nothing. It's just I'd rather leave the horse here if we're going to go exploring.'

'What's wrong?' Tog insisted.

'All right. It's this place. The way my father spoke about it, I thought . . . I thought we'd be safe. But it's like everything else. I just want something to be easy. For once. I want to meet someone who doesn't mean to slit my throat. Have something that's not taken away from me. Not have to fight. Not have to . . . You know.'

'Yes,' said Tog. 'I know. Let's hope our luck's changed now, eh?'

The others had gone on ahead but Allanza came tiptoeing back. 'Quiet,' he whispered. 'There's another building ahead. And there's a light coming from it.'

The path ran alongside a high, roughly plastered wall with a large, double wooden gate set into it. It was stiff but did not squeak as they squeezed through.

A courtyard. An overhanging roof, supported by columns, making shelter all the way round the walls. Wet leaves flat and black on smooth stone flags. A square pool brimming with dark water.

Across the courtyard another door stood ajar and light fell from it on to the ground.

Tog approached the door and listened. Inside he could hear voices talking so softly he could not make out the words. Warm air, deliciously scented, drifted out to him. Nothing that smelled that good could be bad, surely.

He squared his shoulders, lifted his chin and, holding his breath, pushed open the door and crossed the threshold.

'*In principio erat Verbum et Verbum erat apud Deum et Deus erat Verbum.*'

The words were spoken by a man who was holding a small silver goblet above his head. His robes were white, his skin was very white, as was his vigorous cropped hair. He was standing in the middle of the huge room lit by oil lamps. To his left stood a woman in long white robes, to his right a small, plump man in a shorter, rougher tunic who was holding a metal tray.

'*Hoc erat in principio apud Deum.*' Tog knew the lines and could not stop himself saying them. The woman gave a little scream. The small man gave a start and stepped between Tog and the woman, holding the tray up as a shield. The man recited two more verses and placed the goblet on the silver tray as it was held up for him. Then he turned his attention to Tog.

He was so clean, Tog thought, that he glowed. He was as clean as a baby he had once seen, cleaner even than the woodcutter after his spring bathe in the bay – a ritual that involved him rubbing himself with handfuls of sand until his skin was red and glowing. This, however, was a different sort of cleanliness. It was the man's state and somehow connected with his pale blue eyes, his rudder of a nose, his thin, firm lips, his clean jaw.

He looked at the servant. 'And who is this?'

His voice was no heavier than it needed to be. A bit sneery, maybe.

'I have no idea, My Lord. Not a village boy – I know them all – but a—'

'He speaks the mother tongue.'

'Like a jackdaw, Lord. Borrowed. Stolen. Learned by rote. Be off with you. Go! Go!'

'I speak good Latin,' Tog said in Latin. 'We are lost and need to find shelter.'

'He has friends,' the servant said. 'Cut-throats. Thieves. My Lord—'

'He needs shelter. He is lost. We have a duty. Have you come far?' the man asked.

'Yes, Lord,' Tog asked. 'Very far.'

'And did you meet – I only ask – did you meet on the Eastern Marches with a commission from the Emperor himself? Did you meet my son, the Centurion Petrus Caetius Ventus?'

'No Lord, I . . .'

'No? I would have thought—'

But the woman interrupted, moving up to him and putting a hand on his arm.

'You cannot expect a mere boy to know the affairs of men, my dear,' she said. 'And besides, he has another mission.'

'My dear?' The man raised his eyebrows looked at her closely. 'Ah yes. I believe you said . . .'

'Exactly, my dear. He is to be our guest at dinner tonight.'

'Our guest. That is correct. His room is prepared and the baths are ready, are they not, Gaius?' He spoke slowly, his eyes locked on to his wife.

'Indeed, My Lord,' the servant said wearily. 'At your request.'

'So see to it, you booby. And our guest's . . . retinue. See to them as well.'

The servant sighed heavily. 'At once, My Lord.'

He pushed the front door open wide. Allanza, Kai and Jenna flinched, then stepped forward. 'This way, gentlemen,' the servant said. 'Madam.'

He stepped aside. 'A girl,' the woman said. She looked unexpectedly stricken. 'Almost starved to nothing. Come, my dear, Gaius will look after your friends. You will come with me. Bring milk. Bring honey. Bring cakes. Are the baths still warm? Yes? No? Warm them then, Gaius. Warm them. Make sure our guests lack nothing.'

She led Jenna off. Meanwhile Tog was gripped by the

forearm and frogmarched off in the other direction, with Allanza and Kai following.

Tog tried not think too much about what had just happened in the room and concentrated on his surroundings. The sharp angles amazed him: angles where ceilings met walls, where walls met floors and each other. Ahead, the tiled corridor seemed to narrow to a point. The air was different too. It was still and scented and warm in a strange, choking way.

'Where are you taking us?' he asked.

'The master asked that you be washed and that's what I'm going to do.'

'I can wash myself,' Tog said.

'If your present state is any indication of your washing skills, no you cannot,' the servant said. He ran his hand through Tog's hair. 'Hmm. Do you know what soap is?'

'Is it something you eat?'

'No. It's something you can wash with. Now, here's the kitchen. All of you sit there. I'm the only servant left here. Try to keep things going as best I can but it's hard and getting harder. The villagers used to treat us with awe but I can see the respect going, draining away like sand in an hourglass. And now with warbands roaming the land it's only a matter of time before they end up here. Of course

238

there's nothing left to steal – that all went years ago – but people will talk and anything that stands out in this day and age . . .'

'The man and woman: who are they?' Tog asked. 'Are they really Romans?'

'Aulus Caetius Vetus and Spuria Rutilia Atella: the last Romans in Britain,' the servant said. 'At least I don't know of any others and God have mercy on their souls. I don't know how much longer they can last.'

He put down three flat discs and loaded each one with oatcakes. Honey came in a jar, buttermilk in a pitcher. He talked while the boys ate. 'To be honest, I don't think anyone cares about them any longer. When the legions left ninety years ago, his grandfather refused to leave with them. Had a British wife, farmed British land, drank beer instead of wine . . . (You can dip the cakes in the honey, if you like, or you can use that thing called a spoon to carry the honey to the cake and drip it on.) By all accounts the estate supported a small army as well as the slaves and brought some peace and stability to the neighbourhood. It's why the monks came here in the first place, I believe. They knew there was a good Christian Roman on the hill above their Island: a good Roman with a few spears to his name. Then my master's father took it over but he died quite young – a winter fever – and Aulus, that's my master, took over the estate forty years ago when I was just a lad. Even then, the estates were rich but . . . one thing went wrong, and then another and by the time you fixed the first, a third had gone wrong . . . His faith meant he had to give all the slaves their freedom of course, and that didn't help. I wouldn't take it – my freedom, I mean. Couldn't see the point. The others drifted away and when they came back, months or years later, looking rather like you, there was no work for them. (No, no, the idea is that you lift the beaker to your mouth and tip it slowly. Lapping doesn't really work.) The fields gone over to weeds, the walls broken, the cattle stolen . . . He started giving them the land to work – said it was a sin to see it go to wrack and ruin – and they took more, and more and more . . . Now, there's just a couple of acres left: a garden that I tend, one cow on her last legs. We have oats to see us through the winter, and honey and, to be honest, not much else.'

'And who is his son?'

'Petrus Caetius Ventus? He left twenty years ago. Died in one of the Emperor Zeno's wars. My master doesn't remember much of the present but the past . . . the past is very real to him. Insists we keep the front door open so he can return at any time. I try to make sure things are kept in order but what with the cooking and the heating and the cleaning and everything, I'm rushed off my feet. You're in luck anyway: the baths are still hot from the morning.'

'Hot?' Tog asked. 'Hot baths?'

'Trust me. Most of the glory of Rome was to be found in her bathhouses,' the slave said. 'And your names are?'

'Tog,' Tog said. 'Allanza and Kai. The girl's called Jenna.'

'I'm Gaius. Well, Gair probably but it changed to the nearest Latin name. When in Rome, you know . . .'

'Call me Toga,' Tog said.

'What? Toga? Oh, I see. Tog. Toga. Very good. Very good indeed,' and he repeated his funny, dry little laugh. 'Strictly speaking, it should be Togus, of course, that being the masculine ending.'

Half an hour later and Tog knew what it was like to be cooked. Gaius stripped the boys, led them into an oven, sat them on stools and as soon as they started to cook, showed them how to scrape away their filthy sweat with a curved metal tool. The dirt flowed off them in black rivers.

Gaius kept up a stream of commentary. The metal thing was called a strigil and technically, the warm room they were in was called the caldarium. However, because he hadn't had time to get a new fire going, the caldarium, which should be hot, was tepid and the next room, the tepidarium, which should have been tepid was cold. He added that he did not think they had lived long enough to get so much dirt on them.

Tepid or not, the caldarium was unimaginably hot and it was a relief when Gaius started to pour water that was merely warm over Tog. The slave then encouraged them to rub their skins with rough pads called sponges. This too felt good. In fact, it all felt good to Tog apart from the servant's attempts to do something with his hair. This hurt. When that was over, they jumped into a deep pool of cold water that made them scream. Then they were given rose-flavoured water to drink, handed light, closely woven tunics and led through to the hall where the Romans were waiting.

Three long, battered couches had been arranged into a rough triangle and more oatcakes set out on rough wooden stools by each one. Aulus and Spuria took one each, Tog, Allanza, Kai and Jenna sat in a row on the other. Allanza kept on nudging Tog, raising his eyebrows and nodding at Jenna whose hair had been oiled, plaited, twisted and piled up on her head like a crown. Glistening blue threads shimmered through it when she turned her head. She sat bolt upright, her hands on her lap. She looks at home, Tog thought with a shock.

When Spuria signalled, Gaius would pour out more beer and each time she spoke, her husband would rearrange his features into an expression of polite enquiry, and nod, looking at his wife out of the corner of his eye for cues.

Suddenly he interrupted: 'Of course, the Emperor is a barbarian and everyone should know it but he's done quite well, supported, of course, by true Romans like our Petrus. But then, that was always our duty: to shine light into the darkness and bring order to chaos. And when the bastards don't listen, we chop their ears off.'

He laughed crudely, then blinked at Tog in some surprise. 'Who is this man?' he asked.

'Our guest, my love.'

'Then he must see the pictures.'

He rose, beckoning the others to follow him and led the way through a curtained archway.

Heavy, choking air comprised of heat and an overpowering scent, wrapped itself like a blanket around Tog's head. The room was lit by lamps in the wall. The Roman took one down and invited Tog to take another. He held it over the floor, cupping his hand above it to reflect some light downwards.

In the middle of the floor, a man on a flying horse plunged a spear down the throat of the writhing monster whose claws were hooked into the horse's flank. The monster was green, the horse rich chestnut, its wings white, and the blood that poured from its flank was red. Jenna knelt to try and touch the horse but as her hand touched it, the whole scene – horse, man and monster – flattened itself, lost all shape and substance and Tog was left staring at a picture in stone.

He looked at the Roman who said, 'Fascinating, isn't it? The rider wants to fly upwards to the gods but the monster won't let him. He flies at the monster, kills it, but now his horse is too tired to fly to heaven. The rider reaches out but overbalances and as he tumbles back to earth, sees his precious horse reach heaven alone. So our souls can only reach heaven by losing the vile weight of our flesh.' He held back the curtain. 'But move through. Here is the real mystery.'

The next room was smaller. Four lamps set in metal brackets, one on each wall, gave a smoky, glamorous light that made the picture on the floor glow mysteriously.

It was a man's head. The first thing to strike Tog were details: the fine, determined mouth; rather regretful, dark eyes; long black hair. Sun's rays blazed from his head but it was the sign above that transfixed Tog: a blade above his head and the golden cup hovering above.

Suddenly he was back in the old king's tomb where he had found his sword. He thought of the baby lying there, the leathery skin cracking over its little bones, the bronze sword placed crossways above it and above that, the half coin, golden and shaped like the bowl of the cup. He thought of the sword itself and the man in the blade. It was the same pattern, here in this room, presented in stone. Past, present and future wrapped themselves around him in a shroud that smelled of incense and grave dirt.

But the Roman was speaking. 'See the blade that pierced the side of our dear Lord! Behold the cup that saved his blood!'

Then his voice dropped, and became almost dreamy. 'After the Christ's death, his followers took the cup to the ends of the earth. For centuries his killers searched for it, conquering vast continents in their quest. At last they narrowed their search down to a small green island surrounded by a wild grey sea but such was the power of the cup that when they finally found it, it possessed the seeker and he became a follower of the Christ. That island was Britain. All we know is that the cup went north, beyond Hadrian's Wall, beyond even the wall that Antoninus built from coast to coast and—'

'My Lord! My Lord.' Gaius burst into the room. 'Attackers! People! I was feeding the cow when I heard sounds. I peered around the garden wall and saw at least four men, whispering. Up to no good! We must lock the doors! We must protect the mistress! Quick! Quick! We must act fast!'

Oh no, Tog thought. At least four men. We've been followed. When is it going to end?

'We can fight,' he said.

At least there were weapons. Because the master of the house was convinced they were friends of his son, he ordered them to take what they wanted from the armoury: Allanza and Kai a sword and spear each and Jenna a dagger and a short bow which she strung expertly.

Tog kept his sword and tried out a small wooden sparring shield on his arm. As he lifted it off its hook, a cobweb stretched and broke.

He walked round the dark, damp rooms with Gaius, closing shutters. Outside lay a misty, overgrown garden and beyond that, a weedy field. Shrubs and huts made perfect hiding places in the gloom. There was no sign of anyone, but it could not be a coincidence that Gaius had seen four people. It had to be Penda, Helori, Sebbi and Alric, with the women hanging about in the background as reserves.

'Is there a way up to the roof?' he asked.

'Steps are in the courtyard.'

'One of us should go up there and keep a lookout.'

'I'll get you a cloak. It'll be cold up there.'

* * *

Up on the roof, Tog shivered and tried to get comfortable. A parapet concealed a tiled roof but when he set foot on it he could feel the beams below flex and didn't think they could hold his weight. So he was stuck in a sort of narrow gutter, jammed with dead leaves and broken tiles, and because he didn't want to stick his head up above the low line of the parapet, he was forced to squat in the damp mulch and wonder what the others were doing inside. The moon, a sliver off half full, was behind high, thin clouds but gave enough light to see. All colours were between black and white.

A quick circuit had made Tog think that the best place to wait would be the right hand side of the building, where overgrown, ornamental bushes provided cover.

He lifted his right hand. In the gloom his clean skin seemed to glow with an unnatural, ghostly paleness. A smear of mould stood out like a scar. Tog looked at the bushes. Listened. Heard a stream he hadn't noticed before, a rustle that might have been the wind stirring the leaves in the courtyard except the wind was too light and the leaves too wet. Something else then. He peered over the edge of the parapet. Below him Alric was working almost silently at a shutter with a knife. That wasn't what Tog heard.

What he heard came blundering out of the bushes led by Sebbi. It was big and it was black and as it moved, it swayed its head from side to side. Tog noticed how it didn't seem to have a neck and the whole body seemed to narrow into a snout as sharp as an axe head. Alric shook his head and they moved off. Clearly they had wanted to get into the house silently. Crouching behind the parapet Tog shadowed them round as Alric tried another window – then watched them as they gave up on that. He couldn't follow them around the courtyard – the cloister roof was too steep and slippery – but he guessed they would be looking at the main gate which Gaius had closed and barred earlier.

He ran down to the stairs and tapped on the front door.

No answer.

He knocked again, slightly louder this time.

No answer.

He stood on tiptoes to look through the grille but all he could see was an empty hall, lamps flickering on the walls, no people.

At that moment, the main gates started to creak. Tog stared. The gap between them, a black line, seemed to be growing and shrinking and the doors moving. Tog ran lightly across the courtyard and put his hand on them. They were held by a heavy wooden bar that lay across them and the problem seemed to be that it was rotten. As the doors were pulled, it creaked and gave, but it was just a matter of time before it snapped completely.

There – it went again, and this time the gap that opened was wide enough to see the stranger, and all the men, armed, hauling on a rope that was fed through the door handles and lashed to the bear's harness. That was where all the power was coming from: the massive weight of the bear, straining and heaving against the doors, urged on silently by Sebbi. The bar gave again, and hung in its metal brackets. Tog ran back across the courtyard and banged on the door as hard as he could, shouting to be let in.

Where were they? What were they doing?

Behind him, he heard the bar give with a small, rotten snap. He turned to see the gates swing open.

They advanced towards him. Tog retreated until he felt the studs of the front door press into his back.

'Behold: the prodigal is run to earth.' Penda held the others back with a gesture. 'And looking different: almost human and perhaps he doesn't smell quite so bad now. Nice silky hair, smooth skin, hands as soft as a princess. How did we overlook you? How could we have planned to sell you? As I live and breathe, I do believe I'm half in love with you.'

Penda had a bruise that covered the right side of his face and closed that eye completely. Alric walked one side of him, Helori the other. Sebbi was silhouetted in the doorway, unhitching the bear from the doors.

'Get back,' Tog said. 'You've no right to be here.'

'No?' Penda asked. 'Not invited? I'm hurt. I'm crying inside and I don't think I'll ever live the shame down. Still, we're here now and may as well make the most of it, eh?'

'They know you're coming,' Tog said. 'I was up on the roof and saw you.'

'But I'm afraid that was your big mistake. You see,' Penda dropped his voice, 'you should have waited until they let you in before you told them. I worry about your so-called friends, Tog. You see, to me, when your friends leave you outside to meet your enemies and lock the door and don't even answer when you knock, I'm afraid that means they've thrown you to the dogs. Woof woof.'

Alric put his tongue out and panted. Helori threw his head back and howled.

'I'm not scared. I know you're just cowards.'

'Yes, but a pack of great big, grown-up cowards with a bear,' Penda said. 'Ever had a Saxon sword in your guts?'

'Let me fight the bear,' Tog said.

'Single combat? Sebbi? Did you hear that? All right. Roll up. Roll up. Watch the bear eat the brat. That's right, sir. Step this way for your fight to the death.'

Tog swallowed. Would the bear remember him? How could he buy time?

'I don't want to kill the bear,' he said. 'I had the chance last time and . . .'

'Stop stalling. Sebbi?'

With a leer, Sebbi led the bear round the side of the pool on a long chain. As the bear swung its head from side to side its chain clanked. There was a dullness about its fur that Tog had not remembered. Claws clicked on the courtyard's flagstones.

'On, on,' Sebbi urged. He hefted a coiled leather whip in his free hand and dropped the chain. The bear moved a few paces further, head swinging from side to side as if it were uncertain what to do next.

The bear's eyes fixed blearily on Tog. It stopped swinging its head and reared up half-heartedly. Sebbi cracked the whip and the bear reared up then lowered its head, sniffing at Tog.

He felt frozen. He might as well be crushed. He saw Sebbi lift his arm again but instead of a whistling crack of the whip, there was a dull thrum followed by a *thock* and Sebbi was looking at his ribs, under his arm, where a black feathered shaft protruded. He staggered. The door behind Tog was flung open and with a roar, Allanza, Kai and Gaius burst out, yelling. Jenna was behind them with a bow.

They were carrying flaming torches in one hand, swords in the other, and each rushed an attacker. Allanza swung his torch at Alric who stepped back coolly, his sword raised. Gaius brought his down on Penda's head. He ducked but the torch connected with his shoulder and exploded in a shower of sparks that sent him rushing away, swearing and beating his smoldering clothing. *Thock*. An arrow suddenly sprouted from his arm. He swore and collapsed gently on to his knees. Helori, who was easily holding Kai at bay, looked up for a second and Kai thrust the torch into his groin, then followed up with whirlwind of stabs from his sword. One got through, as far as Tog could see, because Helori cursed, and retreated. Jenna sent off two more arrows in as many heartbeats and in that time Penda and Sebbi had been disabled and Helori stabbed. Penda roared, the bear reared up and Gaius, reacting as if there were fifty years of stored anger inside him, rushed it, his sword drawn and pointing at its ribs.

'No!' Tog threw himself at Gaius's arm but at that moment, the bear decided to defend itself. Its paw swept round in a massive blow, catching him on the side of his head. He saw with startling clarity the bear, very black and very shaggy against the sky, its head crowned with a ring of bright stars. Then the stars exploded inside his eyeballs and he felt himself fall into a pain in his side that was wet and hot, sharp and blunt.

He frowned at the sky, then passed out.

* * *

Tog woke up in a warm room.

When he tried to move two things happened. Firstly, his head split in half and the separate halves rolled off the bed and crashed on to the floor. Secondly someone or something shoved a red-hot poker in his side and stirred it around. When he closed his eyes, it hurt and when he opened them it hurt worse. The only thing that didn't hurt was the small hand on his forehead. That just made him feel sick but it hurt too much to say anything. Jenna's blurry face smeared itself on to his eyeballs.

She got up and walked across the room.

Tog passed out.

The second time Tog woke up, he could feel the sword in the bed with him. Someone had noticed that his head was split in half and had tied it together with a leather band around his forehead. The only problem was that the band was being drawn tighter and tighter and now his brain was bring squeezed out of his ears and nose, and his tongue, he was sure, was sticking out. He managed to go '*ghhla*' and someone put warm, honeyed water in his mouth.

The man with the poker had stopped stirring it around inside him and was just running it up and down his skin. If anything this was worse.

'He's getting too hot,' a voice said. 'That means the

wound is filling with poison. I don't know how to deal with that.'

Tog said '*ghhhla*' in order to get more water. He felt a pressure on his side.

'What do we do?'

'They say the monks know how to heal – some kind of magic they have. It's less than half a day away. But how can we get him there?'

'I'll ride and he can be strapped to me.'

'We'll have to bind him up tight, then.'

Tog was made to sit up, a pad was pressed on to the burning hole in his side and bandages wound round him until he could hardly breathe. He was lifted out of bed and immediately began to shiver so hard that his eyes were shaken open. There was Jenna, there was Kai, and Allanza was carrying him but where was he? He was looking back at the bed but he was gone. Only a red stain was left behind, like the stains on the flagstones in the courtyard that jolted past his eyes.

He went absent.

Allanza was carrying him to the stable yard where Kai was mounted on the horse, Jenna holding it steady. Allanza was putting him down behind Kai as gently as he could, but with every movement he felt a horrid wet pain in his side, a sort of warm slackness that was his life leaking away.

Then Gaius and Allanza were lashing him to Kai with strips of fabric.

The first step the horse took sent a jolt right through him. The second was even worse and from then on, the pain squeezed reality out of his head, so one minute he was back in the earth tomb watching Jenna give birth to a bloody monster on the stone slab, the next he was flying with the swallows on the day he had been to the Bloodstone with the woodcutter. From high in the air he could see Britain and it looked like a bear.

Something was singing, an endless figure of four or five notes that was always the same and always different. As the sound wormed into Tog's mind, he realized that he was back on the awful rock in the middle of the slave camp and the moon was shining in his eyes. Then the moon turned into a great breast and dropped milk into his mouth. The milk was ice cold and numbed the pain. Where it overflowed his mouth, it twisted itself into a great white dragon that writhed under and through the earth. Under and through everything, in fact, like the music made into cold, white dragon flesh.

Tog needed to shout and so he opened his mouth, and spat out a huge roar. The whole land of Britain heaved. Its spine of mountains flexed. Rivers boiled. Forests tumbled and lay like wet bear fur. Tog flexed his claws. The writhing dragon beneath him screamed and pierced his side with its burning, sword-like bronze teeth.

He opened his eyes and the dream receded, leaving behind a simple and very clear thought. Where was the stranger?

They were picking their way downhill, Allanza by his side, and Jenna walking by the head of the horse.

'*Ghhla*,' he said.

'He's woken up,' Kai said.

'Did he say anything?' Allanza asked.

'He made that *ghhla* noise. Still, it's better than him dribbling down my back.'

'Should we give him a drink?'

'We should push on. We're almost there.'

'*Ghhla*,' Tog said more urgently.

'Almost there, mate. We'll get those monks to make you better.'

Tog tried to gather his strength. They were descending a hill, heading towards a low golden mist that hugged the ground. He smelled wetness all around. Round, green hills rose to the left and right but straight ahead was the largest hill of all: a sloping shoulder of land that climbed from the golden sea to a steep-sided peak, crowned by a great standing stone. It was the Island. He had got there. Now he had to warn them.

'The stranger wasn't in the courtyard,' Tog said, summoning up all his strength. 'He must be planning an ambush.'

'What's he saying?' Allanza asked.

'*Ghhlaghhlaghhla,*' Kai said. 'He must be feeling better. Whoops!'

The horse slipped and a shock wave of pain passed through Tog's body. He went absent again.

VIII

Waxing Gibbous

Tog tried to imagine himself moving forwards under the blanket of mist but instead saw dark lines spreading out from the Island – a dark sun, radiating dark rays.

By the shore lay a dark boat. Tog saw Jenna approach it and now he noticed that a single figure, cloaked and hooded, stood in the back. He knew what he must do – he fumbled in his tunic and found a gold coin. He signalled to Allanza and as they gently lifted him down, he made it clear that they must give the boatman the coin.

Laid in the boat, his friends bowed over him.

'When are you coming?' he asked.

'Soon,' Jenna said. 'But this part of the journey is for you alone. Only a few may pass to the Island and few of them want to return to these shores. You have been through much to get here.' And she bowed her head.

The boat glided off across the smooth water. Swans dipped their heads as it passed. Tog's head was raised on soft pillows and he could see that the Island was green and fair, with orchards hazed with early white blossom. On the greensward were gathered a company of men to greet him and a tent had been prepared, and from it fluttered a flag: a bear crowned with stars. As the boat drew near to the shore Tog saw that the crowd was made up of all the peoples he had met on his journey: Pict and English, pigsey and Briton, pirate and soldier. And his friends were gathered there: Allanza, resting his great hands on a mighty broadsword, Kai intent and quizzical, and Jenna. A silver crown was woven into her raven tresses and her markings flickered up her body. He turned and saw that he was mistaken in thinking that he had been taken to the Island by a boatman. It was a woman standing in the stern, her hand steady on a single oar and as he looked at her she smiled, and he was not afraid.

Her skin was very pale and her eyes were dark and he knew her to be a witch.

'What is happening, My Lady? Why are these people here to greet me?'

'Why Tog,' she laughed. 'They are not here to greet you only. More to honour you, for where others have failed, you have triumphed. A bastard once you called yourself but here I can now reveal who you really are. All you must do is step from the boat on to the Island where you will find peace.' Air was thick. Happiness was smothering.

Kai's voice grated in his ear. 'Oh no you bloody don't, mate. You're not going all dreamy on us now. I know what that means.'

A shocking slap of cold water on his face jerked his eyes open. He felt cold, tired, wet, but oddly the pain in his side was lessening. He was lying on cold earth. Bullrushes bobbed their heads and tall brown reeds hissed in the wind.

'We almost lost him,' Kai said. 'If he stops breathing again, someone pinch him.'

Straight ahead across black ruffled water, Tog could see the Island. It seemed to float. He was transfixed. The Island, he thought. I'm there. I've made it. He closed his eyes, then heard Allanza say, 'Is that thing over there a boat?' and opened them again.

Allanza was jumping up and down, waving his arms. Jenna was standing by him. She looked away as his eyes met hers, then looked back. He managed to smile and to his amazement, she smiled back. He closed his eyes again, feeling madly happy, then heard Allanza's voice again.

He forced his eyelids open. A boat lay just off shore with

two bearded men in it and Allanza was trying to negotiate with them.

'To the Island, right? THE ISLAND. To the MONKS to make him BETTER. Take him and then come back for us, all right? First TAKE him and then come back for US. This is PAYMENT for TWO journeys. RIGHT?'

He was holding out the sword and the men took it.

This really is the end, Tog thought, as Kai and Allanza lifted him into the boat. They laid him down on a pile of fishy netting, staring up into an eye-watering sky.

Tog's mood changed as the boat moved away from the shore. He felt incredibly, worryingly weak. He could have moved before, he was sure of it, but now he simply could not. And hadn't someone just given his sword away? That wasn't right! He should have stopped it and now something terrible was happening on the shore. Horsemen were attacking his friends. Kai and Allanza were knocked down and one horseman picked up Jenna by the waist and swung her on to his horse. Tog thought he was tattooed but it was hard to see through the misty air. Perhaps it hadn't really happened. His eyes closed because he was too weak to keep them open and by the time he had gathered enough strength to open them again, the shore was hidden behind banks of reeds. Something – he imagined an eel – was alive under his back and the boatmen were talking.

'Take him to the Island, to the ol' monks?'

'Not unless I'm silly. This is one for the Lady.'

'That's right. And the liddle man. See 'im dance in the blade, did you?'

'I sees him.'

Tog tried to struggle up but felt a hand press him down. 'He's twitchin'.'

'Knock 'im on the head like a little fishy?'

'Better reason with him first. You lie calm, sweet apple.' A cold rough hand that smelled of woodsmoke and fish stroked his cheek.

'That's the way, sweet froggle'

'That's the way, little fish.'

'With us, little sweet fruit.'

Tog lay still as the boat glided across a stretch of still water then passed an islet with houses on stilts standing behind a boggy foreshore. Tog's boatmen hailed people on the shore who waded into the water to look at him. They had long hair, were dressed in well-worked skins and wore fine necklaces of fish bone.

'One for our Lady?' they called.

'Little chap for the Lady,' was the answer.

'Bless you, boys, bless you. She'm be pining.'

'We knows it, lover. We knows it.'

The boat sped on through another maze of reeds, one

man in the bows directing the other with small hand movements, then it was back out in open water and skimming towards a roundhouse that stood alone on strong wooden poles.

Behind it, the Island rose up so close that Tog could see long grey buildings, trees and small figures in dark robes. From this angle, the stone on the hilltop was as thin as a blade.

The boat glided to a halt at the far end of a long jetty that led to the roundhouse.

'Lovely work. Tie us sound.'

'Tie us true.'

'This way, sweet apple.'

'This way, little eel.'

Tog didn't like the way that all the things they called him were edible. He was in a sweat of pain and fear as they carried him towards the house.

'Lady, sweet Lady, gifts for'm!' the men called out.

A door was opened by a woman with messy hair.

'A gift for the Lady is always a good gift.' It sounded to Tog like a well-worked formula. Her voice was low, as if she had practised being soothing and calm.

'No gift too great for the Lady of the Lake,' the men chanted.

'He came from where?'

263

'Three friends brought him for the monks to eat this Eastertide when their God needs the blood to come alive. He'll do better with you, our Lady. He hurts and needs mending.'

'Easter isn't exactly . . . Oh, never mind. Bring him in and lay him down. What's this?'

'That's the little shining man of legend, no doubts about it. We wants'm, m'Lady, we wants'm bad but the best gift is the wanted gift.'

'It can't be. Wait. So it . . .'

Tog vaguely registered the shock on the woman's face. She gathered herself. 'Thank you dear hearts, and bless you. You will be rewarded.' The men laid Tog just inside the doorway. 'Oh boys, you couldn't tie him up for me, could you? You'll find some lashings on the back of the door.'

Trussed up like a chicken, Tog heard the slap-slap-slap of their feet as the lake men bolted along the jetty and paddled off as fast as they could in their boat.

Tog's cheek was squished into the floor. If he rolled his eyes down, he could see water between the floor's wooden slats. If he rolled them up, he could see the woman. Better a woman than cannibal monks, he supposed. Maybe.

He could see bundles of herbs hanging from rafters, snake skins, and what looked like a partially disembowelled

264

goose. The woman was bent over the table, looking closely at the sword and seemed to be talking her thoughts out loud.

'Lost for all these years, then back at Easter. That can't be an accident. And the high king dying . . . it's too good to be true or the worst of all worlds. And how does a creature like *that* come to have *this*? He's clean mind you. Cleaner than you, you old witch.'

This set her laughing and she bent over him.

White teeth, blue eyes, black hair, Tog thought. Her hand felt cool on his forehead and the memory was still with him when he realized that she was taking the dressing off.

She bent down to sniff it. 'I can see your wound's been dressed, and carefully too. Hello. This tunic's got a fine weave. So, you've been visiting our Roman friends on the hill, have you? Did they have the sword? No, surely they would have said. Still, we can find out about that later. Now, I asked the lake men to tie you up because I need you to lie still. And don't worry about the monks. They won't really eat you. In fact, they'll try to cure you but the truth is, I taught them everything they know so you're better off with me.'

Tog tried to say Easter but only managed a soft '*earghh*'.

'Easter's two days off but there'll be time for talking later.

Hello. What's this?' Her fingers started probing his head. 'Pulpy. Were you knocked out? In all honesty, that's probably what's causing a lot of the problem. What was it? Ran into a wall? Headbutted a cudgel?'

'*Brgh.*'

'A bear? Well, well,' she said disbelievingly. 'Been passing out? Feeling sick? Thought so. That could all come from the knock you got to your head. Actually I'm relieved. I think you're going to get better from that and the side wound hasn't penetrated your gut. I'm going to clean this one and see how things go. If your brain doesn't get any better, I might have to drill a hole in your skull to let the darkness out, but it may not come to that.'

While she was talking she walked across the floor to a row of stoppered, earthenwares flasks on a shelf. She lifted stoppers, sniffed before finally settling on a flask. 'The ointment'll hurt so I'm going to give you this first.'

She fumbled in her apron pocket and pulled out a small wooden box, which she opened and seemed to palm something. Suddenly she pinched Tog's nose with one hand, dug fingers into his jaw muscles with another and while his mouth was open in paralysed shock, dropped something into the back of his mouth before tilting his head back and clamping his jaws shut. Tog felt something slip down his throat, leaving a brown, musty taste behind it.

He protested furiously.

'It's better this way. Trust me, I'm a witch.' The woman started pottering again. In rather less than a while, Tog found his murderous thoughts had been replaced by languorous benevolence. He no longer wanted to kill her, nor did he want to move from the floor or even be untied. When she lifted his head to look into his eyes, he opened them wide and laughed rather stupidly. When she started to prod and push in his wound, he felt the pain but was disconnected from it. Admittedly, when she dipped her fingers into the ointment bottle and started smearing the foul-smelling concoction in his wound, he shouted out because it burned worse than hot fat, but after a while the pain stopped. The witch cut his bonds and in the course of the day, he uncurled like a bracken frond in the spring, and slept.

He woke in the night, sweating. In his dream, he was with Allanza, Kai and Jenna. They were asleep in a clearing in the forest. He had to wake them because he could hear the Saxons in the woods but when he opened his mouth his tongue and jaw turned to thick rough stone. He gripped the sword but his fingers ached dully and they were thick and stony, and the dull, heavy grey was aching its way upward. His arm was so heavy it dropped off.

Later, he crawled on his side to the door and looked out

through the gap underneath. Dawn outside: a swan drifted by, dipped his head through a patch of pondweed into the still black water but when it straightened its neck again, it was still gleaming white as if the water had not been there. A sooty black moorhen scooted from its nest and tried to scare it away and it drifted off.

Tog wanted his friends. He'd done his job and brought the sword to the Island. Now, suddenly, he just wanted to hand it over and get away. He heard the witch stir, get up, blow on the embers of the fire. He rolled over and looked at her. She lit a candle, came over to him, laid her hand on his forehead, felt around the wound and nodded.

'No heat. Good. Now drink this. Comes from the Island's spring – holy water with a hint of the Christman's blood, if the monks are to be believed. Me, I prefer to think it's anything else.'

The water was cool and a bit rusty.

'I want to see my friends,' Tog said huskily. 'How long have I been out? Why am I here?'

'All in good time. All in good time. You were talking in your sleep, mystery boy.'

'So?'

'In Latin.' She pursed her lips. 'You weren't brought up by the Romans, Aulus Caetius Vetus and Spuria Rutilia Atella, or I'd have seen you.'

'Have to get to the Island,' he rasped.

'Wrong. Very wrong. As wrong as you can be. You have to get *away* from the Island. If the high king or anyone else close to him catches you with that sword, they'll hang you from the nearest tree. Trust me on that. It will bring back . . . unwelcome memories.'

But Tog found comfort in the idea that he had a job and needed to finish it. While this had made his life very complicated in the past, now it seemed to make it simple. He shook his head. 'I've got to,' he said.

'You— Oh, I don't suppose it matters much. You're not going anywhere for a while. Can you listen?'

He nodded and heard her settle, then begin to talk.

'Very good. Try to keep awake because I am going to tell you exactly why you shouldn't be setting foot on the Island with that sword, and exactly why the high king is one person you want to avoid.'

'Right. Off we go then. Many years ago, the high king married a Cornish queen and they had a baby. You don't know how hopeful everyone was back then. The high king was forward thinking, modern, Christian and represented the very best of Rome. He could read and write, and wanted to bring in new laws that would apply to everyone. His big idea was that if everyone followed the same path, it wouldn't matter if they were northern or southern, English or British, Irish or Pict. The queen was a bona fide home-grown, traditional royal witch and beautiful too, so the people would love her. And if they could bring together the best of the old and new, and mix it together, then there would be hope for the country. Traditionalists and reformers would feel they had someone on their side but at the same time they could both look forward.

'But it didn't quite happen that way. The traditionalists thought the high king wanted to force his ways on them, while the modernizers feared that the old British traditions that Rome had more or less stamped out were going to be revived. Result? A breakdown in relations due to irreconcilable differences. Except . . . there was a baby.' Her voice trailed off, her eyes drifted to the fire again and she fell silent for a while. Then she shook herself.

'Where was I?'

'The baby,' Tog said. He was interested now the witch had mentioned the high queen and felt he was on familiar ground.

'The baby. Yes. It died of course. The supporters of the queen have always claimed the king murdered it, while the king's people say the queen killed it by magic. Now, this is where the story gets interesting. One winter's night about fourteen years ago, one of the lake people is hired to row two of the high king's bodyguard off the Island in secret. It wasn't that unusual – the king has a specially trained bodyguard he uses for his secret, dirty work. The lake man picks them up from the Island in the dead of night and asks them where they want to go. "West," one of them says. "Far as you can go." The laker sits in the back of the boat and paddles. Now normally, these bodyguards are as tight as oysters in a storm but there's something about that night that loosens their tongues. Maybe it's the way the boat glides; maybe they think the boatman's stupid; maybe it's the dark; whatever it is, they start to talk.

'Now, my man doesn't hear much but what he does catch really pins his ears back. One of the men says, "Angry was he?" The other replies, "You know him: more cold than angry." Then the first one asks, "And he really thinks it'll work?" and the other says, "Orders is orders. It's his baby. He can do what he wants with it and he never wants to see the sword again. Do the baby, lose the sword. Make sure he never shines again."

'Well,' the witch continued. 'The laker took them as far as he could and dropped them off at the road to Cornwall. A few months later we heard that the queen's baby had died and no one has ever heard of the sword since, until now, and that's why the high king won't want to see that little sword again. It'll be like opening up a grave he thought was good and closed. He's not a forgiving man. People who do things in secret never are usually.'

She got up, stretched, and threw the door open just as a skyful of starlings smoked past, unfolding and folding, darting and swooping, darkening and lightening. When they had gone, the dawn seemed stranger.

'Those two soldiers. Did they ever come back?' Tog asked. His throat felt small and pinched. He knew exactly what the witch meant about a grave being opened.

'No. In fact, there were rumours that they had deserted, though that was probably just one of the high king's stories. He sent them on a mission to kill his own baby and told them to make themselves scarce after that. Or maybe they stayed away, just in case he regretted what'd he'd done. They're clever, these bodyguards. Have to know their Bible, read, write and talk about three languages, including Latin. Look like monks except they wear black. What's the matter?'

But Tog couldn't answer. Something inside him had cracked and he was flooding with awful feelings: grief, loss, anger . . . Tears scalded his cold cheeks. His chest heaved. The wound in his side stabbed him but he welcomed the pain because it was somehow his own.

Two Christian soldiers had set off from the Island to kill a baby. Once they'd done it, they'd gone native. One had pretended to be a harmless woodcutter; the other

272

had pretended to be a swineherd. One had smelled so bad that no one would go near him; the other was a cantankerous old drunk who bought off the villagers with his whisky.

So he told the witch that he knew both the assassins, that one of them had brought him up while the other one kept guard. He told her that he'd looked on the woodcutter as a father but it was clear now that he had only ever been adopted to act as a sort of disguise, because what was a woodcutter without a poor, skinny, abused brat to kick around?

The witch chewed her hair. 'That is quite a story. Except . . . does it add up?'

'He knew where the baby was. He knew where the sword was,' Tog said. 'He told me where to find them both, and then bring the sword back here. I think that just about clinches it, don't you?'

The witch tilted her head one way, then another. 'I take your point,' she said. 'However, we witches have a saying: never think you have the last word about the human heart. Not unless you have proof and even then take it with a pinch of salt. Now, sit tight. I'm going out to see if ... well, if this fits in with the general madness going on. You know the high king has called all the minor kings to the Island but has chosen this precise time to die on us? However, that's not your concern. Easter's still a day off and you need more rest. Is there anything else you want?'

'My friends,' Tog said. 'It's all I want.'

Tog ate then dozed then woke then ate then dozed. It was good to sleep because he didn't have to think of the woodcutter. His head started to hurt less. He practised straightening up because it distracted him and found he could get on to his hands and knees, then pull himself to his feet using the edge of the table.

He looked around. The roundhouse had more things in it than he had ever seen. For example, the woodcutter had owned nothing but an axe and a cauldron. The Romans had beakers and plates, which was impressive, but the witch had plates, bowls, jars, pots, pans, and all full of herbs, pastes, powders. She even had a transparent flask that seemed to hold its contents – a dead frog – in air. There were grinding bowls with dyes in them and a couple of good knives. The skin of a stag – complete with head and antlers – hung from the wall next to a cloak of otter skins. The woodcutter had told him that priests used to wear them in old religious ceremonies but he always maintained that no one really knew what the ceremonies were and just made them up as they went along. The woodcutter. An assassin with a guilty conscience. Maybe the Lady of the Lake, would like to look after the sword.

He lay down and slept again. The sound of a boat bumping against the jetty produced a spurt of terror. The king's men had found him! Even now, killer monks with dead eyes were swarming out of coracles. He hobbled behind the table and hid behind the deerskin, which was stiff and smelled of dead deer. Peering out from the crusty eye sockets, he heard a voice, and another hush it. A huge dark shape loomed in the doorway.

Tog shrank back, then relief surged through him. He recognized the figure and the others that followed: Borth, Melanius, Kai, Allanza, and finally the witch.

Finally the witch.

He crawled out from his hiding place.

'Tog!' Allanza's face lit up, then he followed the direction of his friend's gaze towards the empty doorway.

'Where's . . . ?' But the words died in his throat. If he asked where Jenna was, he would be admitting she wasn't there.

Kai started to talk fast. 'Arrived here two days ago . . . Waiting for you . . . Bumped into Melanius and Borth at the encampment . . .'

'Where's . . . ?'

'Incredible place . . . So many people from all over . . . Even Crotus, believe it or not.'

'Where's . . .'

'Stroke of luck . . . Some of those tribesmen . . .'

'Where's Jenna?'

'It's no good,' Kai said. 'Someone's going to have to tell him.'

'I will,' Allanza said, but for a while, said nothing and just looked at Tog with his face slightly twisted. 'It's kind of good news, really. When we sent you off, suddenly this troop of picture people on horseback turned up. We couldn't see the problem. I pointed . . . thought she'd be pleased but she ran and they caught her. Picked her right up. Kai and me, we tried to get after her but they rode their horses at us and knocked us down. Then they were off.'

'But why?' Tog asked. 'Her own people. Was she in trouble?'

Melanius spoke. 'She was a runaway. She's whatever the picture people call royalty.'

('Royalty, believe it or not,' the witch muttered.)

'She escaped from their party, made her way to the coast. That's when the slavers took her,' Allanza interrupted.

'But why did she run?' Tog asked.

'The whole camp's talking about it,' Kai said. 'She was being brought down here to marry the high king, or if he was too ill, the successor. Anyone who can secure a treaty with the picture people is going to be a popular choice, apparently. Can you imagine? I mean Jenna! The original wild girl! She's being kept under wraps but I'm sure we'll be able to see her after the wedding.'

The words hollowed Tog out. Inside, everything was sucking emptiness. If he opened his mouth he'd roar like a furnace.

'But we saved her,' he said. Then: 'I brought her here. We'll rescue her.'

'They've taken her to the Island,' Melanius said. 'The only soldiers there are the high king's. It'll be you against a trained army. I'm not letting you throw your life away.'

'I can stand,' Tog said. He got on to all fours, and holding the sword with one hand, he used Melanius to pull himself up. He felt dizzy. Blackness spread across his eyes. He staggered, shook his head like a dog and took a step to the door. 'It's this thing's fault,' he said. 'It's this sword. It's cursed. I can see it now. I should have left it. I should have chucked it away when Jenna said. We should have stayed with the pigseys. We should have gone with the slavers.'

He was in the doorway now. The lake stretched out before him: black water, brown reeds, big sky. Another step and he was on the jetty. He pulled his arm back. His side twitched and tightened, but as he brought his arm forward in a swinging arc, a small hand grabbed his wrist.

'That's not the way forward,' the witch said. 'The sword

was not brought here to be thrown away so lightly. If it has power, now is the time to use it. Bend it to your will. Make it serve your needs.'

'Then we should go to the Island and confront the king.'

'It's too dangerous,' the witch said. 'I know there's going to be a way. Let me think about it. Now I want to talk with your clever Greek friend.'

She beckoned Melanius out and they went to stand at the end of the jetty.

Tog beckoned Allanza and Kai over to him. 'We've got to do something,' he said. 'We can't let Jenna be married off.'

'It could be worse,' Kai said. 'I mean she could be stuck in some Caledonian hovel eating oatmeal. She could be a slave. She could be starving with you.'

Allanza hit him on the arm.

'What was that for?'

'He's right,' Tog said bitterly. 'What could I offer her?'

'You?' Kai was honestly surprised.

Allanza hit him on the arm again.

'But he's just . . . You mean they're . . . ?'

'I don't see why you should have known,' Tog said. 'I didn't know until . . . until she didn't turn up with you. Then it was like . . . I can't describe it.'

'I knew,' Allanza said. 'Right from the start.'

'But that means she came all the way back here even

though she knew it was really dangerous,' Kai said excitedly. 'She really must love you. That means you've got to do the same for her and if we can't rescue her using brute strength, which is ridiculous, we've got to be clever.'

'I know something about the high king,' Tog said. 'He killed his own baby. I know who did it, I know where it is, I know everything. This gathering he's called is meant to be the greatest thing he ever did. If we threaten to tell the tribes, it would spoil everything for him.'

Kai snorted. 'Great, so he'd kill us too. No, we need back-up – other people who know and we tell him if he kills us, they'll tell all the world and sully his reputation for ever. Melanius and Borth are the obvious choices but if they know what we're planning they'll lock us up.'

'Crotus,' Allanza said slowly. 'He promised to protect you.'

'Allanza's right,' Tog said. 'Crotus wants everyone to think he's better than them. He'd say true Cornishmen keep to their word, especially when they've sworn on the royal sword.'

'All right,' Kai agreed. 'But what do we do? If we tell this Crotus, then we've nothing to threaten the high king with. If we don't tell him, he'll kill us.'

What could they do? Tog looked around, searching for an answer. The disembowelled goose the witch used for prophesying seemed particularly useless. A pile of otter skins in the corner. Bowls of ceremonial dye. A knife.

Something stirred in his mind. He thought of the Bible. The woodcutter said that even though it was ancient, it could help you when you were in trouble. How? An image came into his mind of clerks in a monastery hunched over their desks, copying it out, word after word. That was why it was never forgotten, the woodcutter said. People had bothered to do that. While they did it, the woodcutter said, they knew they were making something that could be read in the future. That was the thing about the written word: it lasted.

Once again he looked around.

'I'll need a wing feather from that goose, one of those otter skins in the corner, a knife and the bowl of powder on the table,' he said.

The witch and Melanius were still outside; Borth was still sitting by the door.

To distract him, Allanza joined him while Kai gathered the things Tog wanted.

Tog cut the end of the feather at an angle – something he had seen the woodcutter do – then carefully split the pointed end. That was his pen. A few pinches of the powdered dye went into an empty grinding bowl and he mixed it into a thin, ochre paste with his spit. Then he stretched the otter skin out to make it as flat as he could, dipped the end of the feather into the dye and prepared to make his first letter on the bare side of the skin.

But it was hard. It wasn't just a question of deciding what to say: he had to tailor it to the Latin he knew. But did it have to be in Latin? He had been able to write the word *Jenna*. Could he not make the sounds for British? He must be able to. Think. THINK.

He had to tease the dye into lines as the point of the quill snagged on the skin. He had to be careful how much dye he loaded the quill with because it soaked into the skin and ran, and for the same reason he had to make the letters big.

Painstakingly, the pen scratched across the parchment and the words took shape.

They had a plan. Allanza and Tog could swim, but Tog's wound stopped him. That meant Allanza would take the parchment to the mainland and find Crotus, while Tog and Kai took the witch's coracle to the Island. Allanza would follow as soon as he could. All they had to do now was trap Melanius and Borth in the roundhouse and then escape.

The sun was almost down by the time their opportunity came. The starlings were roosting and Borth, Melanius and the witch went out to look as the flocks swirled across the reddening sky. Kai ran out.

'Something's happened! Tog's passed out! He's right at the back of the house! I'll get water!'

The three adults jumped to their feet and ran into the darkness of the roundhouse. Tog, who had been waiting just inside the door, slipped out, followed by Kai and Allanza, who put his shoulder to it and waited. He watched them get into the little coracle, untie it and push away from the jetty. The coracle was round, flat bottomed with one oar. There was a knack to making it go where you wanted that Kai and Tog did not have. At present, they were travelling in very small circles very close to the jetty. The door rattled against Allanza's shoulder.

'What's going on?' Borth's voice came through the wood.

'Nothing,' Allanza said.

'What are you doing there?'

'The door's jammed.'

'Where's Tog?'

'Tog?'

Allanza braced himself. When Borth hit the door the whole house and most of his teeth shuddered. It gave but he threw himself back against it before Borth could get a foot in the gap.

Down on the lake, Kai had worked out that you had to put the oar in the water and wiggle it from side to side. He had put five feet between the coracle and the jetty, six . . .

Borth hit the door so hard it sprang open at the hinges. Allanza threw himself back against it but the Englishman had got himself in the gap and was bracing himself against the door jam. Allanza pushed but felt his feet slide back over the wooden planks of the jetty.

Surely the others were far enough away now. He let the door go suddenly, heard Borth fall and ran to the end of the jetty as if he were outrunning an arrow. Melanius cried out, the witch swore fluently and then he was in mid-air, legs still running, before smashing into the still, black and freezing water.

Later, much later, when it was over, and after they unpicked the events of the night to work out how things had happened, Tog said to Allanza, 'You know none of this could have worked out without you. If you hadn't done what you did . . .'

Allanza gave an odd, knowing smile. 'You remember when we met? I was a big blubbing slave boy. None of this would have happened without *you*.'

'But you did it,' Tog said.

And Allanza said happily, 'I did, didn't I? But it was touch and go.'

From the witch's house, it had seemed so clear which

direction he should take. He had seen watch fires, heard distant voices, and so been able to plot a course between reed beds to the far bank where the tribes were gathered.

But in the water, everything changed. It was freezing and felt so tight around his chest it was hard to breathe. Sounds died away under the splash of his clumsy swimming and his breathing. The reeds hid the fires, and the gathering darkness did not help.

He repeated the instructions to himself: find Crotus; tell him the sword has a story to tell; give him the otter skin and say he can only unravel it if he hears that Tog is dead.

Sword. Story. Otter. Dead. Sword. Story. Otter. Dead.

He had forgotten to look where he was going. A high reed bed loomed ahead and he had to swim around it. He found himself in a channel of clear water heading in what he thought was the right direction, but then it turned sharp right. He woke a heron that took off, horribly slowly, wings clapping, legs trailing. The sound sent his heart racing, made him think of the black water below him and all the things in it, and he turned once, twice around to see what was behind him. Then he could no longer tell which way he should be facing. He thought he could see a passage through the reeds off to his left but he got tangled up in something clinging and slimy, panicked properly, splashed back, whooping and gasping, and ended up in a sort of lagoon.

Which was wrong. His foot touched bottom but that made him flinch. He thought he saw a gap and swam towards it but a huge shape suddenly exploded from a messy platform on his right and suddenly a force was on his back, beating him, biting him, pressing him down. He felt the bottom and tried to push himself up to the surface where the attack intensified. He dived down again, felt mud swirl around him, kicked something hard yet yielding, broke surface, took a breath of before the swan attacked again, rearing up, blue in the darkness, head striking like a snake, wings bursting against his ears. He backed away, too frightened and breathless to shout out, kicking with his legs, flailing with his arms until his head hit something hard and he went down again, felt something hard scrape across his back, surfaced and grabbed on to the low side of a boat.

Two faces swayed above him.

'He wants to sink the boat?'

'Water'll have him and us too.'

'Where'm he's going?'

Allanza just had enough sense to loosen his grip.

'C-can I g-get in-n?'

'No.' The lake men sounded definite. 'You'll sink'm and

285

us lakers don't swim on account of their fear of the goddess. You follow.'

Allanza hung on to the low stern as they paddled away. The swan lifted his wings and ruffled them as they passed but thought better of attacking a boat. Another boat joined them, and another.

Allanza, who had been hoping to make a secret landfall, was soon surrounded by a flotilla of dugout canoes laden with lake people, candles and offerings – beakers, fishbone necklaces, reed hats, water-vole pouches – which showered down on the hero who had chosen to go swimming with the goddess of the wet water. When he crawled up the muddy shore, tired and feeling very exposed, cheers came from the boats while a crowd of tribesmen from all corners of Britain, united in their disdain and curiosity, remained silent.

Allanza asked a man wearing checked leggings and braided hair if he knew Crotus. He laughed at Allanza's accent and said something in an incomprehensible dialect to his companion. Other people looked him up and down and shook their heads.

Allanza peered at the tents pitched by the lakeside. Each was surrounded by wakeful guards who drew their weapons when he tried to approach. The mood was brittle, cruel and watchful. He blundered on, feeling more and more useless.

By the edge of encampment was a large covered cart and a tent surrounded by soldiers wearing Roman helmets and metal breastplates and a lot of leather.

Allanza paused to look, then shrank back, shocked: standing by the cart he could see Melanius and the witch.

Were they looking for him? No. They were waiting to go into the tent. How did they get here so fast? He must have been ages in the water. Who was in the tent? He backed away but still hung around until he saw someone who didn't look too vicious and asked him, speaking very slowly and clearly, who the cart and tent belonged to.

By some miracle the man was happy to talk. 'Why, that's the high queen. I hadn't heard of her either but the word is,' and he lowered his voice, 'that she's still married to the high king, if you follow the letter of the law, that is. Of course, no one's seen her for ten years or more and they're saying it's because she's grown a huge scaly tail and won't come out for fear that people can see that she's really a dragon. No wonder the high king won't have anything to do with her.'

Allanza thanked him and backed away. Tog had mentioned her once. Tintagel sounded familiar. Wasn't that where Tog was from? Yes, but he was running from there, wasn't he, which meant she must be bad. Did that mean

Melanius and the witch were betraying him?

He looked at the sky again. The moon was sinking. Dawn couldn't be far off. Dawn meant Easter. Easter was the day everything happened. He went from tent to tent, trying to ignore the curses of the guards and the suspicious looks from people who were milling around. He was getting desperate now, horribly aware that he had been sent on a mission and had failed. What was worse, he was back at the queen's encampment. There was nowhere else for him to search.

But all had changed. Instead of a circle of soldiers lit by flaring torches, a solitary guard was leaning casually on his spear, keeping an eye on two men huddled on the cart's steps.

Master and servant. Crotus and Pyrs.

The old man lifted his head as Allanza approached across the bruised turf. His face had grown even thinner and greyer and the moonlight deepened the lines in his face.

'Pyrs. Tell me I'm dreaming, I beg you.'

'You're dreaming, My Lord.'

Allanza frowned, then remembered his mission. Sword. Story. Otter. Dead. Sword. Story. Otter. Dead. 'There's a sword and a story,' he began.

'Yes, indeed.'

'Tog has gone to see the high king.'

Crotus frowned. 'The poor lad is confused, Pyrs. It must be the cold. Quick, quick, fetch him a blanket. No, I forgot. We only exchange warmth for what is most precious.'

'And we have no blankets left, My Lord,' Pyrs said.

'Ah yes. We have lost our blankets.'

'Tog's in trouble. He needs protection. You promised,' Allanza blurted out.

'Did I promise, Pyrs?'

'My Lord will remember.'

'The oath was forced from me. Does that count, Pyrs?'

'My Lord in his wisdom will know.'

'Alas, he does. What kind of protection does he need, exactly?'

'He's going to . . . if the high king kills him, you have to read this.'

Allanza reached into his tunic and took out the sopping, rolled-up otter skin.

'It's inside,' Allanza said. 'The writing. A message.'

They had been relying on the otter skin's waterproof qualities to protect the writing. What they hadn't expected was the effect of the wet bundle of fur. Crotus's smile was sudden and terrible, and a dry clacking noise came from his throat. Allanza thought he might be dying before he realized that he was laughing.

He prodded the sodden bundle. 'What do the wise men say about misfortune, Pyrs?'

'That every cloud has a silver lining, My Lord.'

'Indeed. My misfortune was to lose my guard last night when they took everything I own and left me here. This however is the silver lining. You're not making this up?'

'No,' Allanza said.

'Open it, Pyrs.'

'No! Not yet!'

Pyrs cut the ties around the skin and held it up. 'I can see letters,' he said. 'I can read it. And who wrote it?'

'Tog, of course,' Allanza said.

'What does it say? What does it say?'

'If you read it, its power will go. It's meant to give us power over the high king,' Allanza wailed.

Pyrs read: 'VE BABBY N VE TOOM IS VE HI KINGS BABBI HE HAD IT KILT I KNOW HOO DID IT ND WAIR ND WI.'

Crotus went very still, then his head started to nod. 'So. The brat seems to think he can answer a question the whole country has been pondering these last fourteen years. And now we are supposed to do what, exactly?'

'Wait,' Allanza said. 'Tell everyone if they kill him. That's what he said.'

'Well, that sounds very clear but very stupid,' Crotus said.

'It's what he wants.'

'I cannot allow it. If by some chance he gets as far as the high king without being strangled by one of his bodyguards, he will surely be killed as soon as he speaks these words. It follows then, that if I allowed him to do this, I would be failing in my duty. Do you understand?'

'I think so,' Allanza said.

'We must go to him. I hate the little brat but I swore to protect him. That is what makes me a British king.'

Allanza felt trapped. On the one hand, there were his instructions from Tog. On the other, the old man seemed to be talking equally good sense.

'They're on the Island,' Allanza said. 'They're there now.'

The king stood and put his arm round Pyrs's shoulder. Allanza stood on his other side and together they lifted him free of the mud, made a chair with their hands and carried him to the lake shore. It was like carrying old sticks in a loose sack.

A couple of boats were still hanging around, the lake people hoping that Allanza would repeat his swimming trick. For the love of him, they said, they would carry him, and his ill-favoured friends to where they wanted. Allanza saw lights burning in the roundhouse but only had eyes for the eastern skies. The huge black bulk of the Island was a flat shape against the sky. The moon was down but the peak was clear and stark, the stone on its summit ringed by stars. Was it his imagination, or was grey creeping into the black on the horizon? Easter was almost upon them.

'Monks'll be wakin' now,' one of the rowers observed. 'Great ones for not sleeping, them be.'

'Do you know anything about the picture people?' Allanza asked. 'They're staying on the Island.'

'And we puddle'm over sure enough. Them be on the high ground, up aways but that's not where you'm to head.'

'But did they have a girl with them?'

The lake men laughed. 'And two people a-sitting on her but she didn't stop yammering, nor pinching nor biting. Fine girl. But the High King of the World, him's at the nasty well, straight ahead and up the hill. There's a hurry of his own all to do with 'im, a cause the sickness what's gripping hard in his belly as his god eats him from the inside out.'

'Who? What?'

'The high king. Him that's eaten the Christman's flesh and drunken of the Christman's blood – now the Christman's set up home in his vitals and's eating him from the inside out, sins an all. Only question is, which gets ate first: the sins or the man.'

They ran the boat aground on the Island. ''Ere we go, gentle now. Up the hill to the lights, that's where you want to go.'

Across a sheep-cropped lawn, bare apple trees scratching the air. Past stone buildings and a small wattle and daub shed. The ground steepened, then grew boggy and all the time the Island's strange, irregular peak grew bigger and blacker.

Built into the side of the hill was a simple, square building, Roman in shape. Light glowed through the hide window coverings. Somewhere nearby a little stream chattered.

They heard voices, rising and falling, growing louder and softer, but all the time, the hubbub seemed to grow denser. Suddenly Allanza heard a single voice shout out, high and clear. 'No!'

It was Tog. Leaving Pyrs and Crotus to stagger up the hill on their own, he ran the last few feet and crashed through the door.

Climbing into the coracle opened Tog's wound and he could only hunch in the back while Kai tried to work out how to steer it. He heard them shouting from the witch's stilt house – something about the danger he was in, but the witch had told him all about that and he didn't care. He just had to stop the high king, this old, dying man, from marrying Jenna – or marrying her off to his successor.

Kai worked out how to make the coracle go more or less in the direction he wanted, Melanius stopped shouting and someone started to whistle: a long, low sound that carried over the water.

The witch calling for a boat.

Kai paddled as hard as he could between banks of reeds and rushes. They heard voices on the shore and rowed away from them, then found a narrow channel that led them to a muddy patch of foreshore. They hid the coracle in the reeds, and Kai helped Tog up the bank.

Twenty or thirty paces inland a dark clump of gorse offered cover. A monk passed, humming a psalm. The night grew darker. Then, at last, a glimmer of light, and the edge of the moon appeared above a low, rounded hill on the far side of the lake: first a crescent, then a half, then three quarters and finally the full moon floated free.

Full moon. Easter. Time to move. They found the path the monk had followed through an orchard. A whitethorn looked like a bloom of frozen smoke. A sheep bounded off, a low wall cast a straight black shadow. They crouched behind it and spied out the land.

Straight ahead stood a group of buildings. The door

from one opened and two monks walked purposefully out, one carrying a small lamp.

The monks headed for a little shed and went in. Tog and Kai scurried across the grass and peered through an open slit window.

The monks had put the little lamp on a low wooden table and were kneeling in front of it. The table itself was covered in a heavily embroidered cloth. A single battered golden cup stood on it. The monks stood, crossed themselves and backed away.

'And if he dies?' one asked. He had a tired, cruel face made of lines and planes. The other's was as smooth and bland as a sea pebble. Both had their hoods down, showing that their hair had been shaved back to the crown of their heads.

'We have just prayed to our Saviour, who built this chapel with his own fair hands, that he lives,' the other reminded him calmly.

'But if the Lord God decides in his wisdom to take him to his bosom,' the first one said. 'If he dies . . .'

'If he dies . . . we still have the Pictish wench. We must baptise her to make her decent. She is the cornerstone of the alliance and perhaps far more. Do you know the legends . . . ?'

They left.

'The monks must be the high king's advisers. They're

heading for him,' Tog whispered to Kai. 'We've got to follow.'

The monks moved quickly. Even with Kai's help, Tog struggled to keep up as they followed the bobbing lamp away from the main building and then along a track that angled up the side of the hill with the lake on their right.

Tog felt the lack of time like a lack of air. If the high king died before they could get to him, what then? And what if the witch managed to whistle up a boat from one of the lake people? And if, after all that, he was caught by ruthless monks before he saw the king? What then? He felt breathless and forced himself to hold air in his lungs. 'Stop sighing. You're as loud as a cow,' Kai hissed.

The path climbed, then rounded the shoulder of a hill and there in front of them was a small stone building. Tog and Kai left the path and made their way through a patch of gorse bushes. They saw one of the monks talk to a soldier and heard him say, 'King's orders. He can't stand the dark.'

The monk knocked on a plain, wooden door and bent his head. There was a pause. He said something. Bolts shot back and he was let in.

'Can we get to a window?' Tog asked.

The little building had a window on each side – but each was lit by a smoking torch and guarded by a well-armed soldier, complete with spear, sword, shield and helmet.

'A diversion,' said Kai. 'It'll have to be me.'

Tog felt too weak to protest. 'What will you do?'

'I'll think of something. You get as close as possible because I don't think you'll have much time.'

At the front of the building Tog wriggled forward until he felt that his nose was touching the pool of light cast by the burning torch. He watched while Kai got closer, closer still, paused, then leapt to his feet and ran past the guard on the door, shouting and leaping in the flickering light like a madman. The guard started, shouted 'Hoy!' then lumbered off. Kai stopped, jabbered nonsense in a high-pitched voice and disappeared into the darkness, the guard following.

Tog hobbled to the door, pressed himself against it and knocked.

The low voice, a finger's breadth of wood away, took him by surprise.

'*Rex quondam*,' it said.

Latin, and not just any old Latin. Surely those there were the words he had seen carved on the tomb's stone in the nemeton.

'*Rex quondam*.' The voice again, more insistently this time. Tog racked his brain. He translated silently. *King in the past . . . King in the future.*

'*Rexque futurus*,' he answered.

297

Bolts rattled. Tog drew the sword. The door opened. Tog stepped in and stuck the sword up into the guard's throat.

'Where is he?' he said. 'Where's the king?'

Somehow the guard did not look scared. He swivelled his eyes down, then round. Tog followed his gaze.

The room was bright and smoky. Bare stone walls, stained with soot. Bare stone floor. On a bed across from the door a freckled, fox-faced man sat up on a narrow wooden bed. He was playing with a bracelet of round stones, shuffling them between his fingers, click-click-click. His mouth formed silent words and his eyes were turned inwards.

The two men Tog and Kai had followed were by the bed. The thin faced man was kneeling and half turned. His robe was brown and a heavy wooden cross hung around his neck on an iron chain. A monk. The other was wearing the black robes of the king's bodyguard, like the guard at the door, and there was something ominous in the way he appraised Tog.

'How did he get in?' he asked.

'He knew the password.' The guard sounded professionally offended rather than shocked.

'How?' The question appeared to be addressed to the world at large and when the world did not answer, the man pushed his bottom lip out. 'Well, boy?'

His eyes were as glossy as wet pebbles.

'I read it,' Tog said.

The man in the bed looked up, and looked away quickly but Tog noticed how his eyes had snagged on the sword.

'He lies, Mailgwin. He says he reads.' His voice was weak but unexpectedly deep.

'It is unpardonable, My Lord.'

'I am not lying,' Tog said. Now he was certain the man on the bed was the king. 'I have demands. For the king.'

The king looked pained, then said, 'The longer you keep your little sword at my guard's neck, the more certain I am he will kill you. Drop it and you will be safe. I promise.'

Tog lowered the sword and the guard stepped back but kept close.

'I keep my word,' the king said. 'I am not in the mood for killing. Please tell me why you're here.'

'There is a Pictish girl on the Island,' Tog said. 'She is going to be married to you tomorrow. It's wrong. It'll kill her. You must let her go free.'

'It would kill her. I see. And if you thought it would help save the country if she did get married?'

Tog swallowed. 'I don't know. It's none of her business. I'm not here to discuss it. If you marry her off, I'll tell everyone about something you did. Once people know, no one will listen to you ever again.'

The king's stare seemed to strip the flesh from his bones. 'Which thing? Oh, don't be afraid to talk in front of these good people. General Mailgwin helped me commit most of my sins; the good abbot Hyacinth has heard me confess them. But before you go further, know this: it is not in my power to do anything about the girl. It has been agreed. It is the result of many years' negotiation. It is a contract that cannot be broken. My dream, to unite the people of Britain, depends on the marriage of the high king to the Pictish princess. Without it, the whole plan will fail. The country will fail.'

'But what you did was wrong,' Tog said.

'Do you really think I care?' the king shot back and his voice dripped with such contempt that Tog flinched. Then he smiled, his face softening for an instant as he looked up at Mailgwin. 'He thinks kingship is about being good. Why does he think I sinned? Why does he think I lie in agony while my sins consume me? Doesn't he know that I sinned to make Britain strong? Boy, know this. The worse I am, the more my people will respect me and the more I must suffer for my people. And while I wonder how you found out what you know, I do not greatly care. What's that?'

Shouting outside. The clash of metal. Mailgwin and the guard leapt for the door but before they could reach it, it burst open, smashed against the wall and suddenly the room was full of people shouting.

There was Melanius with his sword at the abbot's throat, Borth holding the guard back, but dwarfing Mailgwin was a filth blackened figure with arms like tree roots and hair like flattened worms, and the source of all foul smells in the world.

'Hogman?' Tog gasped. He was so amazed by the sight that it took a while before he registered that Kai and the Lady of the Lake had slipped in and were standing beside him.

His lip framed the question, 'What?'

The Lady of the Lake said, 'She likes an entrance,' then put her finger to her lips and nodded to the door.

The woman who stepped into the room was huge, dark eyed, bare shouldered. A chin held high, just beginning to thicken; an imperious breast armoured with amber plates; white, ringed hands by her side. Mountainous hair, black as jet, was twisted into thick gleaming hanks and secured with golden pins.

Her presence was like a force. Everyone stepped back. Melanius, Borth and the hogman put their swords down, as if the presence was enough to keep the peace.

The hogman brought her a chair. She lowered herself into it, opposite the end of the bed and stared silently at the king.

'What is going on, Abbot? Anyone?' In pushing himself more upright, the king seemed to be shrinking into his pillows. His voice rose in pitch, outraged yet impotent. 'Why have you brought this woman to me?'

Melanius cleared his throat. 'My Lord, before we do anything else, may I ask permission to talk with the boy on his own?'

'No. I will not have secrets. You have been plotting. This is not the court of the Emperor of Byzantium, Greek. You have no power here.'

The king knew Melanius? Tog leaned forward. This was interesting.

Melanius bowed. 'I know, My Lord, that this is not the great hall of the emperor in the greatest city on earth, nor is it the court of the great Clovis, with a hundred lords and their ladies. But no matter. You are the High King of Britain and I am at your service.'

'It is not a service to bring the witch queen into the royal presence,' the abbot rasped.

'They are still married,' Melanius said gently.

'A detail,' the king said. 'I will . . . what's the word again?' he asked the abbot.

'Divorce.'

'I will divorce her.' The king coughed, then winced. Pain lines deepened on his face. 'In fact, what is stopping us from doing it now?'

'I would suggest the boy might be able to offer one compelling reason,' Melanius said. 'It might save you . . . pain, trouble, complexity. Have you ever known me to lie?'

'I know you call yourself a merchant but are a spy for the Emperor of Constantinople,' the high king said. 'I do not know if that makes you a liar. Very well. You have my attention briefly. Tell me about the boy. He says he knows things about me, and that gives him power over me. Can this be true?'

His eyes slid around the room, resting on everyone but the queen.

'I met him on the road from Tintagel one month ago,' Melanius said. 'He was in the company of two others: the Pictish girl, whom you know, and a Breton. He had rescued them from slave traders. As interesting, to me at any rate, who has studied the history of this country, was the little sword that he had.'

'We noticed,' the king said. 'He waved it in my face like it was . . . a twig.'

'How long must this go on?' The queen's voice was rich and harsh at the same time, like gritty cream, and although the words were spoken slowly, they had a sudden quality. 'I am no diplomat. I will not skirt around the truth. I will say my piece.'

'You will pay me respect! May I remind you that you are here in my court and on my terms!' The high king's voice rose into a screech and he seemed to be fighting for air.

'Your terms,' the queen said dismissively. 'You are in no position to make terms. Even as your own god eats you, the world changes. Buried secrets rise from tombs. Your kingdom is failing. Achievements turn to dust in your hands. All those years ago when you thought you were winning yourself a future, you were putting it in my hands.'

'When I did *what*, all those years ago?' the king asked.

'Careful, My Lord,' the queen said.

'I want to know.'

The queen spoke calmly and triumphantly. 'When you thought you had built the foundations for your new Britain in blood and bones. When you sent two assassins to my castle to kill my child and hide the old king's sword.'

No one moved. The only sound came from the torch flames softly beating the air. The king looked down for a moment but when he looked up, Tog noticed that his face had sharpened.

No longer defensive. No longer shifty. Interested.

'Ah. That. Now I remember,' he said. 'One small

correction though: not your child, our child. When I sent assassins to kill *our* child.'

'Yes, My Lord. That. But would it interest you, My Lord, to know what really happened?'

The king's expression was unreadable as he nodded.

'Your men betrayed you,' the queen said. 'They were so disgusted, that like true Britons they came to me on their knees and told me what you had ordered them to do. My Lord, they did not kill the child. He lived, My Lord, and was brought up in secret. Your blood and my blood still course through his veins, My Lord, but he was brought up true to his traditions, a Cornish boy, raised on Cornish soil, true to British traditions.'

She paused and Tog heard himself say, 'But the royal baby's in the tomb. I saw it. A little baby. It's dead.'

'It was put there to deceive,' the queen said. 'My child, the royal child, was brought up in the shadow of the castle in secret by the king's own assassin. And today destiny has brought him to this little room where he stands before you with a sword in his hand. Your guilt, My Lord, your shame.'

Tog felt her dark eyes on him and looked dully around for this child, then he looked down at his hand and the sword that was in it.

Time wrinkled.

There was a *before* he understood anything and there was an *after* he understood everything. Between them there was an empty gasp of surprise.

'Son,' the queen said to him, and now her voice was cracked and waxy like an old black honeycomb. 'Son, come to me.'

Tog found that he was standing in front her and her white, ringed fingers, were on his shoulders and her thumbs were digging hard into his back. She leaned close to him so that her mouth was in his ear. *'Now. Now. Man of Cornwall, you are stone and you are bronze. He tried to kill you when you were a baby. This is your destiny. The sword is the blood of the stone. Let it drink the blood of this man. Do it. Do it now.'*

Her voice became his thought. Tog raised the sword, saw the light gather on its point; in the blade he saw the little man begin to writhe. His heart was stone, his mind was silver, and destiny danced on a sharp, bronze edge. He was one with the metal now. He was the blade.

He looked at the man on the bed but even as he hardened his muscles to strike, something in him rebelled. His arm dropped as heavy as stone.

'Do it,' the queen hissed.

He looked at her. He looked at the sword.

'No,' he said, more loudly than he meant to, because she

306

flinched. 'No. This is your destiny, not mine.'

'Do it!' the queen shouted.

'NO!' Tog shouted back and then he was pushed to one side as someone rushed past him. He saw the queen rise like a wave, her hair falling in thick black torrents, and topple forwards, a thin, shining point of light in her hands.

Then she stopped, frozen in mid-air, the golden hairpin a finger's breath away from the high king's eyes, and Tog saw Allanza, his hands wrapped in her thick black hair, pulling her back like a rider pulling back a horse.

The queen dropped the hairpin, subsided and started to scream.

Borth picked Allanza up from the floor.

'Good,' he said.

'What's going on?' Allanza asked.

'Tog's just realized he's going to be the next high king,' Borth said.

'Who's that woman?'

'His mother.'

'Tog's a king?'

'High king. It's different.'

'He'll make a good one, won't he?'

'In a perfect world, yes,' Borth answered. 'But it's not over yet.'

The king subsided against his pillows. The queen was back on her seat, as still as a mountain. Only a light flush on her upper slopes and the rivers of hair down her back showed that she had ever moved.

The abbot leaned over the king. 'I counselled execution years ago to stop something like this happening. Shall I order it now?'

'Oh no,' the king said. 'I said earlier, I have had enough of killing. Anyway, perhaps she was right to want to me dead.'

'My Lord?'

'She thought I wanted to kill her son. Is that not reason enough?' He turned his attention to Tog. 'And you, boy. You did not kill me even though you thought I had tried to murder you. Why not?'

'It wasn't my quarrel,' Tog said. 'It was between you and her.'

This time, when the king looked at him, there was interest in his eyes.

'My assassin, the man who brought you up, must have done a good job. Do you think he found peace in his little woodcutter's hovel?'

Out of the corner of his eye, Tog saw the queen sit straighter in the chair. 'You would have to ask his friend, the hogman,' he said. 'But in the end, I think, perhaps, he must have been proud of me. He trusted me. He taught me well.'

He looked behind him. The hogman's face was unreadable but to Tog's surprise, he saw that Crotus had somehow crept into the room and was leaning in the doorway, breathing hard.

The king hooded his eyes and nodded. 'Then I chose well,' he said.

'What do you mean?' the queen asked, her voice slow and harsh. 'Your men betrayed you.'

'In which case, why did one of them risk his life to bring you here?' the king said. 'Let us review the situation and look at the facts. Fourteen years ago, you claim I sent assassins to Cornwall to kill my son. Correct?'

'Correct,' the queen said.

'And we have one of the assassins in the room at the moment? This man Leminauk who worked as a swineherd in the vicinity of Tintagel?'

'Correct,' the queen said.

'And he was collaborating with another of my assassins, Bediwir, who posed as a woodcutter. But they did not kill the child. They came to you and told you what had been asked of them and together, the three of you, made up a plan. And this plan was that you would not *kill* the child.

Instead one of my men would bring the child up himself in secret while the other guarded him. You would have to keep well away from this child. I am a suspicious, untrusting, cruel man who would always hold in the back of his mind the tiniest doubt that he had been betrayed. My spies would tell me if the queen was taking too great an interest in one of her village brats and I would have the child killed again, only this time I would make no mistake.'

'Correct,' the queen said.

'Have I left anything out?' the king said.

The queen narrowed her eyes.

'I *have* left something out. It concerns the body in the tomb – something my son noticed.' He acknowledged Tog with a nod. 'If he is our son. Whose was the baby? Could it have been that of the wet nurse who fed him? Could that have been the baby in the tomb, put there to deceive me?'

A silence.

'You are guessing,' the queen said finally.

'My Lady, you are deceiving no one but yourself.'

'Someone must have told you this.'

'But it was a secret. How would I know unless I was told it all those years ago by one of your plotters?'

'You lie.'

'Christians never lie. I sent those two men to you. I even sent the wet nurse. I knew how much you hated and distrusted me and more importantly, I knew that sooner or later your hatred of me would infect your feelings towards the child – unless you were convinced that I hated him more. Just one look that reminded you of me would rekindle your hatred. Is this truly a son of Cornwall or has he been infected with the inspiration of Rome? Is this a guardian of our dark traditions or will he be drawn to the light of Christian truth? The only way to save him was to make you think that you had saved him yourself.

'So that is what I did. I sent two men posing as assassins but their job was never to kill him. Their job was to take him from you and bring him up themselves.'

There was a pause, then the queen said: 'But the boy was brought up Cornish.'

'You should have kept a closer eye on him,' the king said and turned to Tog. 'Young man, you were directed to the tomb in the woods by the woodcutter, were you not?'

Tog nodded.

'And what was on that tomb?'

'A stone,' Tog said.

'And what was on the stone?'

'Writing.'

'And in what language was the writing?'

'Latin.'

'And what did the writing say?' the king asked.

311

'In Latin or British?' Tog asked.

A spasm of real pain crossed the queen's face, but she recovered.

'Tales,' she said. 'Tall tales.'

'Shall we ask the man you call the hogman?'

'He will say what he needs to live and you have made the rest up. Perhaps I have made my story up. Perhaps this creature really is just a woodcutter's bastard.'

'He knows,' the king said. 'He speaks Latin; he knows his Bible. However, there is one final piece of proof. In the tomb, young man, you found the sword, the baby and something else. Can you tell me what it was?'

Tog didn't have to think. 'A coin. Half a coin, My Lord.'

'And now you can give that to me. You see, I have the other half and when they are joined together, it will show that the plan was mine from the outset. And the queen was tricked.'

'But I don't have it, My Lord.'

'Didn't Bediwir tell you how important it was?'

'No, My Lord. He died before he could say anything much and that's another thing . . .'

'You don't have it?'

'I thought the sword . . .'

'The sword is nothing! You have given away the thing

that was most precious. You have failed. You have—' the king cried shrilly but it was too much for him and he began to cough.

'I gave the coin to Crotus,' Tog said. 'It was payment.'

Crotus was led forward, Melanius holding one arm and Pyrs the other.

He looked up and sideways at each of them, like an old crow gauging the wind.

'A Cornishman,' the queen said triumphantly.

'He swore to help me,' Tog said.

'I swore to protect you,' Crotus answered. 'I think you will admit that things have moved on.'

'Do you have the coin?' the abbot asked.

'I lost everything,' Crotus answered. 'All was stolen. My tent. My oxen.'

'A Cornishman,' the queen repeated.

'But one thing I retained. I took it as payment in good faith but now I return the high king's property.'

'And you confirm you had it from the boy?'

'I confirm it. I had it from the boy and the boy said he took it from a tomb.'

The Lady of the Lake muttered rather too loudly, 'He knows which side his bread is buttered.'

He did not look at the queen as he handed the coin to Tog. The king reached into his loose shirt and pulled out half a gold coin hung on a golden chain. He gestured for Tog to approach. Tog leaned over the bed, smelled the king's sour bed sweat, and pressed his half coin against the king's. The fit was good. Then the abbot went down on his knee and bowed his head, and then the black robed soldier. By his side, Crotus, Pyrs and Melanius knelt, and when Tog turned he saw Allanza, Kai, Leminauk and Borth kneel. Then the queen knelt and the high king bowed his head.

Then the high king started to cough and did not stop.

IX

Full

Tog and Kai were waiting on the hillside outside the Picts' camp. Time – horrible, yawning, freezing lengths of time – had been spent in the misty dawn while Melanius made what he called representations to them after waking them up, assuring them it was not an attack, promising them it was important.

The picture people had chosen to set up camp on a long, narrow ridge that stuck out into the lake. To get to them, you crossed a marsh, sweated your way up a steep hill, before braving a picket line of giant, naked, tattooed warriors who had animal skulls woven into their hair and carried crossbows – a weapon that could fire a short, heavy iron-tipped arrow a quarter of a mile straight into someone's eye.

As well as the most defensible spot on the Island, it was also the second holiest. Halfway along the ridge was the thorn bush that the Christman's uncle had planted when he brought the young Christman to Britain before he was famous. There were rumours that the Picts were using the holy thorn bush to dry their clothes, but as so many of them went around naked, this was hard to believe.

'Why can't I go there myself?' Tog repeated.

'It's called protocol,' Kai yawned. 'It means there's a right way and a wrong way of doing things.'

'Suppose you're doing something for the first time?' Tog asked.

'Then I'm sure there's protocol for that. Ask Melanius.'

'I never imagined he was a spy. It's a lot to take in. He actually knows the Emperor.'

'And I know you should keep your back straight. Don't twist yourself around your wound. If the Picts smell fear, they'll be on to you like wild animals.'

'Stop talking rubbish,' Tog said, with some heat.

Kai opened his mouth to answer back, then stopped.

'Sorry, My Lord,' he said.

Tog rolled his eyes. 'Don't take me so seriously. Do you know what the hogman said to me? He knelt at my feet and said he was my dog to kick or love as I pleased. If you did that I'd be sick.'

'You couldn't order him to wash, could you?'

'I could send him to the Romans. I could order him to guard them and then Gaius could bathe him. I could do anything. It makes me feel like I'm floating. I never used to feel like that. Suppose I've changed. Jenna might . . .'

'She's royal too.'

'So she'll feel the same as me.'

'I wouldn't say that. She's got far too much class.'

'That's it. I really am going to cut your head off.'

Kai laughed. Kai understood. Tog felt drenched by happiness, friendship and luck. His throat tightened and he stared into the low morning sun to make his eyes water and remembered how Kai had once put his head in the smoke of the fire to hide his grief. At the time he had thought nothing of it. Now he saw just how sad Kai must have been, but it didn't make him feel sad. If anything he felt fuller and better for having realized it. Happiness could wrap itself around even the saddest memories.

The tent flap billowed. 'This is it,' Kai said. 'Good luck.'

Tog had one last look around. Below, ghosts of white mist twisted above the lake. Above, the sun was like young gold. Beyond the tents, apple trees were covered in pale blossom. How had this happened? How was he here? Then the flap was pulled back and Allanza came out, followed by Borth and Melanius.

Melanius approached him. 'My Lord, there are matters to discuss. I am not . . .'

'Not now. No more protocol or whatever you call it. Look!'

The Picts had appeared: a small, wiry man wearing a lot of gold; a tall, thin, doomy-looking woman wearing a lot of gold; the bodyguards, not wearing anything much. There was a commotion inside the tent, lots of shouting and then Jenna fought her way into the open air, slapping at the hands of two servant women who were trying to hold her back.

She laughed at the bodyguards' naked behinds, saw Tog, dropped her jaw like his and fired a sharp question at her father, who whipped round and said something sharp back. Jenna ignored him, pushed past her bodyguards and stood in front of Tog.

Her eyes searched his face, she touched his cheek, then the wound in his side. She was wearing gold up to her elbows, gold round her neck, gold in her hair, and gold round her waist.

'What have you done?' she said. 'Why are you here? Are you hurt? You've changed. You look different.'

'I'm still me,' Tog said. 'But it's very confusing.'

Jenna's eyes glistened. 'What's going on? What did Melanius want? When he came they sent me away.

They didn't let me listen. It's to do with . . .' She looked down. 'I want to be dead. You know I've been promised to the high king.'

'I know. I . . .'

'Then why are you here? I can't bear to see you. You don't understand. You can't. I've got to marry an old man. Sick. He's not . . . you.'

She tried to pull away but Tog caught her arm. 'Jenna, it's you that doesn't understand.' He swallowed. 'The high king . . . You *can* marry him.'

'I can't! How can you say that? You stupid pig!' She punched him on the chest, then backed off, shivering.

'Jenna. It's me, or will be when my father dies.'

'Do not . . .' she said, 'do not tell me lies with your mouth.' It sounded as if she had no breath in her body.

'But it's true,' Tog said. 'That was my mission, although I never knew it. I'm going to be king and you . . .' He could hardly say it. 'You have to marry me.'

Her eyes burned him. Now it was his turn to look down.

Jenna said, 'If you're lying, I will kill you dead.'

'I am telling you the truth,' he said, raising his eyes, managing to look straight at her, finding he could not look away.

'I have to marry you?' she asked.

'Yes. I command it. I decree it. I order it. But only if you want.'

She kissed him on the lips and her tongue darted around his, as fresh as apple, as fast as fire. The bodyguards, who had followed, made a sort of rumbling noise.

Her father cleared his throat. Jenna pushed Tog away. His face was flushed and she was smiling.

'Do I look stupid?' she asked.

'No,' Tog answered.

'You do.'

And her smile flashed brighter than anything Tog had ever seen and his heart lifted as if it had eagle's wings.

Jenna's father then made a long speech in Pictish, and at the end of it he hugged Tog and kissed him three times. Tog bowed, trying not to wince, and the Pict gripped his wound and kissed him again. Somehow, though it hurt even worse after that, it was a different sort of hurt.

Suddenly, he found there was something he had to say to Jenna and walked her over to a gnarly apple tree that was coming into bud. He pushed a curl back from her temple, and looked closely at the golden oak leaves woven into her hair. A golden snake, two-headed, coiled round her neck and rested on her collarbone. When she moved her arms, bracelets shifted with soft, metallic kisses.

'You know I haven't got anything to give you,' he said.

'I would not care but it is not true,' Jenna said. 'You will be king.'

'But what you did . . . what you gave me . . . When you came to the Island with me, you didn't know who I was. All you knew was that you were getting closer and closer to the one place in the world that you didn't want to be. You could have run away at any time. Right at the end, you could have got away on a horse – but you didn't. You didn't.'

Jenna narrowed her eyes and looked at the horizon with a little smile on her lips. 'No,' she said simply. 'I didn't. I could not.'

Melanius had drawn away and was deep in conversation with a small man with a limp, but before Tog could ask who he was, he saw the abbot Hyacinth striding across the grass towards him, looking significant and with dark, papery bags under his eyes.

He gave Tog a quick bow but did not meet his eyes. 'If you have finished courting your painted lady, the high king is dying,' he said curtly. 'He has called you.'

He strode off, the dew-soaked hem of his habit slapping against his bare shins. Tog was forced to follow.

'Is he still in pain?' Tog asked as he caught up. 'Because the witch may have something . . .'

'A witch can have no Christian cures.'

Tog followed him down the hill, and up another. The sun was rolling up the eastern shoulder of the tor and the stone on top was black.

Hyacinth was tireless; Tog was exhausted and in pain. Kai and Allanza walked behind, uncertain whether or not to eavesdrop.

'I was told,' Tog panted, 'that the sword used to be kept in the stone up there.'

'I do not know of these things,' Hyacinth said. 'The high king wants the tribes to see you. He wants this to take place in the chapel of the Christman our Saviour. It is the chapel he built with his own fair hands when he walked these hills. The tribes will be gathered outside. You will be inside. They will be ushered past you. Then you will come out and we will baptize you in the lake. It will be a great day.'

'What about the sword?' Tog managed to get out.

But the abbot ignored him and they did not talk until they arrived at the little square building where the king was lying. Tog entered the room. In the daytime, clean air was allowed to blow through it from the unscreened windows and it was bright with the early morning light.

The king was whey-faced, his eyes bloodshot. He gestured to the bed and Tog shuffled closer, uncomfortable with the intimacy. His father's breath was thin – the dregs of a life, leaving – and he rambled.

'Close to death,' he breathed. 'Listen, don't speak. No more friends. From now on, trust no one. People want peace. Strong king, peaceful people.'

The king's face changed suddenly. Lines in it deepened and his eyes bulged. He gripped his stomach and writhed. Hyacinth stepped forward, but the king pushed him away.

'The girl. You are married? Not yet? Keep her close. Watch her secrets. You can . . .' He spat. 'Where Rome failed, you can . . . succeed.'

'I don't understand.'

'Peace is not a feeling. It is a state of calm. Power brings calm. Only power. It's hard.' Suddenly he gripped Tog's arm. 'Pain. My pain is penance. Your penance . . . the way you were brought up, humble, with woodcutter, ready to change . . . the world. Your suffering, my gift, to you. Wasn't I . . . brilliant?'

Outside Kai and Allanza were waiting.

'Are you all right?' Allanza asked.

But Tog couldn't answer. It was as if his head was full of voices all talking at the same time so loudly that they drowned each other out. There was so much to think about but he didn't know where to start so he put his head down and headed to a small grove of young trees nearby. In the grove there was a glade and in the glade a raised stone pool brimmed with rusty water.

Tog lay down on the grass, his head propped on a pillow of moss, and looked at the sky though the lattice of thin branches. The sun was warm on his face and bright, so he closed his eyes and listened to the water as it trickled over the edge of the pool. A silvery sound. A tinny sound. Silver and rust. Bronze and tin. He saw the shining man against his eyelids, twisting in the sound.

Oh little shining thing
My little tinny thing
Make me a king.

Oh little shining man
As your start was stone
Water is your end.

Who's the little blade?
I'm the blade.
Who is the blade?
I am.

He opened his eyes. Crotus was kneeling by the pool, chanting quietly to himself. As Tog pushed himself up on to his elbows, he turned and seemed to taste

Tog with his yellow eyes.

'Who's the little blade?
I'm the blade.
Who is the blade?
I am.'

he sang. 'So, the young prince is trying to escape already.'

'I just wanted some time on my own.'

'Very wise, but you will never be on your own, ever again, for as long as you live, which may not be long. Tell me, are you pleased with your fate?'

'According to the high king, it's my fate to be a sort of new Christman.'

Crotus dipped his hands in the red water and washed his face. 'The old king dies at Easter, the new king is reborn in his blood. It's an old story, older far than the Christman's and it has been told every spring since the world began. When you saw the man in the blade, did you not see the Christman with his crown of light, or thorns, or whatever you want to make of it? The same story. And now you are part of it.'

'What would happen if I just walked away?'

'You would starve, or become a slave. No blame though, no blame. The high king would not be the first to die without a successor. The tribes would leave this place, go home, start to fight, get weaker, weaker, then another would come to try and unite them. It makes no difference, really. All is change and all stays the same.'

'But you helped me. You gave the high king the coin even though he's not Cornish.'

'I did what was needed,' the old king said with a flash of his old malice. 'I thought that perhaps you might give the country a year's respite, a month's, a week's. A week where Briton does not kill Briton would be a good week.'

'Just a week?'

'Just a week.' He lifted his eyes. 'The high king is . . .'

'Dying.'

'Any famous last words?'

Tog felt his voice shake but his fierce desire not to break down in front of Crotus allowed him to answer.

'He was rambling. He said he was brilliant. He said I could succeed where Rome failed.'

'In what respect?'

'Jenna, I suppose. Marriage. Peace. Peace between the tribes. If the high king can be united with a Pict, anything is possible,' Tog said.

'He is right. You have conquered her. For three hundred years Rome tried to conquer the north. It never succeeded. But enough of high politics. I heard you were wounded in a sword fight. As a king, you must watch your back at all times. You must trust no one.'

The stranger! Tog thought. How could I have forgotten about him when I'm still hurting from that attack? Where is he now? He heard someone crashing through the trees and turned, fear like cold, tight skin, but it was Allanza, red-faced and excited.

'They're arriving! The tribes are arriving! You've got to be there! No one knows what to do. They're waiting for orders.'

Tog looked at Crotus but he had subsided. Sunlight passed through bare branches, glittered on the spring water and dappled him into the earth. Allanza was hopping from foot to foot, not knowing whether he could insist on an answer.

For a second, Tog's mind was as blank as the sky, then it seemed to brace itself.

'There's a little church . . .' he began, then paused. No, he had to get this right and the little church felt wrong. 'The tribes shall gather on the tor. I shall see them at midday. Tell them that. I shall tell the abbot to be there with the monks and if he's very good, they shall sing.'

Crotus and the stranger and everything else were driven from his mind.

After that, things moved fast.

Mailgwin approached Tog and asked if he would like to

inspect his guard, about fifty men, standing in loose ranks. As he walked past them, one or two of them glanced at him but they kept their eyes on Mailgwin, who said, 'We need orders, My Lord.'

Tog recognized a test. 'The tribes will be meeting on the top of the tor,' he said. 'We need to make that happen.'

'The abbot wants . . .'

Tog looked at Mailgwin and found he had an overwhelming urge to make an impact on his professional soldier's face. 'It won't work,' he said. 'Not all the kings are Christian and don't want to be either. The abbot thinks that if he baptizes me, it will impress them. I don't. Now, should I be up there waiting for them, or should I arrive once they've all assembled?'

Mailgwin raised his eyebrows, then he bowed his head and scratched his chin. 'If you're up there while they arrive one by one, it won't make an impact. On the other hand, if they're on top of the hill and you arrive, it will look as if you're coming to them. However, if you go up there now, we can hold them down here until just before midday. Then we'll all come up together, and approach from the north so you have the sun behind you.'

Tog nodded. 'That's good.' Then he watched as the soldier's eyes were drawn to something over his shoulder – something that made shock register on his bland face.

Two pigseys were approaching him, followed by a gaggle of monks.

Mailgwin crossed himself. 'Are those . . . ?'

'It's all right,' said Tog. 'I know them.'

Mailgwin crossed himself again.

Then the abbot came out of the king's house and announced that the high king was dead, and there was huge embarrassment because it seemed so clear to everyone that he had smothered him.

The pigseys were a sensation. The traditionalists were awed because they half believed the pigseys were magical; the modernizers and Christians were impressed because they didn't believe in magic and so had convinced themselves that pigseys didn't exist.

The pigseys climbed the hill with Tog and showed him how the little sword had been designed to fit into the standing stone and how, with a little twist, you could lock it into place, and with another twist, unlock it.

The tribes arrived. There was Cerdic of Wessex, Elifer of Ebrauc, Pabo of the Penines, neighbour Gerren of Dumnonia, Aircol of Dyfed, Aesc of Kent, Geot of Lindsey. They walked up to Tog, one by one, put their hands on the hilt of the sword and said they were his dogs, in a variety of different ways. A Scot from Ireland and a

Briton from Strathclyde nearly came to blows over a question of some stolen cattle until Jenna's father stepped in and whispered something to each of them. Then they both went down on their knees in front of Jenna and kissed her hand, looking up into her face with something like wonder. Indeed, all the northern kingdoms – Fidach, Ce, Circind, Goddodin, Fidach, Fotla and the rest – were polite to Tog but treated Jenna with reverence.

And it made him proud.

Tog received smaller kings like Crotus but their names blurred and their faces blurred and he felt that they were more interested in each other than in him. He put the sword into the stone, pulled it out again and held it up in the sunlight. The monks chanted. The abbot made him and Jenna hold hands and announced that now Tog owned everything Jenna possessed and she had to do everything he said. The monks chanted some more and only Tog heard one of the pigseys say in his sibilant, matter of fact voice, 'Thiss will not work properly.' The other agreed. 'The old king hass died, yet there iss no blood on the stone nor the earth. Yet the queen . . .' He saw Tog looking at him, paused and said, 'The queen is the . . .' Tog could not quite catch me word Crow? Cure?

The queen will be the cure. That was a thought to hold on to, Tog thought. A cure for me. A cure for the country.

He remembered how Crotus had said that even a week of peace was better than none and right now it was good enough to be on top of the tor on a fine spring morning, the sun as fresh as a daisy's eye, a wind blowing in from the sea, the world spreading out around him and a sword in his hand that was shining.

When Picts got married, their families abandoned them for ever. Jenna's parents left in a barge immediately the ceremony was over. They tore some clothes symbolically and flattened a couple of pewter bowls, which they threw into the lake, the lake people respectfully turning their backs so no one could accuse them of diving for them later. Jenna cried dutifully on the jetty, her father looked tearfully haughty and her mother covered her face. That was that. Jenna watched them go, shoulder to shoulder with Tog, her fingers twining and untwining around his. He could feel her thin body tremble and put his arm around her. She shook him off.

'You have to work now. I am a princess. I know. Call your generals. Make them see you. Talk to them now, before the feast makes them drunk and fatty.'

'About what?' Tog asked.

'Ask them what they are doing and what their plans are. When they answer, nod and tell them to carry on. Then say you want to go riding and need an escort. This is what my father did. It is what kings do.'

He did. The generals told him about their various duties and he promptly forgot everything they said, although Kai seemed to be taking quite a lot in. Then he was shown a crossbow that a Pict had treacherously sold and this time, although he didn't follow the long debate about its pros and cons, he could tell Allanza was thinking about it all very hard. After that they went riding and although he could barely stay on the gigantic horse Mailgwin gave him, everyone pretended he was the best horseman they had ever seen and complimented him on his natural seat. What wasn't good about that? Then there was a feast with people getting drunk and fatty, as Jenna had said they would. Then nightfall and Jenna on her own, and falling asleep in a state of happy wonder, Jenna in his arms, Latin chiming in his brain.

Duo ubera tua sicut duo hinuli capreae gemelli qui pascuntur in liliis, he recited to himself. *Your breasts are like twin deer that are fed on lilies*. It was the first of a series of wonderful discoveries to find out that Jenna's were not, but now, as he drifted over the borders of sleep, he realized that the woodcutter had spent his last night alive trying to teach him about love. It made him feel humble, grateful, awed.

* * *

Then he woke. Their room, a small, square retreat built for contemplation, looked very bare in the moonlight. His mind too was moon bright: clean and cold.

What had woken him? A thought or a noise or the moon?

He sat up.

'Come back,' Jenna muttered. 'It's cold.'

Her skin was a landscape of dips and rises, shadows and light, swirling with signs and pictures it would take a lifetime to read. He had a lifetime to read them. At the thought, his heart jumped.

'I can't sleep,' Tog said, dropped a tunic over his head, wrapped a cloak around him and went outside.

He shivered. Straight ahead the ground was dotted with shrubs, and the sheep trails criss-crossed the hill's contours in a lazy maze. He saw a flutter of grey against the black as a figure climbed the slope and there was something in the way it moved that bothered him. It was furtive but familiar. Horribly familiar.

He began to wince across the grass, the dew at first refreshing then just chilling his feet. As the ground steepened, he rowed his way up the hill, one hand pressed into his side, which was still sore, the other grabbing turf.

At the top the peak flattened out and he limped towards the stone.

No guards and the sword was gone.

In a state of near panic, Tog collapsed with his back against the stone, breathing in the sicky smell of crushed lichen. He heard a horrid wet chunking sound and looked round the back of the stone. Silhouetted against the moon, a hooded monk was on his knees, slamming the sword into something over and over again.

He was singing the song:

> Oh little shining thing
> My, little tinny thing
> Make me a king.

> Oh little shining man
> As your start was stone
> Water is your end.

> Oh little shining thing
> My little tinny thing
> Make me a king.

The stranger. So that was the thought that had whispered through his head in the night. Above, beyond and behind everything that had happened to him, no one had answered the question: who had been trying to kill him for a solid month, all the way from Cornwall to the Island?

Behind him the moon glinted off a river that wound through the flat lands. On the horizon, a dim line of silver marked the sea. The song changed to a psalm. The stranger sang psalms when he thought he was alone, Tog said to himself. He was a monk. He always had to be a monk. A monk is about the only person in the world who can go around with his face hidden and not saying a word. He must have raced back after the fight at the Romans' villa and had been here ever since.

'It's you, isn't it?' Tog called out from behind the standing stone.

The wet noise stopped.

'He wouldn't die,' the stranger called out. 'The other guards went really easily but not him. It's this chap.' He held the little bronze sword up so the blood ran down the blade and spiralled around his wrist. 'He's a thirsty little beggar.'

'You should put it back in the stone.'

'Going to make me? You and whose army?' The stranger found this funnier than Tog. With his hood up, he looked like any other monk. With it down, the wounds in his face looked dark. As they healed, they pulled the corners of his mouth up into a permanent, almost wistful smile.

'Why did you want the sword so much?' Tog asked.

'Oh my God. You're too stupid to live,' he replied. 'You

have no idea of what you're up against. No idea at all. And it's never going to stop. I can sell this sword to the highest bidder, or I could use it to bargain with. It's the way of the world. You fight or you get fought. You screw or you get screwed. You kill or you get killed. This little man is going to help me.'

'It's not just a sword. It's *the* sword. It's got its own destiny worked out. You can feel it working through you.'

'Destiny.' The stranger said derisively. 'The high king used to talk about destiny. He told me about the sword. Went on and on about what he'd done. God, how he bored on about it. Night after night. I just sat there and listened.'

'Who are you?' Tog asked, suddenly aware that he was missing something big. 'If you weren't the high king's man . . .'

'Who am I? *Who* am I? Who am *I*? Who are *you*? No, I'm serious. Tell me. What have you just found out about yourself? That's really important.'

'I'm the high king's son.'

'Right. And that makes you special, does it? Now let me tell you a little secret. I was never the high king's man. I was his boy. Like you. He. Was. My. Father. That shocked you, didn't it? I'm an accident of birth and you're an accident of birth, except your accident proved a little bit luckier than mine because in my case, instead of raping a queen and marrying her, he raped a serving girl and didn't. He always kept an eye on me, I'll give him that, and when he found out that I was clever enough to learn Latin, he decided I should become a monk. Well, I went along with it. In some respects I was good at it because bastards like you and me, we do whatever we have to in order to survive. In fact, I convinced him I was so holy that the old fool started to confide in me. He told me about this thing, this wonderful hidden treasure he was going to produce like a magician, just when it looked like he's lost the kingdom and lost his grip. And who did he choose to go down to Cornwall to escort it back? Yours truly.'

'That's how you knew where I was?' Tog said.

'I knew about the woodcutter but I didn't know what the treasure was and that old drunken bastard wouldn't tell me. I never guessed it was you.'

'So you killed him because you wanted it for yourself.'

'We fought; he lost. So then I just had to follow you.'

'But you bribed those soldiers to kill me.'

'That was just meant to scare you. You weren't meant to get away, but hey, all's well that ends well. All I had to do was follow you, after all. Big stroke of luck for me that you haven't told anyone to look out for a man with two holes in his face. Before I kill you and claim the sword, the kingdom and your little Pictish bit, can you tell me why?'

337

'It's simple,' Tog said. 'I forgot. Compared to everything else that's been happening, you just didn't seem that important. Except, in another sense, you are. You see, if you hadn't been chasing me, I'd have never made it here, and if I hadn't made it here, I wouldn't be high king. So thanks. I mean it. I suppose in one sense, I owe it all to you.'

As intended, the stranger lost his temper and attacked.

Same old moon up in the sky, same two idiots fighting on the ground, but this time, Tog thought, he's got the sword. We circle round each other, moon shadows touching. Forget everything, except everything you were ever taught about how to win when you're wounded. Keep your body stiff so you don't tear the wound any more but if he thrusts, like that, twist away and forget about the damage. When he darts forward, step back, that's right, wait for the quick second strike and when it comes, fall, and kick out for his knee as hard as you can. It hurts like hell but you can feel his knee-bone scrunch sideways. He goes down, then recovers. Stagger back and brace yourself against the stone, show him your injured side and pant a bit. When he swings the sword round, swivel, and slip sideways so the blade sparks against the stone where you were a moment before. Grab his arm below the elbow and above it, then bend it backwards until it breaks at the join.

He screams. The sword drops. Kick him away and pick it up. There. Feel the old blood stick in your palm. Watch him as he comes forward and . . .

The stranger grabbed the blade and pressed the point against his belly. He smiled knowingly through the tears. His old trick.

'This is where you find out the truth about yourself,' he said through bared teeth. 'It's just you and me, boy, and you know you can't do it.'

Tog killed him. The sword passed quickly through the soft wall of the stranger's belly, then turned upwards to pierce the heart. The stranger died, not knowing that he'd been killed, a slightly smug look on his face.

Tog shuddered. Blood clung to the sword's edge. Is that destiny? he thought. Does it just live on the point of an old bronze sword? And if I kill again, is that destiny? And again? And again?

And now he'd done it once, he saw how destiny was too easy a little word, too much of an excuse. I killed him, people said. It was destiny.

As if that made it better. As if that made it *right*. And what did it mean?

Suddenly he was running. Something carried him down the slope, something that seemed to lift him above the tussocks and roots so that he neither fell nor felt tired.

He arrived at the lakeside, chest heaving, feeling bright and hollow.

Over the lake, the silver mist hung low and the full moon drenched him in light. The water was very still; there was no wind. In the distance a duck squawked in distress and a lake man cried out.

The wood of the jetty creaked as he walked along it. He hefted the bloody sword in his hand, then looked out across the water. It was time to do what he couldn't do before. It was all in the rhyme of course.

Up above him, he felt the slow wheel of the things in the sky: the hunter chasing the bear, the dog running after the hunter, the seven dancing sisters, the twins and the bull and the crab. The woodcutter had showed them, and many others besides, to him, and explained how the ancients thought that life on earth was bound up with life in the heavens, as if people were joined to the old sky gods with starbright thread. But as they glittered through the thin mist and moved slowly across the sky, Tog felt them to be very distant and very stiff. Nothing ever changed up there, he thought. The hunter never caught the bear, the dog never licked his master, the seven sisters danced for ever, and ever, and ever.

It seemed to him then, that while he might be

smaller than an ant compared to them, he could do something they could not even dream of.

He would not have a destiny. He would have a future.

The sword wanted each life to be forged in the bloody pattern of the one before.

The high king wanted him to suffer as he had suffered.

But Tog was different. He might suffer, but he didn't want others to suffer. He might have to kill but he would never seek the slack justification of destiny. The thing was, he had been given love and in ways he could not understand, he knew that love could give him the strength to break the shackles of his past and forge a new future for himself.

Destiny might have set him on his journey, but love had kept him going. So he pulled back his arm and threw the shining man as far as he could into the lake.

As your start was stone
Water is your end

The moonlight flashed quickly on him as he turned and then he was gone, hitting the water with barely a splash as a twist of mist, as thin as a wrist, rose up to meet him, the shining man no longer, just a little old sword.

Read on for Tog's next adventure in *A Heartless Dark*.

Out now . . .

They all looked up. A full moon, yellow as old teeth, had cleared the hills in front of them. 'That's the fires on the other side of the forest,' Nm said. 'Burn day and night they do – something to do with the ghosts. Makes the moon that colour, red sometimes, like blood you know.'

The boat lurched and their stomachs hollowed as a wave slipped beneath the boat. Its saw-toothed edge nibbled the banks as it disappeared into the darkness ahead of them.

'What was that?' Tog asked.

'More to the point, who are they?' Facing backwards as he rowed, Kai nodded behind them.

The two craft, narrower and thinner than theirs, were forging through the water so quickly that their bow wave glimmered white in the moonlight.

'Row, lads!' Nm shouted.

Tog and Kai took up their positions, measured the stroke set by Allanza and Gerwyn, then dug their oars into the water. Not too deep, not too shallow, watch the oar behind your shoulder, not too deep, not too shallow.

'Who are they?' Tog gasped.

'Pirates.'

'Pirates you were waiting for.'

'Shut up and row.'

'We'll never outpace them,' Tog said. 'Who are they?'

'It was a misunderstanding.'

'You stole the boat,' Tog said. 'I knew it. You just wanted us to row you away from trouble.'

'I sold the cargo and didn't exactly tell the owner,' Nm said. 'Now row. They won't spare you, you know. They'll either kill you or sell you. They're always looking for slaves up at Castlebright.'

So they rowed. It was a strange race: silent apart from the creak of wood, the splash of oars and the rush of water. At first they held their own, even drew away but as soon as the pursuers realized they had increased their speed, they responded. The two pursuit craft drew closer. Tog saw Nm's head turn from left to right as he scanned the banks, looking for a place to put in but there was a sheer mud wall on the right and forest on the left.

'How many are there?' Gerwyn gasped.

'Six in each boat. Too many to fight,' Tog answered.

'Ditch the boat and swim?' Kai said.

'Don't leave me, mates,' Nm said. 'They'll kill me.'

'And while they kill you, we'll be getting away,' Kai said. 'Woah!'

Again the boat lurched but this time, Kai and Allanza missed their strokes and tumbled backwards. The boat tipped and a white wave ran along the bank like a crease; Kai's oar slid from its rowlock into the river.

They rowed on but with only two oars, it was hopeless. The pursuing boats were long and low with sharp, raised bows and surged closer, then separated and started edging up on either side.

Tog crawled to the bows where the packs were kept and unburied a bow. He fumbled the wrappings open, strung it, notched an arrow, then very deliberately stood to show himself and his weapon. The boats steered away but kept up with them. Tog let off an arrow, could not see where it went, so notched another. But then Nm shouted out a warning and he saw the other boat was sliding closer. He swung the bow to cover it, then swung back to the other. Stalemate for the time being, but their situation was hopeless and he knew they were being toyed with.

What now? He looked at the shore but there was nothing to see and anyway, they would be boarded long before they got there. He was struck at how quiet it had become as the boats glided down the still river.

Quiet apart from a sort of gentle hissing sound.

'I'm just beginning to remember something, lads,' Nm said. 'I knew the moon meant something! The old god, he's down there in the water looking up and when he sees that moon, he wants a bit of it and goes chasing after it at the spring tides. Sometimes it's a little wave like the first one, sometimes it's a bigger wave like the second and sometimes it's a giant wave the height of man and it comes crashing down the river in a wall. And the reason you know it's coming is because it hisses. Row. Row. ROW!'

The panic in Nm's voice infected the rowers. They started to pull again. The hissing grew louder and now, when Tog looked back, he thought he could see something – a darker line above the river, fringed with white. Their attackers responded. Both had been standing off but as their prey seemed to take flight, they both picked up speed. Both were turning sideways on, heading towards him to present as small a target as possible. Tog watched as they moved past, then looked back.

The hissing grew to a roar and mingled with the groan and crack as low lying branches were torn away by the wave. Was it possible that their attackers hadn't noticed?

The boat rocked. The river shrank into itself, as if it were drawing breath, and the shore line rose. Behind them a wall of blankness seemed to be rushing towards them – not a blankness but something equally unlikely: a wave that towered over the boats and was bearing down on them with incredible speed. Now the attackers saw the danger and tried to respond but they were too late. They were sideways on when the wave struck. It lifted them, knocked them over, then they were gone as Tog felt the stern of their boat lift and the wind start to tear his hair.

'Row! Row!' Nm shouted again, then 'Hold on!'

The wave, instead of knocking them over, picked them up and carried them forward on a rushing slope, so fast the trees on either side of them blurred. Tog heard someone shouting, then realized it was his own wordless yell of excitement.

'Bend coming!' he called.

Nm pushed the rudder over but it made no difference. One minute they were in the middle of the river, the next they were rushing towards the left hand bank. Nm cried out, swung the rudder still further, and ducked as the boat surged into the branches of old willow tree.

Tog was too slow. One branch knocked his head, the other scooped him out of the boat like a stiff, rough arm and dumped him in the river. The water closed over him, eddies caught him, a small wave lifted him, dumped him on the bank, and dragged him off. He felt a tree root under his hands and hung on as a series of diminishing waves lifted and pulled him, lifted and pulled him, lifted and pulled him . . . then stopped.

Suddenly, everything was weirdly silent and he was totally alone in the river by a forest that was full of ghosts.